THE
BIRTHDAY
PARTY

ALSO BY SHALINI BOLAND

THE BIRTHDAY PARTY

SHALINI BOLAND

THOMAS & MERCER

Published by Thomas & Mercer, Seattle

www.apub.com

Amazon, the Amazon logo, and Thomas & Mercer are trademarks of Amazon.com, Inc., or its affiliates.

EU Product Safety contact:
Amazon Publishing, Amazon Media EU S.à r.l.
38, avenue John F. Kennedy, L-1855 Luxembourg
amazonpublishing-gpsr@amazon.com

ISBN-13: 9781662529511
eISBN: 9781662529504

Cover design by The Brewster Project
Cover images: © Vovantarakan / Shutterstock; © Ebru Sidar / Arcangel

Printed in the United States of America

To my daughter, who gives me endless inspiration
(in both my life and my writing)

Prologue

You take her small, cold hand in yours and spin her around on the ice. She's giggling her head off. Making silly faces, her dark eyes flashing up at you, but she can't see you inside the grinning cartoon costume. All she sees is a huge cuddly dog with big eyes and a fluffy brown-and-white coat. Your hands are the only part of your body that are uncovered. To her, you're part of the birthday experience. Part of the fun. She trusts you. It makes you sick, but at the same time, it shouldn't. This is a sign that everything is going to plan.

The ice-rink music is muffled inside the costume. Mariah Carey's 'All I Want For Christmas Is You' interspersed with laughter and screams. The lyrics are apt. But you're becoming distracted. You need to focus. You blink the sweat from your eyes. The temperature this evening is below freezing, but you're hot and clammy. Your breath trapped inside the heavy costume, settling on your skin and prickling like chilli sauce. You imagine how red and blotchy your face must be. Focus.

You've been practising your skating skills over the past few weeks. But you're still wobblier than you'd like. The last thing you need is to fall. To draw attention to the both of you. To have an accident.

This has to go as smoothly as the ice you're gliding across as you head towards the barrier.

Away from the rest of the birthday party. From the life she knows.

To a new beginning.

For both of you . . .

Chapter One

'Oh no,' I gasp.

Sasha's feet leave the ground, her small, bundled-up body flying backwards as though in slow motion before she lands heavily on the ice.

My breath hitches. 'Sasha!' I croak, skating over to where my eight-year-old's best friend has fallen. 'Are you okay?' I don't think she's hit her head, but I can't be sure.

She stares up at me, dazed, the floodlights leeching the colour from her face.

'Are you okay?' I repeat.

She nods slowly, blinking.

'It's a good job you're wearing all those layers,' I say. 'Did you hit your head?'

She sits up, patting the back of her red bobble hat. 'I don't think so.'

I help her to her feet, relieved that it doesn't appear to be anything too serious. What a responsibility it is having all these children to look after on the ice. Thank goodness she's okay. 'Let's go and check you out anyway.'

'Sasha!' The girls all crowd around, some giggling nervously and others wide-eyed and worried. My husband, Theo, gives me a *what on earth have we got ourselves into* look. And I shoot him one right back.

'Can you keep an eye on the rest of them while I take Sasha off the ice for a minute?'

Theo nods. 'Right, come on, you lot, follow me over to Frosty the Snowman. Carefully.'

I help Sasha to her feet and hold her hand as we skate-walk over to the side. My eyes are watering in the frigid evening air as I remove my gloves and then carefully take off Sasha's hat before feeling the back of her head for any lumps and bumps. This is all I need, an injured child on my daughter's birthday. Maybe an ice-skating party wasn't such a good idea. But Georgia was adamant. It's all she's talked about for weeks. Chattering non-stop with excitement.

It's hectic having a December baby, trying to juggle Christmas with her birthday celebrations, but I can't deny that it's always a magical time with everyone in a festive mood. Thankfully, there don't seem to be any bumps on Sasha's head, so I replace her hat and give her hand a squeeze before pulling my gloves back on.

'Can I go back now? I want to see Frosty the Snowman too.' Sasha gazes up at me with a hopeful expression, the tip of her nose red, her eyes glistening. The early evening session we're booked on has cuddly cartoon characters skating around, interacting with the kids. Glancing back across the rink, I smile at the sight of Georgia pulling at the leg of a cartoon dog, trying to get its attention.

I look down at Sasha once more. 'Are you sure you're okay, sweetie? You came down quite a cropper.'

'I'm fine,' she replies, nodding.

I wonder if I should text her mum, Liz. Let her know that Sasha took a tumble. She said she'd be close by, doing some late-night shopping in town. I pull my phone from my pocket, then put it back again. It's an ice-skating party, falling over is all part of the fun, and I don't want to worry Liz for no reason. 'Let's just sit for a minute, Sasha, okay? And then we'll go back out.'

'Okay,' she replies. My daughter's best friend sits obediently next to me on the cold bench, hugging her knees and staring longingly across the rink where our little birthday group is loosely clustered around Theo, who's holding the fort. I hope he can manage them all. The rink is getting busier now, the music louder, the screams of excitement more frantic. It's a real winter wonderland in Bournemouth Gardens, with garlanded trees, decorations and lights strung all the way down to the beach. There's a Christmas market, the Alpine Bar and lots of little stalls selling hot chocolate, warm doughnuts and candyfloss. People come from far and wide during December to enjoy the festivities.

It's nice to be able to catch my breath for a few moments. It's been a crazy-busy day leading up to this evening. You'd think that as an events planner I'd take my daughter's birthday party in my stride. But give me a black-tie corporate event in a posh hotel with two hundred guests over six young children any day of the week.

At the moment, I work for a charity, organising fundraising events such as auctions and fun runs. But as I soak up the atmosphere of the gardens tonight, I'm envious of whoever got to organise such a landmark event. I'd love to sink my teeth into something like this. Or reach my ultimate goal of creating big weekend festivals. Seeing everyone having a great time and knowing I was a part of making that happen.

Sasha tugs my hand. 'Can we go back now, Natalie? I love this song!'

'Yes, just a second.' I look up at the ice rink once again, trying to do a headcount of the girls. There's Cleo, Naomi and Faye, but where are Georgia and my niece, Elle? I can't spot either of them.

I get to my feet, a beat of worry surfacing. Hand in hand, Sasha and I weave in and out of the skaters towards our little group, who are clamouring around a large, fluffy snowman who takes turns spinning the girls around to their delighted squeals.

'Is she okay?' Theo asks.

'Where are Georgia and Elle?'

'They're right he—'

'Mummy!'

My legs are grabbed from behind and I almost topple over. 'Georgia, is that you?' I turn to see my daughter's smiling face. 'Are you with Elle?' I glance behind her. 'Are you having a good time?'

'Awesome!' Georgia turns to her friend. 'Sasha, are you okay?'

'Yes, I'm fi-ine.' Sasha rolls her eyes and then laughs.

'Have you seen your cousin?' I ask again.

'Umm . . .' Georgia glances around and shrugs, shaking her head before taking Sasha's hand and skating off. 'We'll have a look for her!' she calls back to me.

My sister's daughter, Elle, is over a year younger than my own and they're quite different. Georgia is bubbly and outgoing, while Elle is a timid little thing. I wasn't sure tonight would be enjoyable for her, but she's taken to it quite well, holding on to the dolphin-shaped skating aids to keep her balance. I hope she hasn't fallen over.

Theo and I are both scanning the rink now, the skaters seeming to flash past us even faster, blurring before my eyes.

'She's wearing jeans and a pink coat and hat,' I say. 'When did you last see her?'

'She was with me a few minutes ago when you left the ice.' His eyes darken with worry.

'So what happened?' I ask, trying to stay calm. 'Did she skate off? You must have seen her.'

'Umm. I mean, one minute she was here and the next she was . . . I don't know. I was trying to keep track of five girls, and it's busy.'

'I know, but she's younger than the others,' I say, irritated that he didn't realise Elle needs a little more supervision. 'We need to keep a closer eye on her.'

'Sorry, but I was doing my best.' Theo's mouth hardens into a straight line.

I can sense we're about to get snappy with each other, which isn't like us. I know it's simply that we both want Elle to be safe. We're fighting off a creeping panic. 'Well, she must be here somewhere,' I reply briskly, trying to change my tone and reassure myself at the same time. 'Can you skate round and look for her while I stay with the girls?' Theo's a better skater than I am, so it makes sense for him to go.

He nods and takes off around the rink, while I do another headcount of the children, hoping to spot Elle in among them, but there's no sign of her . . .

'Girls,' I say, my voice raised to carry over the music. 'Can you keep an eye out for Elle, please?'

When Theo returns after a few minutes, I've almost convinced myself he's found her, but he's shaking his head. 'I can't see her anywhere.'

'Are you joking? But she was here a few minutes ago.' My gaze sweeps the area once more, taking in the waist-height barriers and the thick crowds of people beyond the rink enjoying the evening festivities. If Elle's not out here on the ice, she could be anywhere. My heart begins to thump uncomfortably and my body grows hot, my mind spinning out. Where is my six-year-old niece? *Where is she?*

Chapter Two

Theo and I take turns scouring the rink for a little girl in pink, but the more I look, the more it seems like every little girl is in a pink coat, and none of them is Elle. We've asked the girls to stick together but to keep an eye out, and they're beginning to get worried. I'm afraid there might be tears soon, and not just theirs.

'Have you lost Elle?' Cleo asks accusingly, her eyes narrowing beneath her white pom-pommed hat. Cleo is the alpha among Georgia's friends and can be quite a bossy little madam. Her accusation has caught me off guard, as if she can see right through to the fear at my core.

I don't answer. Instead, I address all the girls as brightly as I can. 'Okay, first person to spot Elle wins one of those amazing helium balloons.'

Five heads swivel in the direction of the ice-rink café where a balloon seller is flogging ludicrously expensive metallic balloons of Disney characters. This galvanises them into more positive action and distracts them from their fear. Cleo, unsurprisingly, takes charge, shrilling out orders and pointing with a white-gloved finger.

'Any luck?' I ask Theo as he glides back towards us after making four or five laps of the rink. Although it's patently obvious that he hasn't had anything of the sort as he's on his own. I'm glancing wildly around, trying to think of where else she might be.

'I don't understand it.' Theo rips off his beanie and rubs a hand across his dark hair. 'She was with me one minute, and then . . .'

'I'm going to speak to the people in charge,' I say, laying a reassuring hand on his arm. 'Can you stay with the girls?' Before he has a chance to answer, I'm skating over to a bored-looking teenager in a hi-vis vest. 'Excuse me.'

She turns and raises a pierced eyebrow.

'Hi, my six-year-old niece seems to be missing. She was here a minute ago and now she's not on the ice.' Saying this out loud makes my throat constrict. How can this be happening?

'Oh, right.' The girl frowns. 'What's her name? What does she look like?'

'She's called Elle and she's wearing blue jeans, a pink coat and a pink hat. She has brown hair and brown eyes. She's only little. About this high.' My voice cracks as I say the words and hold my hand out to indicate her height.

'Okay.' She nods.

'Okay, *what*?' My tone is stressed but I'm too upset to modify it.

She pulls a radio from a clip on her belt and holds her finger out to shush me while she speaks into it. 'Hey, Ant, we've got a lost six-year-old girl called . . .' She raises her eyebrow again.

'Elle,' I repeat.

'. . . called Elle. Wearing jeans and a pink coat and hat. Apparently, she was on the ice a few minutes ago, but now her mum can't find her, okay?'

'I'm her aunt, but that doesn't matter, what are you . . . who are you talking to?' I ask, stumbling over my words.

'I've told my boss. He'll put it out on the tannoy. Get the public to look out for her, okay? Get them to come forward if they've seen her. He'll tell all the staff too. We'll find her.'

'This can't be happening,' I mutter.

'Don't worry, kids get separated from their parents all the time, but they always turn up. Have you tried the café or the toilets?'

'No. Of course, I'm so silly, she must be in the loos. I'll go and check.' Relief courses through me at such an obvious answer. She went to the toilet but forgot to let us know. I push away the thought that Elle wouldn't have gone on her own. That she's far too clingy for that. She never strays. Unlike my daughter, who's always wandering off. For now, I'll allow myself the luxury of hope. Because the alternative is too scary to contemplate.

'Let me know if you find her so I can tell my boss,' the girl says with a worried smile. 'Give me your number then we can call you if someone else finds her first. My name's Jenna.' She taps the name badge on her vest.

'Okay, thanks, Jenna. That's a good idea.' I give her my details and then head to the bench, where I start removing my skates with trembling fingers. She said that they always turn up. So it'll be fine. She'll be around here somewhere. She has to be.

Theo appears in front of me. 'What did she say?'

'Hang on. Listen . . .' I point towards the speaker as the music suddenly cuts out and a man's voice starts describing Elle. Saying how she's lost. Telling members of the public that if they spot her, they should bring her to the entrance of the skating rink.

The announcement comes to an end and Kelly Clarkson's 'Underneath the Tree' resumes, blasting out across the rink. It seems wrong to play such an upbeat tune while Elle is missing. Like the interruption was an inconvenience. As if Elle's disappearance isn't as important as everyone else having a good time.

'This is a nightmare,' Theo says. 'We can't leave the others, but we have to find her. What are we going to do? I mean, should we . . . call the police?'

I swallow and take a breath, trying to clear my brain. 'I'll get my boots and check the toilets and surrounding area. She can't have gone far.' I daren't voice the horrible thought that she might not be lost, that she might have been taken by someone. Surely I'm panicking over nothing, and we'll find Elle in the next few minutes. But my heartbeats have started clattering wildly out of control and I think I might be sick. Where *is* she? Should I call my sister? What will she say?

Jo and her friends have gone into town for a night out. How can I tell her that I've lost her daughter? Sweet little Elle. But I'm getting ahead of myself. Of course we're going to find her. Of course we are.

I get to my feet and plant a kiss on Theo's lips. 'See you in a bit. Keep in touch on your mobile.'

'What shall I tell the girls?' Theo asks, trying to sound stoic, but his eyes are unable to hide his growing concern. I hate seeing him like this.

'I don't want to freak them out. Just . . . tell them that we need to find her, but that it'll be fine and she's . . . just a bit lost!' I screech the last bit.

'Hey, hey, we'll find her, okay. Of course we will,' Theo says, his resolve strengthening in the face of my panic. 'Like you said before, she won't have got very far.'

'What if—'

'Shh, we're going to find her.' But Theo's face is taut, his eyes as disbelieving as mine at the situation we're in. 'Go,' he adds. 'I'll keep looking here.'

'Check behind the barriers. Maybe she . . . I don't know . . . fell over the side or something.' But the barriers are crowded with spectators. Surely someone would have seen my niece if she had fallen. 'Theo, ask the people watching if they've seen her. They might not have been paying attention to the tannoy, but they might have noticed a girl in a pink coat.'

'Okay, I will. You go check the toilets.' I think we're both relieved to have a plan of sorts.

On shaky legs, I head to the exit to exchange my skates for my boots. I pull them on with numb fingers, constantly glancing around, looking for a little pink coat in the crowd. In the hope that any second now Elle will burst out of the crowds, running towards me in tears because she couldn't find us. But she's not here.

Of course, there's a million-mile queue for the toilets, but I don't have time for etiquette, so I walk straight in, ignoring the mutters of protest.

'Elle!' I call out. 'Elle! Are you in here?' I bang on each of the cubicles in turn. I'm desperate to hear her voice calling out to me. Desperate to hear her cry *Aunty Natalie*.

An older woman with short grey hair, snowflake earrings and a Christmas jumper taps me on the shoulder. 'Are you the mum of the little girl who's gone missing? I heard it announced on the loudspeaker just now.'

'I'm her aunt,' I squeak out. Everyone is looking at me now. I clear my voice and speak up to make myself heard over the whoosh of hand dryers and piped music. 'If anyone sees a little girl with brown hair in a pink coat and hat, can you please bring her to a member of staff here?'

A teenager exits one of the cubicles and her gaze lands on me as I finish making my announcement. 'I think I saw that girl.'

Hope swells in my chest. 'You did? Where?'

'She was on the ice with a cartoon dog. The big brown-and-white one.'

'She was?' I grab her arm, desperate. 'When was this?'

'Um, not long ago, maybe ten minutes or so. I can't remember exactly. But she was really cute. Giggling and stuff.'

'Whereabouts on the ice?' I realise I'm rattling off questions like machine-gun fire, but I can't help it. I need to find my niece.

'Um. Just skating around, I guess.'

'Near the barrier?'

'I can't remember exactly. I only caught a glimpse, you know.'

I nod, relieved that someone saw Elle, but worried that she's still not been found. 'Okay, thanks.'

'We'll all look out for her. I'll tell my friends.'

I realise I'm still holding on to her sleeve and let go, blinking back tears at the reality of the situation. At the fear that my niece is actually missing right now, and strangers are offering to look for her. I *have* to find that cartoon dog. 'Thank you,' I gasp before tearing out of the loos and racing back to the edge of the rink.

I scan the ice for the cartoon dog. I can see a snowman, two elves, a Santa Claus, and a reindeer. But no dog. I head over to Jenna again.

'Did you find her already?' she asks with a hopeful smile.

I shake my head. 'No, but do you have a cartoon dog on the ice?'

'A dog?' She frowns. 'No. It's all Christmas-themed characters today. No dog, sorry.'

'Someone saw Elle skating with a brown-and-white dog earlier. I need to speak to the person in the dog costume.'

'Are you sure it wasn't a reindeer? Look.' Jenna points to the far end of the rink. 'It's brown, so maybe they got confused.'

I shake my head. 'I don't know. But I'm sure I also saw my daughter with the dog earlier. It definitely wasn't that reindeer. Maybe I should go back and ask the teenager in the loo, if she's even still there.' I'm trying desperately not to give in to the mounting panic in my brain. I don't know what to do for the best. Where to look, who to talk to, what to *do*! 'This is a nightmare,' I mutter. 'Where is she?'

'Um, let's talk to Charlene,' Jenna replies, looking disconcerted by my freak-out. 'She's the one in the reindeer costume tonight. Maybe she remembers.'

Theo spots me and skates over with the rest of the girls. I pull him aside and fill him in on what the teen in the loos said about Elle skating with a dog character, but Theo says that doesn't ring any bells.

'Georgia . . .' I crouch down and lay a reassuring hand on my daughter's shoulder, trying not to convey any of the fear I'm feeling. 'Do you remember skating with a big brown-and-white dog earlier?'

'Umm . . .' She frowns, and then scowls. 'Yes. I tried to catch up to it, but it just skated away. It wasn't a very friendly dog. Not like the other characters.'

'Did Elle skate with it?' I ask.

'I don't know.'

'Girls!' I clap my hands to get their attention. 'Did any of you see a brown-and-white dog character skating with Elle?' I don't even know how I'm managing to talk normally. My chest is tight and I can barely breathe.

Georgia's friends all stare at me blankly, shaking their heads.

Theo and I talk to Charlene – aka the reindeer – next, and to all the other characters one by one as they skate over to us, removing their cartoon heads to reveal hot, sweaty faces. But they all say the same thing – that none of them remember seeing Elle. Although Charlene says she does recall seeing the dog briefly and wondering at the time why no one told her they had a new character on the ice.

'Theo?' I beg, growing more and more panicky, wanting to believe that he must have the answer, that I'm not alone in this. 'Please just think if you might have seen the dog with Elle?'

'I already said I didn't,' he replies, his tone letting me know that he too is at his limit, that he's as desperate as I am. 'I mean, it's not something you'd forget, is it? A bloody huge dog skating around.'

I push my gloved fingers into my forehead, trying to make sense of what's happening, and what I need to do in order to find my niece as quickly as possible. But my brain feels impossibly slow.

'I want to find her as much as you do,' he adds, his eyes imploring me to fix this, just as mine are reflected back at him. Right now, we're both drowning in dread and anxiety, hoping the other has the answer.

'Jenna,' I say, fixing the ice-rink employee with a pleading stare. 'Are you absolutely one hundred per cent sure you don't have a dog character? Maybe it's new and no one told you.'

'I know everyone who works here, and I know all the costumes. We definitely don't have a dog character.' She looks at me pityingly.

'So who was in that costume?' I ask, my stomach dropping.

'I'm sorry, I don't know.'

Chapter Three

It's been thirty minutes since Elle went missing on the ice, and fifteen minutes since we had to abandon Georgia's birthday party early. We were all supposed to go for a pizza afterwards, but of course that's out of the question now.

I leave my sister a voicemail, trying to convey my urgency without telling her exactly what's happened. It's not the kind of information I can leave in a message. Jo isn't good at handling stress. I've already sent her a couple of texts and WhatsApps to contact me asap, but they're all still sitting there unread. I don't even know which pub or bar she's gone to. I've texted her best friend, Ollie, but there's no reply from him either. I just wish she'd look at her messages. I've also messaged the other mums and asked them to do an early pick-up.

On the one hand, I desperately want Jo to call me, but on the other, I want to have found Elle first. I want to be able to leave another voicemail for Jo saying *Don't worry, ignore my message.*

Theo's waiting with the girls while I tear through the lower gardens shoving Elle's photo in front of the staff in the food concessions and to other random people, asking if they've seen her or the cartoon dog, but no one has. I reach the edge of the gardens and make my way across the road, past the taxi rank and up through the town. It doesn't help that the place is packed solid with visitors and shoppers dawdling along with friends and family, enjoying the lights and the Christmas stalls. I weave around thick clusters of them as they laugh and gossip, clutching shopping bags, cups of mulled wine and bags of roasted chestnuts.

As I battle through the festive crowds, I don't feel like I'm even here. My heart rate has gone supersonic and a cold sweat blankets my body. To top it off, it's started snowing – something that would have been magical for Georgia's party, but now makes me worry for Elle. What if she's lying somewhere, freezing and hurt? Everyone seems to be pointing at the whirling flakes, smiling in wonder at this rare event. As a southern seaside town, we hardly ever see snow. But to me it's a distraction, making it even harder to look for my niece.

I keep showing Elle's photo to the stallholders, hoping each time that someone will have seen her. But always the answer is *No, sorry.* I gabble at them to call the police if they spot her. To please keep an eye out. My vision blurs under the bright lights as I duck into a few shops, scanning, scanning, scanning for her pink coat. But she's not in any of them. Next, I make my way to the main square and into the heaving Alpine Bar. After a quick scout around, I'm pretty certain she's not in here either.

Am I wasting my time doing this? I feel like she's not going to be anywhere. I check my phone but there are no messages. My pulse races with anxiety and my head swims. Maybe I should have headed down to the seafront rather than the town? What if I'm searching in completely the wrong place?

I step back into the main square and stop to catch my breath, hands on my hips, bent over at the waist, trying not to lose it. I need to calm myself. Freaking out isn't going to help Elle. I need to be logical. To think where she might be. Would she really have wandered off this far? Unless she truly did get lost and can't find her way back to the skating rink. *She could be freaking anywhere!*

This is no good. I think I'm too far away from the ice rink. I decide to retrace my steps and head back to where Theo and the girls are waiting. Jogging there, thankful the ground is not yet icy as wet snowflakes fly into my face. I cast my gaze left and right, praying to spot my niece, wishing for this nightmare to be over. But all too soon I spot my husband and his disappointed expression, mirroring my own. The girls are huddled together next to him, sipping from cardboard cups as they wait for their parents to collect them.

'Mummy!' Georgia cries, stumbling over to me and wrapping her arms around my legs as though she hasn't seen me for days. Usually, she wouldn't dream of calling me something as babyish as 'Mummy' in front of her friends. But none of these seven- and eight-year-olds are feeling very grown-up this evening. They're all in shock.

'Are you okay, sweetie?'

'Where's Elle? Is she going to be okay?'

I crouch down and straighten her hat, pushing a wisp of hair out of her eye. 'Don't worry, we're going to find her. She's wandered off and got lost, that's all. Like you did that time at Legoland – remember?'

'Oh, yes. That was scary. I lost you in the gift shop, but then Daddy bought me a yellow foam sword and we had a play fight. Maybe we could buy one for Elle when we find her. Or she could have mine because I don't play with it anymore.'

'That's really kind of you, Georgia. I'm sure she'd absolutely love that.' We walk the few steps back to our little group and I check on each of the girls to see if they're okay. They're dispirited; even the whirling snowflakes don't get a mention from any of them.

'Nothing then?' Theo asks quietly as I shake my head in response. 'I bought the girls hot chocolates. They were getting cold.

Here's a coffee.' He hands me a cardboard cup. I don't feel like drinking it, but at least it's warming up my hands.

'Thanks. I need to call the police, don't I?'

'I think so, yeah.'

We stare at one another in shared horror at what's unfolding. As I press 999 I feel like I'm having an out-of-body experience. I wish I'd called them earlier, but I was so sure we'd find her. So sure we wouldn't have to do anything as drastic as calling the authorities. The man on the switchboard tells me to wait at the rink and they'll send a couple of officers to talk to us. I hate to call the police before telling Jo what's happened, but what choice do I have? It could be hours before she gets in contact.

Theo swigs the last of his drink, crushes the cup and tosses it into the bin. 'Maybe I should go looking next?' he says. 'I'll head down to the beach.'

'There are some more Christmas trees and decorations that way. Maybe she went to take a look at them,' I say, but I don't feel convinced.

'Okay. Message me when the police get here.' He gives me a quick kiss and jogs away towards the seafront, stopping periodically to speak to people.

Now it's me standing with the girls, waiting for the police to arrive. I'm sure I can hear the wail of a police siren in the distance, but surely it's too soon for them to have got here. I step away from the children to leave yet another frantic voicemail for my sister, exhaling clouds of air into the frigid night, stuttering out my words into the phone.

The siren is growing louder, and my heart gives a jolt when I see a squad car slowly blue-lighting along the pedestrianised path, the crowds peeling off to the sides as it approaches, the siren more intermittent now. It comes to a halt outside the ice rink and all eyes are glued to it, a momentary hush falling over the gardens before the crowd noise starts up again.

I realise my heart is banging against my ribcage. Is this really happening? I suddenly feel as though I've overreacted by calling the police, and that Theo is about to show up holding Elle's hand and we'll feel guilty for wasting police time. *Please, God, let that be the case.* I glance down towards the pier to see if I can spot him, but the crowd is too thick.

Two uniformed male officers exit the car. They look so official in their dark clothes and heavy shoes, their hats and hi-vis coats. People move aside for them as they approach the rink entrance, and I notice a woman in jeans and a bomber jacket get out of the car and walk over with them. I look towards the pier again to see if I can spot Theo, but he's out of sight. I quickly text to let him know the police have arrived and then I raise a hand to the officers as they approach.

The girls look up at the officers, wide-eyed and nervous. Georgia sidles closer to me again and takes my hand.

'Natalie Edwards?' the plain-clothes female officer asks.

'Yes,' I reply thickly, feeling like I'm in one of those TV police dramas. Their arrival does nothing to quell my bubbling fear. It does the exact opposite. The police means that this is serious.

Chapter Four

I shiver and stamp my feet, taking a sip of lukewarm coffee as I look at the police officers. The woman is about my age, tall – well, taller than me anyway, which isn't hard – with red hair pulled back into a low ponytail. Her colleagues are male, one older and one much younger.

'My name is Detective Sergeant Lucy Gilligan. You reported your six-year-old niece missing, is that correct?'

I swallow. 'Yes.'

'I'm so sorry, that must be worrying for you. Could you tell me the last time you saw her, and when you first noticed she was missing.'

I tell her and her male colleagues everything as best as I can remember, including the sightings of Elle with the brown-and-white dog character. One of the male officers is taking notes, both of them highly focused on what I'm saying.

'And you said you were here with your husband,' the DS says. 'Where is he now?'

'We've been taking it in turns to search the area. He's just gone down to the beach and pier. But one of us has to stay with the girls until their parents arrive.'

'Okay, that's good. Have you asked the ice-rink staff to check their security cameras?'

'Oh, no, I definitely should have done that!' I curse my stupidity.

'Don't worry, we'll speak to them, and we'll check the council CCTV along with the beach webcams.'

I exhale heavily. It sounds so scary, but it's also reassuring to have proper help.

'Can you give me a good description of Elle and what she's wearing this evening?'

I start describing my niece, and notice that as I'm talking the male officers are both speaking into their radios, relaying and receiving information. I take my phone from my pocket and pull up a photo. 'Here's a picture I took of my daughter and Elle this evening when we first arrived.' I pass my phone to the officers with trembling fingers, a stab of emotion constricting my throat and stinging my eyes at the sight of my sweet, smiling niece.

'Can I take a copy of this?' the DS asks. I nod and the younger male officer snaps a picture with his mobile before handing my phone back. 'What did this dog character look like?'

I think back to when I saw Georgia skating after it, pulling at its leg to try to get its attention. Could it really be something to do with Elle's disappearance? Or is it just a coincidence? Someone in fancy dress just innocently skating around? 'Like I said, it was brown and white, a full head-to-toe costume, it looked a bit like a beagle with floppy ears. But it wasn't expensive-looking like the other characters. If you look . . .' I turn and point at the ice rink. '. . . they're all big, fluffy, heavy-duty costumes. But the dog suit looked cheap. I think it was thinner material rather than thick fur. A zip-up costume. Like you could see that there was a person inside.'

'Could you tell if it was male or female?'

'No. I only really caught a glimpse.'

The younger uniformed officer is still relaying the information into his radio and it all sounds pretty frantic. The other officer has headed into the ice-rink entrance and is now talking to one of the staff members.

'Can you help us find her?' I ask the DS, my voice shaky. 'It's been almost an hour now.'

'An hour? Okay, my colleagues are on it. We'll get POLSAR down here asap, and—'

'POLSAR, what's that?'

'Sorry.' The DS shakes her head. 'Search and Rescue. They'll do a thorough search. If she's here, we'll find her. We'll also bring the sniffer dogs to try to pick up Elle's scent.'

I feel woozy at the talk of sniffer dogs. This isn't real life. What's happening? Everything seems to be receding – my hearing, my vision, it's like someone's just turned off the TV.

'Natalie? Natalie, are you okay? Would you like to sit down for a bit? There's a bench over there.' The DS places a hand on my upper arm, but I'm suddenly conscious of the girls staring at me and I don't want them to be even more alarmed than they already are. The last thing they need is to see me fainting. I inhale deeply and feel my faculties returning.

'No, no, I'm fine. Honestly.' I glance around to see if Theo might be on his way back now that the police are here, but there's no sign of him. Why isn't he back? He must have seen my message by now.

'These are all precautions,' she continues. 'Nine times out of ten, the child is simply hiding. We're going to do everything we can to find Elle, okay? If the weather conditions allow, we'll also deploy the search helicopter, but with this snowfall, visibility is quite poor, so I can't guarantee it. Where are her parents?'

I explain that I've been trying to get hold of my sister, who's a single mum, but she's currently out with friends. The thought of

23

telling Jo what's happened makes my chest tighten in horror. How can I tell her that I've lost her daughter? That she's disappeared on my watch?

'And the father?' the DS asks.

'Out of the picture,' I reply. 'Jo doesn't know who it is.' I don't know why I let that last part slip out. I'm not thinking straight.

The officer nods, keeping her expression neutral. 'Okay, we'll also need to have a word with your daughter and her friends.'

As she's speaking, I see Cleo's dad and stepmum rushing along the path towards us.

'Dad!' Cleo races towards them and her dad picks her up in his arms. I can hear him asking her a dozen questions at once while she attempts to answer them between gasping sobs.

Her stepmum comes up to me and gives me a hug. I don't know her very well, but she seems quite nice, and it honestly feels so good to have someone hold me even for this brief second. 'I'm Rachel. We came as quick as we could. We're dropping Naomi and Faye back home too,' she says, giving each girl a little reassuring smile before turning her gaze back to mine. 'No luck finding your niece?'

I shake my head. 'Not yet.'

'We need a word with the girls before you leave,' the DS reiterates in an official tone.

'Of course,' Rachel replies before giving me a supportive squeeze on the arm.

She and the two officers move away down the path with the girls to get their stories. Now it's just me, Georgia and Sasha standing together. I put an arm around each of them and rub their backs to warm them. Theo's been gone a while. I better text him again or, better yet, call him. I really need him here with me right now. *Why isn't he back yet?*

As I unlock my phone to text him, it rings and I see that it's Jo calling. A mixture of relief and terror floods me as I slide to answer.

'Hey, sis, what's happened?' Jo's shouting into the phone to be heard over the background noise – music, shouting, laughter. She must be in a bar.

'Jo, where have you been? I've been trying to get hold of you.'

'I'm in the pub. Only just saw your messages. Are you okay? What's going on?'

I start to speak, but I can hear her talking to someone else. 'Jo! Jo, are you listening?'

'Sorry, just getting my drink at the bar. Go on . . .'

'Can you come down to the ice rink?' I ask, unable to tell her about Elle right now. Maybe I'm hoping that by the time Jo gets here, we'll have found her. Or maybe I'm just delaying the horror. I tell myself it's because it's not the kind of thing I want to tell her over the phone. That it's better doing it face to face, where I can comfort her and answer all her inevitable questions. 'Whereabouts are you?'

'You want me to come *now*? I'm up at the Triangle. You haven't fallen over, have you? I told you you were mad to go ice-skating, you've always had crap co-ordination.'

'Jo, just get here now, will you?'

'Blimey, all right. Is Elle okay? Is it Georgia?'

'I'll tell you when you get here.'

There's a pause at the other end, and then her voice changes from light and breezy to more worried. 'You're scaring me, Nat. Just tell me what's going on.'

I can't tell her this on the phone. 'You're breaking up,' I lie. 'Just get down here, Jo. The entrance to the ice rink.'

'Fine. I'm on my way.' She ends the call.

My hands are shaking and I suddenly feel faint. If anything happens to Elle, Jo will never forgive me. I'll never forgive myself.

'Natalie, you poor thing, what can I do to help?' I glance up from my phone to see that Sasha's mum, Liz, has arrived. It seems like days since I last saw my friend, but it was only just over an hour ago that she dropped Sasha and a couple of the other girls off at the party. She gives me a brief, warm hug and then bends to hug Georgia and Sasha, who flings her arms around her mum. 'I couldn't believe it when I saw your message. Shall I take Georgia so you can concentrate on finding Elle?'

'Oh, Liz, would you? That would be so helpful. This is all . . .' I lower my voice and turn away from the girls for a moment. 'I need to find Elle, but it's Georgia's birthday and I don't want her to . . . I can't—'

'I know, Nat. Don't worry. I'll keep Georgia calm, take her back to mine. She can stay the night, unless I hear otherwise from you, okay?'

I swipe a hot tear from my cheek. 'Thanks, Liz. You're a lifesaver.' Liz and Steve live in the next road to us in Southbourne so it will be easy to bring Georgia home if she gets too upset.

'No need to thank me. Call if you need anything else. Steve is at home, so I can send him out looking for Elle too if you like?'

'Thanks, I'll let you know. The police will need to talk to Georgia and Sasha before you go.' I indicate down the path to where DS Gilligan and the younger officer are currently talking to the other girls.

'Fine, no problem. Where's Theo?' she asks, glancing around.

'He's gone down to the beach to look for Elle. But he's been gone ages.' I throw my hands up. 'It's impossible. There are too many places where she could be. I mean, we don't even know if she's still in the area. If she's on her own or if she might have been taken—'

'Don't even think that. Kids get lost all the time and they always turn up.'

'I know,' I reply with a gulp. 'You're right.'

'Where's Jo?' Liz asks. 'She must be beside herself.'

'She was out with friends. She's on her way here now.' I clench my hands and bring them up to my mouth. As a single mum, it's been tough for Jo raising Elle alone in her little rented flat. With the girls so close in age it's logical for Theo and me to help out, sharing school pick-ups and having Elle for dinners, outings and sleepovers as Jo works shifts so it's tricky for her to have a regular routine. As it's Georgia's birthday, I was happy for Jo to take some time for herself this evening. To go and have fun. I said I'd bring Elle to the party and keep her with us overnight. But look how that's turned out. I've gone and lost her daughter. I can't believe this is happening. 'What am I going to do?' I whisper.

'They'll find her,' Liz says briskly. 'She probably just wandered off. It's so busy tonight. So easy to get lost. Either the police will find her, or someone else will and they'll take her to the police station.'

'I know, I know. You're right.' I nod several times, hoping that by the time my sister gets down here, we'll have Elle back safe and sound. 'The DS said that most kids in this situation are hiding.'

'Well, there you go!' Liz replies.

I force out a panicked smile, even though I know that hiding doesn't sound like something Elle would do. We join the police, who are asking all the girls the same questions they asked me and taking everyone's details.

Then, in a whirl of hugs and goodbyes, Liz takes Georgia and Sasha off with her, expertly calming them down, telling them everything will be all right and that Elle, the silly sausage, has got herself lost, but the police will find her soon and everything will be fine.

I'm just about to call Theo again when he finally arrives back by my side, without Elle.

'Where have you been?' I gasp.

'Looking for Elle.' He sounds a bit put out by my tone.

'You were gone ages.'

'Yeah, well, it's a big beach.'

'Don't be like that, you know what I mean. I messaged you ages ago to say the police are here and I've had to talk to them on my own while looking after the kids and I'm freaking out!' I feel a tear slip down my cheek.

'Hey.' Theo puts an arm around me and kisses the side of my head. 'I'm back now, okay? And we'll find her. Don't worry.'

'Why were you so long?'

'Because I wanted to find her. She loves the beach, so I was sure I'd see her sitting on the sand, or on the steps of one of the beach huts. A couple of times I thought I did, but it was just shadows.'

'The police will want to speak to you now. DS Lucy Gilligan seems to be the one in charge.'

'Fine.' Theo's expression clouds over.

Part of me wonders if he delayed coming back on purpose because he doesn't want to talk to the police. My husband is a respectable guy with a good career as a sales manager for a sportswear company. But he's got a bit of a past. Just after we met at university, when he was only twenty, he was arrested for dealing marijuana. He was completely innocent, just had some on him for personal use, but he got some terrible legal advice and ended up getting tried in a higher court where the judge made an example of him, sentencing him to twelve months in prison. So, he wound up with a criminal record and was unable to finish his degree in sports psychology.

I suppose he could have continued with his studies somehow, but it just never happened. He's since worked his way up in sales and enjoys his job, but I know there's always that little bit of *what if?* Consequently, he's always been nervous and distrustful around the police, and I occasionally see glimpses of his past in his rejection of authority. Not that I blame him, because that was a horrible time in his life. In both our lives. All those police interviews and nights of not sleeping due to stress. His solicitor had assured him he wouldn't get a custodial sentence, so when the judge ruled, it was a massive shock. I visited him in prison every week, and we never told anyone in my family about it. He was mortified, and didn't want people treating him any differently.

Despite all that, Theo is normally the one who jollies everyone along. He's the cheeky chappy, life and soul of the party. The person who will take control in a crisis. But that hasn't happened this time. Right now, he's gone quiet. Aside from having to deal with the police, I know he must feel terrible that he was the one on the ice looking after the girls when Elle went missing, but I can't reassure him that he's not to blame. Not without sounding like I do blame him. Which, of course, I don't. I wish I hadn't snapped at him earlier. I take his hand for a moment instead, trying to convey that I'm here for him, that it's not his fault.

Moments later, a couple of the officers come over to interview Theo, and he tells them what happened. But I can see his discomfort in the way he glowers and responds defensively to their questioning.

It feels like a waste of time anyway, because their questions have uncovered nothing new. No one saw Elle walking away from the rink. The only suspicious link in all of this is the person in the dog suit. Did *they* take my niece? Who was inside that costume? And, more importantly, where are they now?

Chapter Five

At an opportune moment, you skate over to the furthest corner of the ice rink, away from the lights and behind the crowds. You lean over the barrier to retrieve the backpack you stashed there earlier. You have to do this quickly, before anyone notices she's missing. You shield her from prying eyes and tell her that she's won a prize — a black puffer coat, the same as all the big kids wear, and a fluffy white hat with sparkles. You draw them out from the backpack to show her.

Her face lights up, but then she immediately frowns. What about her pink hat and coat? She loves them. They're her favourites. You tell her not to worry. You'll keep them safe. For now, she can wear the special new ones.

This is a tricky moment. Will she accept the new clothes?

You exhale as she nods and sheds her hat and coat, replacing them with her new ones.

You swiftly remove your cartoon dog head and jam on a baseball cap. It feels good to get some cold air on your cheeks, but you feel exposed. She looks up at your face in surprise. As though she never realised you were a person rather than a cartoon dog.

Next, you leap the barrier and lift her over too. Now you set about removing both sets of skates and hand her a pair of pink trainers. All the while, you talk about how her family are going to be so excited when they see her dressed in her new coat and hat and trainers. You slip out of the dog costume, roll it up and stuff it into the backpack along with her discarded hat and coat. You slip both pairs of skates into a thick plastic bag. Now you hand her a plastic bottle of cola. She takes a few sips. And then some more.

You're all smiles, but in reality you're sweating, your heart beating too fast despite the fact that it's going well. It's all going to plan. For now, at least.

Chapter Six

Two more squad cars show up and the area is suddenly flooded with uniforms. I stand in the gardens watching the skaters leave the ice rink early. It's a slow process as each of them is interviewed by an officer as they depart. The music has been switched off and the atmosphere is hushed and strange despite the chattering crowds. A police cordon has been erected around the whole area, the adjoining café included. As families, couples and teenagers trickle out through the exit, I see parents hug their children tightly, kissing their cheeks, and I catch snatches of conversations: 'It's about that girl who went missing.' . . . 'Apparently she's wearing a pink coat.' . . . 'Look at all the police!' . . . 'They think someone took her.' . . . 'Do you think they'll reopen it this evening?' . . . 'Will we get a refund?'

Theo squeezes my hand, but he doesn't say anything. We're both beyond issuing each other platitudes. We just need Elle to be found. Now that the police have interviewed Theo, he's going to have another search around while I wait for Jo. She should be here any minute and I'm dreading giving her the news.

'I'll try along Westover Road and up past the Royal Bath this time,' Theo says, rubbing at his dark-stubbled chin. 'Unless you want me to stay with you while you tell Jo?'

'No, that's okay. It's better if you keep looking.' Tempting as it is to have Theo with me when I break the news, it will be better if I do it on my own. Jo and Theo aren't each other's biggest fans.

'Okay, no problem. Shall I message some of our friends to come down and help search?'

'Umm.' The thought of messaging everyone else to tell them about Elle is terrible. It makes it more real somehow. But it makes sense to do it.

'Nat?'

'Sorry, yes, that's a good idea. I'll do the same. Liz said she'd ask Steve, so I'll follow that up. Let Liz know we're still searching. The more people we have down here, the more chance . . .' I tail off.

Theo knows better than to hug me right now. I need to be strong, and his sympathy will undo me. Instead, he says, 'Don't forget, the police are out in force now too, and all those skaters and spectators will have heard the tannoy announcement.'

I take a fortifying breath of cold air, watching the officers interviewing the ice-rink staff in the café and checking CCTV. Surely someone will have seen something. Or they'll spot her on the cameras. 'Okay, you go,' I say to Theo. 'I'll let you know when Jo gets here.'

We both glance skyward at the sound of a helicopter drawing closer. The snow has eased off now and there are patches of clear black sky above, dotted with icy stars. I realise the temperature is plummeting fast.

'That must be the police chopper,' Theo says, as its wide-beamed searchlight sweeps the ground below. 'If anyone can find Elle, they can. Thank goodness she's wearing that pink coat and hat. She'll be easy to spot.'

'You're right,' I reply, my spirits lifting a little, imagining the beam locating Elle, illuminating her before the officers swoop in to bring her back to us. It's been over an hour now, but it already feels like days.

'Okay, see you in a bit.' He shoots me a hopeful smile.

'Be careful,' I call after him as he strides away. 'The pavements are icing over.' He waves back in acknowledgement.

I turn away and fix my gaze on the path that leads here from town, and within minutes I spot the blonde-haired figure of my sister dressed for a night out in a tight blue dress and a short faux-fur coat. She's unsteady on her feet, but I can't tell if that's from her towering heels, the icy path, or because she's already had a skinful.

'Hey, Nat. What the hell's going on? Is that the police? It was a nightmare walking down here in these shoes. My feet are freezing.'

'Jo, I don't want you to panic.'

She stops in front of me and tenses up. One of her false eyelashes has come away at the corner and it's flapping ever so slightly. I want to push it back in place, but I know she'll only slap my hand away. I should probably get her to sit down, but other than a snow-covered bench, there's nowhere. And I don't want to go into the café right now, where the staff are being interviewed. So I take her hand instead.

'Nat, you're scaring me. What's going on? Where are the girls? Where's Elle?'

'Jo, we were all skating, having a great time, but Sasha slipped on the ice so I brought her to the side to check her over. She was fine, but when I got back on the rink I couldn't spot Elle.'

'Wasn't Theo with her?' Jo asks.

'Yes, he was with the five of them, but apparently Elle skated off with this cartoon dog and—'

'Skated off? What do you mean, skated off? Like she's gone off with a cartoon *dog*?' Jo yanks her hand out of mine and folds her arms across her chest.

'I don't know,' I say desperately, trying to keep my voice even as my palms begin to sweat. 'All we know is that she's missing.'

'Elle's gone missing? My Elle?' She starts glancing frantically around. 'So all these cops are here for—'

'For Elle, yes.' I gulp and try my very hardest not to cry.

'You're joking, right? You've lost my six-year-old daughter? How long has she been gone?' Jo's voice is growing icier with every word.

'Um, it's been just over an hour.' I've never seen my sister like this before, and it scares me.

'I don't believe this.' She paces away and then walks back, her eyes blazing. 'The one night out I've had in ages, and you've lost my daughter!'

I don't reply. What can I say? My mind skitters over *the one night out I've had in ages* part, but the rest of it is true. I did lose her daughter. And I feel sick to my stomach about it.

'What do the police say?' she adds, looking up as the helicopter does another sweep. 'And that?' She points up at the sky. 'Is that for Elle too?'

I nod wretchedly.

'Who's in charge of the search? Which officer do I need to speak to?'

'There's a new one arrived a few minutes ago. A detective inspector. That's him. Sorry, I can't remember his name, but he said he's the investigating officer.' I point to a man in his forties wearing black jeans, a thick navy bomber jacket and a navy beanie. He's currently standing at the far edge of the ice rink with a few officers wearing hi-vis jackets. I take off after Jo, who's crossed the police cordon and is striding towards him.

'Hey!' the DI calls out. 'Get back behind the line. You're contaminating the scene.'

'I'm Elle's mother!' Jo yells back.

He nods and motions that she should go back, that he'll come and talk to her.

Jo is normally quite passive when it comes to doing anything. I'm usually the one who takes charge, organises and makes suggestions, but in this moment, since Jo's arrived, we seem to have switched roles. Guilt and fear have obliterated my confidence.

Jo turns and walks back towards me, trying to stop her heels sinking into the slushy grass. She's shivering violently.

'Put these on.' I press my hat and gloves into her hands and she accepts them wordlessly, as the detective inspector joins us.

'I'm Detective Inspector Tim Brady. You're Elle's mother?' He sounds very serious and there isn't much warmth to his tone, unlike DS Gilligan's. But I don't care about his manner. All I want is for him to find my niece.

She nods. 'I'm Jo Warren, I've just found out my daughter's missing. What's happening?'

'Look, I don't want to alarm you, but we've just found ice-skate imprints in an area of mud outside the security barriers. One set of prints is child-sized, the other adult-sized. While it doesn't necessarily mean the smaller prints are Elle's, we're getting the dogs down to see if they can pick up a scent.'

'Oh my God.' Jo's knees give way and the detective and I grab an arm each, keeping her upright. I hug her to me and she gives in for a second before shaking me off. 'Did you find anything on the CCTV?' she asks DI Brady.

'Not yet, but my officers are looking. Unfortunately, the area where we found the prints is a blind spot for the security cameras.'

I don't want to voice the thought that maybe if somebody did take Elle, they chose that spot on purpose, knowing they wouldn't be seen on camera.

Jo is standing unaided once more, having pulled her arm from mine, but her face is grey and she's still shivering. She looks like death, and I'm not surprised. I think she's in shock. We both are.

'I recommend you go into the café for the moment. It's below freezing out here, and you'll be no good to anyone if you get hypothermia,' the DI says.

'I don't want to sit in a café, I want to find my daughter,' Jo retorts.

'Of course, and we're going to do everything in our power to get her back for you as soon as possible. I understand you've already met DS Lucy Gilligan?' He waves her over from where she's standing by a newly arrived police van, talking to an officer. She nods and starts to make her way over.

'I've already spoken to the DS,' I reply. 'But Jo hasn't met her yet.'

'Lucy, this is Jo Warren,' DI Brady says. 'Elle's mother.'

'Hello,' she says to Jo. 'I'm DS Lucy Gilligan, but please do call me Lucy. I'm going to be your family's liaison officer, which means I'll keep you updated with everything that's happening with the investigation. I'll be your point of contact, okay?' She sounds much friendlier than she did before. I don't know if that's good or bad.

'Okay,' Jo replies, and suddenly she looks so small, so young, like the fight has gone out of her as the realisation of what's happened dawns. I can't believe I lost my niece. My whole body is freezing, but at the same time, I'm numb. It's as though I know I'm cold, but I'm not registering it. I give myself a shake. I need to concentrate on what's happening.

'Okay, CSI has arrived, so I'm going to leave you both with Lucy.' DI Brady gives us a nod and heads over to the main path, where more cars are pulling up. I realise the whole area around the rink has emptied of visitors now, the fluorescent cordon keeping them away.

'Do you have anything of Elle's that might have her scent on it for the dogs?' Lucy asks my sister calmly.

37

'No. I can go home and get something. I'll call a cab.'

'Hang on.' I delve into my bag. 'I've got her scarf. They're not supposed to wear them on the rink so . . . here.' I hand over Elle's white wool scarf to Lucy.

'This should be perfect,' Lucy replies. 'I'll take it to them now.'

Jo reaches out to touch it briefly. 'She loves that scarf. It's so soft.'

'I'll return it afterwards. First things first, I'll give you each my card so you can put my number into your phones. I'll keep you updated but call me if you remember anything helpful, or if you need anything at all.' Lucy gives a card to me and then to Jo, who takes it in a daze. 'I'm going to head back to the dog handler now, but then I'll need you, Mum, to meet me at the station for a DNA test, and if you could also bring along a hairbrush and a toothbrush of Elle's, okay? Shall we say in an hour's time?'

Jo nods again, and I take her hand and squeeze it. But she immediately extricates it from mine and wraps her arms around herself. Does she hate me right now? I wouldn't blame her if she did. I'm hating myself a little too.

The DS heads off with Elle's scarf in her hand, leaving Jo and I standing together, horrified.

My sister turns to face me. 'How did this happen, Nat? Where is she? Where's Elle? She can't have just disappeared.'

'I'm so sorry, Jo. I . . . She hasn't been gone that long. I'm sure they'll find her.' But I don't sound as confident as I should. I'm not being the comforting big sister I usually am.

There's a five-year gap between us so I've always felt like Jo's second mum. I know she thinks I'm a bit boring and predictable, but I also like to think she knows I'm reliable. That I'll always be there for her. That's why this is so hard to take. I'm not the kind of person who loses children. Who screws up on such a monumentally huge scale. That territory is usually marked out by Jo. *Not by me.*

Chapter Seven

TEN YEARS LATER

The run-up to Christmas has always been an uncomfortable time of year. A reminder of the past. Especially when there's a nip in the air and a frost on the ground. It's triggering for all of us. But it's Georgia I feel sorry for the most. She's almost eighteen now and has had a decade of birthdays tinged with sadness. With awkwardness. With unspoken conversations left to hang in the air. I suppose we could have faced them head on. Talked them through. Unfortunately, we've become more of a 'grit your teeth and get on with it' kind of family. I suppose it's our way of hiding the pain.

Today, Theo and I are home from work early. We're in the living room of our chilly Edwardian house in Southbourne, sitting on the battered cream linen sofa, waiting for our daughter to get home from school where she's in her second year of A levels studying maths, physics and product design. She passed her driving test this summer and we got her a cheap little runaround, which is great as it means Theo and I no longer have to ferry her here, there and everywhere, getting calls at all hours of the day and night when her plans suddenly change, as they nearly always do. It's nice that she has her freedom, of course it is, but it's also something else to worry about. Is she driving safely? Are her friends distracting her? And whenever she's late home, I can't help imagining she's had some terrible accident.

I hear the car engine stop outside, the door slam, and Georgia's footsteps crunching across the gravel drive.

'She's here.' Theo states the obvious while I take a breath and stand up, unsure why I'm so nervous. The doorbell rings and I peer out through the bay window. 'She's forgotten her key again,' Theo says with an eye-roll.

'I hope she hasn't lost another one,' I reply, heading into the hall to answer the front door.

'Hey, Mum.' She dumps her bag and coat on the floor, heading to the kitchen. 'I'm starving. Did you go shopping today?'

'I did. There are blueberry muffins in the cupboard.'

'Amazing.' She strides past, eyes glued to her phone, her dark hair dotted with raindrops.

Theo follows us through and joins us in the kitchen-diner, where Georgia is already tearing into the packet of muffins.

'Hey, you,' Theo says. 'Had a good day?'

Georgia bites into the muffin, a look of ecstasy on her face. 'Mmm, so good. The muffin, not my day — that was boring as usual. Mr Pierce goes on and on about nothing. I swear I haven't learnt *anything* new this term.'

'Well, I hope that's not true.' I pour myself a glass of water.

'It's fine, Mum. I know the course inside out.' She opens the fridge and stands in front of it, staring into its depths as though it holds the meaning of the universe.

Theo catches my eye, and I give him a little nod. 'Shall we sit in the lounge?' he says to her.

'I've got homework,' she replies distractedly.

'Just for a minute. Your mum and I have something we want to talk to you about.'

Georgia closes the fridge and turns to stare, looking at us in turn. 'You're not getting a divorce, are you?' she asks jokingly.

'No!' I reply with an outraged laugh.

'Fine.' She follows us into the living room, no doubt trailing crumbs in her wake.

Theo and I sit down and motion to her to do the same. The central heating clicks on and I'm looking forward to the warmth.

'What do you want to talk about?' She plops herself on the sofa opposite us and curls herself into the corner.

'Well,' I begin, 'it's your eighteenth in a couple of months.'

'I know. It's so weird to think I'm going to be an actual adult.'

'Tell me about it,' Theo replies wistfully. 'It feels like only yesterday we were picking you up from pre-school.'

'We wanted to do something nice for it,' I say. 'Mark the occasion.'

She nods slowly, a wary expression crossing her features.

'So that's why we've booked the top floor of the Hearts Club for your party,' I announce with a skip of excitement, waiting for her reaction.

We haven't properly celebrated Georgia's birthday for ten years. Not since it happened. So this year, Theo and I decided that she deserves the party to end all parties. A proper celebration of becoming an adult. A no-holds-barred event with all her friends and family at a swanky venue in town.

She sits up and stares at us, her dark eyes disbelieving. 'You've booked the Hearts Club? You've actually booked it already?'

'We had to book it a while ago,' Theo says, a note of worry creeping into his voice. 'Make sure no one beat us to it. Is that okay?'

She gulps and gives herself a shake. 'Um, yeah. That's incredible. Thanks, guys. You didn't have to do that. I'd have been happy with a meal out.'

'I know you would, Gee-Gee,' Theo says. 'But we thought you deserved a proper celebration.'

'How many people can I invite?' She's not jumping up and down.

'Maximum is one hundred and twenty,' I reply. 'But we'll also have to invite Granny and Grandpa, Aunty Jo, Ollie and a few other oldies. Don't worry, we'll keep out of your way.'

'That's . . . insane. Thanks.' She gets to her feet and comes over to give us each a hug.

'You can decide on the theme,' Theo adds. 'Whatever you want. It's lucky your mum's a big-shot events organiser. She'll make sure it goes off without a hitch.'

I waggle my eyebrows and buff my nails on my shoulder, but Georgia's response seems a little muted to me. Maybe she's just overwhelmed. She might be worried about inviting enough people to fill the venue. Or maybe it's simply because we haven't made a fuss around birthdays for so long. She's probably stunned that we've offered to do it, and she might also be worried that we'll make it uncool. But I'll give her free rein on the details. Hopefully she'll enjoy planning it with me. It will give us some much-needed bonding time, because lately she always seems to be in her room or out with friends. Spending time with her parents is bottom of the list. Which I suppose it was for me too, at her age.

'So,' I say, 'start thinking about themes and stuff, and tell your friends to save the date. Luckily, your birthday's on a Friday this year, so that's the date we've booked.'

'Great, okay. Thanks so much again, guys.' She stretches her arms. 'Well, I'd better get started on my homework, but the party idea's cool.'

Theo and I nod and smile at our daughter as she leaves the room and clatters up the stairs. But after she's gone, we stare at each other, a little bemused and disappointed. I feel my shoulders droop and my chest hollow out.

'Did we make a mistake?' I ask.

'I don't know. I thought she'd be jumping up and down with excitement.' Theo gets to his feet and walks over to the window, staring out at the sleety rain.

'You know Georgia though,' I add. 'She always takes a while to warm to things.'

'True.'

'She'll love telling all her friends about it.'

'I hope so.' Theo turns around and sighs heavily. 'It's hard being a parent.'

I laugh. 'You think?' But then my mind turns to my sister, who would give anything to be a parent again.

Reading my mind, Theo says, 'When are you going to tell Jo about the party?'

'Soon, I guess.'

My poor sister will miss out on celebrating her own daughter's eighteenth in a year or so, and I can't deny that I'm more than a little nervous to tell her about Georgia's party. Especially as it's on the anniversary of when Elle went missing. I've been looking out for my sister ever since it happened, supporting her both emotionally and financially, and it's taken a toll on my relationship with Theo. But what else could we do? We were supposed to be looking after her daughter, and we failed.

'Still can't believe Georgia's going to be eighteen,' Theo says with a sigh.

'I know. How did that happen?' I slump back on the sofa and hug a cushion to my chest.

'And she'll be off to uni next year,' he adds, sitting opposite me and leaning forward.

I give him a look. 'What?'

'What do you mean, *what?*' he replies.

I frown. 'You look like you've got something on your mind.'

He gives a sheepish grin. 'You know me too well, Mrs Edwards.'

'That's what twenty-one years of marriage will do,' I remind him. 'So? Spit it out.'

He blows air out through his mouth. 'Well, what will we do once Gee leaves home?'

I stare at my husband. '*Do?* What do you want to do?'

'I mean, obviously we'll still be at home and working and stuff, but . . . do you think Jo will still be living here?'

I shake my head and get to my feet, pacing the room. Over the years we've had variations of this same conversation. Theo asks when Jo will be moving out, and I tell him what I always tell him: 'She's my sister, and we lost her child. Surely she can stay with us as long as she needs to.'

'Yes, she can, of course she can,' he replies. 'But will she want to, do you think? And also, is it good for her to still be here? Surely it would be better for her to make a new life for herself. And once Gee goes to uni, I want our lives to be more about *us*. You and me. Not the past. We have to move on, Nat, don't we? Can you stop pacing and sit down? Talk to me about this.'

I'm too agitated to sit. Part of me knows that what Theo's saying makes sense, but I also know that I'll never be able to ask Jo to leave. I just can't do it. And I know that Theo is putting up with her under sufferance, but I hope he'll continue to understand why.

After Elle went missing, Jo was so devastated she was unable to work. She lost her job and consequently couldn't afford to pay her rent or bills. I thought our parents might have offered for her to move back home, but they didn't. So she moved in with us instead. I wanted to comfort her, but she wouldn't let me, and those first few months were hard going. Even though I love my sister and felt responsible for her being in this state, we couldn't cope with her in the house. Not with Georgia in the bedroom next to hers. Not with her asking why Aunty Jo was sleeping all day, or why Aunty Jo was swearing at Mummy. But I couldn't throw her out. How could I?

So, Theo and I came to the decision about eight years ago to increase our mortgage and convert the garage into a one-bedroom flat with its own entrance and tiny courtyard. I'd thought that it would be the answer to all our problems, and it's certainly a huge improvement on her staying in the spare room. At least now we all have more privacy. But it's still not ideal. Jo has never been the easiest person to get along with, and her living in our pockets, coupled with the guilt that Theo and I still carry, has been stressful. Sometimes I feel as though we're trapped in time, unable to move on with our lives. Still tiptoeing around the same issues. I know it's unhealthy, but I'm too scared to do anything about it for fear of the repercussions.

Aside from the cost of renovations, Theo and I had been hopeful at the thought of Jo moving out of the main house into her garden flat. The idea was that it could be a stepping stone until she got back on her feet and found somewhere more permanent. We would help her get through this with some TLC. We thought that the flat would eventually be a great teenager's den for Georgia. But that hasn't happened, and it doesn't look like Jo will be moving out anytime soon. If ever. I just wish Theo would accept that.

Chapter Eight

THEN

I'm in the kitchen with Theo and Jo, a wintry sun streaming in through the sliding doors. But it doesn't feel like our home. Everything feels different and scary. Like I've stepped into an alternate universe where normal rules don't apply. Especially as Georgia isn't here with us.

Liz popped over yesterday to say that she's welcome to stay with them for as long as she likes. I spoke to Georgia and she said she's happy to stay at Sasha's and wants to keep going in to school. That she feels too sad to stay home and do nothing. I'm thankful I don't have to worry too much about her for the time being because I need to be able to support my sister, but at the same time I'm missing having Georgia here, being able to comfort her and comfort myself at the same time. Just thinking about my daughter makes me want to march round to the school and pull her out. Give her a hug and talk it all through. But maybe it's better that she's there, taking her mind off all this.

Right now, the three of us are picking at a breakfast of burnt toast and tea while we wait for the police to come over with an update. The only update we want is to hear that Elle has been found safe and well, but the longer she's missing, the more I fear the worst. The last two nights' temperatures were below freezing, but I daren't let my mind drift into all the terrible possibilities. I have to remain positive.

It's been two days since Elle went missing. Two brutally long days of very little sleep and hours of fruitless searching. How can it have been that long? After the first night, although we scoured the town and beach and gardens until the early hours of the morning, when we were too frozen and too exhausted to continue, I asked Jo to stay with us. She was glad of the offer, saying she couldn't bear to go back home without Elle. Saying that it felt like a betrayal of her to stop searching even for a minute. I had to convince her that it wouldn't do Elle any good if we made ourselves ill. We had to stay strong and keep our energy levels up. But after that first night of searching, Jo's energy has deflated. She's been steadily declining into a stupor. I think it might be delayed shock.

Theo tops up my tea. He's still worryingly quiet, but I don't have the bandwidth to deal with that. I suspect he feels as guilty as I do, but talking about it won't help us right now. I give a start as the doorbell rings. Theo jumps to his feet and leaves the kitchen. A few moments later, he returns with DS Lucy Gilligan. She's wearing jeans and a navy fleece, her copper-coloured hair tied back in a ponytail. Jo and I both stand, eager for news.

'Hello,' Lucy says. 'How are you guys holding up?' It feels strange thinking of her as 'Lucy' rather than DS Gilligan, but she insisted that we call her by her first name. True to her word, she's been keeping us regularly updated with the police investigation. Not that there have been any good developments. Elle seems to have vanished into thin air. The search-and-rescue team and CSI carried out a fingertip search of the area, but aside from the two skate imprints, they haven't found anything of note.

'You had the sniffer dogs out on Saturday,' Jo says, without preamble. 'But they said the trail went cold in the gardens. Did they ever manage to pick up the scent again?'

'I'm afraid not, no,' she replies regretfully. 'The weather wasn't on our side at the weekend.'

'If the trail went cold, does that mean she could have been carried away by someone?' Jo continues, her eyes filling with fear.

Lucy's face softens. 'I know it's difficult, but it honestly doesn't help to speculate – you can drive yourself crazy thinking about possibilities. But please know that we're doing everything we can to find Elle.' She turns to me. 'Is Georgia here too?'

'She's at school. It's been hard on her, what with it being her birthday party and everything.'

'Yes, I'm sure. But it's good she's gone to school. Better for her not to stay home worrying.'

'Yes,' I reply, but I can't help thinking about how my daughter's handling it. On the outside she seems to be coping well, but she's always been a people pleaser, wanting to make things easier for everyone around her. Is that what's happening with her now? Is she in turmoil, or is she genuinely okay? When Theo and I popped over there yesterday evening, she seemed all right, but I worry that might have been a front she was putting on in front of Sasha and her family.

'Will you be returning to your flat in Boscombe?' Lucy asks Jo.

'She'll be staying here with us for a while,' I jump in. 'Until we find Elle.'

'Okay, great.' She turns back to my sister. 'I was going to ask if you had anyone supporting you at home, but staying here is a good solution. You need a lot of good people around you right now. How about grandparents?'

Jo nods slowly. Her relationship with my parents has always been a bit rocky, and I can tell that mention of them has made her clam up again.

'Our parents are on holiday in Austria at the moment,' I say, 'but they're flying home early. Getting back this evening. They live in Southbourne too.'

Jo is so still and quiet. I'm sure she's wondering how Mum and Dad are going to handle this situation. They were shocked on the phone and said they would catch the first available flight back so I'm sure they'll be here for her. But they've always struggled with Jo's personality. Dad in particular found it hard to deal with her during her teenage years. She was his little princess when she was younger, and I think he was dismayed at how she changed after she hit puberty. I never gave them much trouble, so I think they expected Jo to follow the same pattern.

Dad took all her shenanigans personally. Every time she broke her curfew or went out with an 'unsuitable' boy, he really held it against her. Like me, Mum has always tried to be the peacemaker. But she usually takes Dad's side in the end. I really hope they'll give Jo the support she needs. Of course, Theo and I will be here for her, but I need my parents to step up too. Surely they will now, because this situation is nothing like the past. This situation needs us all to pull together.

Lucy types up a note in her phone and looks up. 'Any other relatives? Siblings?'

'No other relatives nearby,' I answer. I don't bother mentioning our older brother, Paul, because we won't be getting any support from him. He's lived in Spain for almost four years, and he and his wife, Susie, don't have anything to do with us. They haven't done since they moved out there. The pair of them are extremely well off and have their own posh friends – well, *Susie's* posh friends. She's lucky enough to have family money, and they now run a holiday rental company.

Susie was always aloof around us, but as time went on she became quite sneery and passive-aggressive. I'm not sure why, because we were always friendly and welcoming. Theo and I can't remember ever doing anything to offend her. We came to the conclusion that Susie doesn't think we're good enough for her. We don't live in the right house or drive the right car. We don't talk with the right accent. Paul has charisma, though, and he's insanely good-looking, which I guess makes up for his lack of wealth. He fits Susie's image of who she should be with.

She definitely wasn't a fan of the whole kids situation, backing away from sticky fingers and wincing whenever one of them cried. Which is fine, because not everyone loves children. But it was a shame for Paul, because he loved Georgia and Elle and they loved him.

Thinking of him, and being in this terrible situation, I can't help but miss my brother. Right now, I'd give anything to have him walk through the front door and back into our lives. The three of us used to be close. He was a buffer between me and Jo. He stopped us clashing. After he went off with Susie, my relationship with Jo suffered.

Paul and Susie don't have children, but I'm not sure if that's on purpose or because they can't. I'm leaning towards the former because of the way Susie acted around her nieces. Of course, it's their business, their choice, but it would be nice to be let in. To be part of their lives. To share their ups and downs. They're our family. It's a shame they decided to cut themselves off from us.

Mum and Dad still see them, but only because Mum insists on flying out there every year for a week. Even then, they have to stay in a separate apartment, not in Paul and Susie's mansion, because 'Susie likes her space'. I'm guessing Mum and Dad will let them know about Elle, but it will be a miracle if either of them calls Jo to see how she is. I feel my blood pressure rising just thinking about it.

'Jo's friend Ollie's also been a great support,' I add. 'He's been here with her most of the time since it happened.'

'Ollie?' Lucy asks. 'Was he there at the ice rink?'

'No,' Jo replies, re-engaging. 'He was out in town with me and my friends.'

'Can I take a surname and number for him?'

'Ollie Camilleri,' Jo says. She pulls up his contact details on her phone and passes them to Lucy.

While there's a lull in the conversation, Theo asks Lucy if she'd like a tea or coffee.

'I'm fine, thanks. Maybe a glass of water, but I can get it myself, if that's okay? I might be here a lot and the last thing I want is for you to be running around getting me drinks. I'm here to support you all.'

'Okay, thanks.' I point to the cupboard with the glasses, not even having the mental capacity to feel weird about this stranger rooting through my cupboards.

She takes one out and fills it at the tap. 'You guys all sit back down and I'll join you. Can I get anyone else a drink?'

We all decline so she comes to join us at the table next to Theo, opposite me and Jo. 'I just want to check with you, Jo, that as per our phone conversation, you're still happy for Natalie and Theo to be involved in the investigation where updates are concerned. Or we can do this, just the two of us, if you prefer?'

'I want them involved,' Jo replies.

'Great, okay. Just double-checking that, as Elle's parent, you're happy for me to share information with all three of you, relating to the case.'

Jo nods. 'I'm fine with that.'

'Okay, so I'll fill you in on what *we're* doing and tell you what we might need from *you*. Does that sound okay?'

We all murmur our assent. It's like I'm in a dream. None of this feels real.

Lucy continues talking. 'We've put out a request to the public on our social media channels asking for any photos or video footage people might have of Saturday evening at the ice rink to see if we can get any shots or video of Elle or the person in the dog costume. We've also asked the person in the dog costume to come forward to help with our enquiries. It could be that they're nothing to do with this and just happened to have caught Elle's attention. But we need to speak to them.' She takes a few sips of water.

'Have you had any responses yet?' Jo asks.

'We've had quite a few, and we're looking through them. Nothing helpful so far, but we're hopeful. I recommend you share our post to your own social media accounts because the more it's shared, the more chance we have of someone seeing it and remembering something from the night that could help us.'

'Theo and I have already posted on Facebook,' I say, glancing sideways at my sister. 'But I know it's been too upsetting for Jo to post anything.'

'I'll share everything though,' she says. 'But I just . . . I can't . . .'

'That's fine,' Lucy reassures. 'Sharing on Natalie's timeline has the same effect. I also want to float the idea of doing a press conference.'

'No,' Jo says immediately. 'I can't do it.'

'I understand,' Lucy replies. 'But we've found that it's the best way to get the word out fast. To get sympathy from the public and make them *want* to help. It doesn't have to be you who does it, Jo. It can be another family member or friend. But it's better if it's family.'

My stomach clenches at the thought, but I know I have to step up for Jo. 'I'll do it, if it helps, and if Jo agrees?' I turn to my sister, who nods several times.

'Great, I'll get that set up as soon as possible. The other thing I wanted to talk to you about, Jo, is a bit sensitive. Can I have a quick word with you in private, if that's okay?'

'Um, sure.' Jo starts to get up, but I motion to her to stay where she is.

'It's okay, Theo and I will make ourselves scarce,' I say, getting to my feet, wondering what on earth it could be about.

'Thanks.' Lucy gives us a grateful smile as we leave the room, closing the door behind us, and head into the lounge. Neither of us sit.

'What do you think that's about?' I whisper to Theo.

'No idea.' He frowns and shakes his head.

'I thought Jo gave Lucy permission for us to hear details relating to the case?'

'Could be something personal.' Theo shrugs.

'I know, but it's weird. I can't think what she'd have to keep secret from us.'

'Maybe Jo will tell us afterwards,' Theo speculates.

'Maybe,' I reply.

Chapter Nine

NOW

Jo and I wrap up warmly and walk the short quarter mile from our home to the high street. I thought it would be nice to try out Trinket, the new bar in Southbourne that everyone's been talking about. It's decorated in a maximalist style, an upmarket Aladdin's cave of jewel colours and gold fixtures, the seating all plush velvet and dark wood.

As we go in, I comment on how lovely it is, but Jo doesn't seem impressed by the decor. She's rarely impressed by anything these days. Over the years, I've tried to get her to go to counselling or to the doctor. I'm worried she still needs help to process her grief. To try to deal with what's happened so that she can live life again, but she's always stubbornly refused. I wonder if she genuinely doesn't want to go, or if it's because it's me who keeps suggesting it. I guess the same could be said for me. Like Theo, I've just buried myself in my work. Why are we always better at giving advice than taking it?

At least if Jo had a career she enjoyed, that would be something. But she's lurched from one short-term job to the next, where she either quits or gets the sack – usually for rocking up half an hour late with a weak apology or for failing to show up at all. She's currently working at the Coach and Horses, a local dive bar where she's washing up in the kitchen. She says she doesn't mind it. That it's soothingly monotonous. But we'll see how long it lasts.

In the early days, I employed her to work at some of my events, but that was an unmitigated disaster where she ended up costing me money and losing several of my clients. Not that I have a right to complain about those things. A bit of inconvenience at work is nothing compared to what she's gone through.

Nowadays, I work for an upmarket hotel chain as their events co-ordinator, organising weddings and conferences as well as bringing in new business. It's not exactly my dream job, but it pays the bills and it can be quite satisfying. I haven't forgotten my life goal to create my own company and host weekend music festivals for families. But things don't always work out the way we want. After Elle went missing, I lost my confidence, my ambition and my mojo. I let that dream go.

Jo sits at a table near the window and stares out at the quiet street.

'What do you want to drink?' I ask. 'They've got a cocktail menu, shall I grab one?'

'No, that's okay. Vodka and Diet Coke please,' she says, without any expression on her face. Again, I wonder if she reserves her lack of emotion just for me and Theo, or whether she's like this with everyone. She still goes out with friends, so surely she can't be this morose with them.

I head to the bar and order my sister's vodka plus a large glass of Cabernet for myself. It feels wrong to order a cocktail when Jo isn't having one. I take a healthy gulp of wine before returning to our table, where Jo is scrolling on her phone. She's pulled her feet up on the sofa, hugging her knees to her chest, like she's on the couch at home. She's thirty-nine but with her dirty blonde hair and petite frame she looks far younger, which is strange because you'd think grief would have aged her. I, on the other hand, am looking every inch of my forty-four years, with a gaunt face and increasing wrinkles around my eyes.

'Here you go.' I set Jo's drink on the table, hating how forced and cheery my voice sounds. *I'd* be irritated with me if I were her.

She looks up and sets her phone down beside her. 'Thanks.'

'Cheers.' We clink glasses, but she doesn't catch my eye. Both of us drink and it feels awkward as hell. I wonder if we'll ever get back to being us. We were never best buddies, but we always loved each other. We could always have a laugh, couldn't we? After ten years, I've almost given up hope of having that easy relationship again.

'So . . .' I say.

She shrugs. 'So?'

I reach into the depths of my brain to search for something non-controversial. 'How's the job going?' is the best I can do.

'It's fine. It's a job.' Jo gives a quarter-smile. 'It gives me a bit of cash so I can get some shopping, go out with friends, the usual.'

I take another sip of my wine and start to wish I'd never suggested coming out. I'd thought it would be a nice change of scenery. Take us out of the house, where we always seem to be sniping at one another. Not that I even see that much of her. She's either holed up in her flat, out at work, or out with friends. I see more of Ollie than Jo as he often pops in for a quick hello or a cuppa after he's visited her.

Jo sighs and fixes me with an unreadable stare. I blink back at her. Finally, she says, 'Is this about you and Theo wanting me to move out?'

I stare back for a moment. '*What?* No.'

'Are you sure?' she asks, her voice tight.

'I'm positive. You can stay with us for as long as you like. Forever, if you need to.'

'Really?' She exhales, her chin quivering.

I'm alarmed to see a tear dribbling down her cheek. She wipes it away, but another one follows it. 'Oh, Jo. Don't cry. Did you honestly think I would ask you to leave? You're my sister.'

'I know,' she replies with a gulp, 'but I'm a shit sister.'

'No you're not.' I shake my head and give a little laugh. 'Well, not all the time anyway.'

She throws a beer mat at me and sniffs. 'I thought that was what all this was about.' She gestures to our surroundings. 'Soften her up with a drink in a fancy wine bar and then go in for the kill.'

'What kind of sister do you think I am?'

She shakes her head but doesn't answer the question. I suppose it was rhetorical, but it would have been good to hear her say something mildly positive about me.

'So, then, why are we here?' she asks.

I want to say something like, *Can't two sisters go out for a drink together without having to have a reason?* But I can't, because she's right. I did bring her here to speak to her about something. Something very specific. There's no point going round the houses, I need to just tell her.

'I know it's coming up to the ten-year anniversary,' I begin.

Jo's face immediately shutters, her eyes hardening and the easiness we shared a moment ago vanishing like a magic trick. She looks like she's barely breathing.

'I just want you to know that I'm here for you,' I continue. 'That I'm still devastated for you.' I want to add that I miss Elle too, but I know those words will only make us both cry.

She nods and bites the inside of her lip. I want to reach across the table and squeeze her hand, but she won't want that so I keep my fingers wrapped around the stem of my wine glass. 'You okay?' I ask.

'Ugh,' she groans. 'It's just . . . you mentioning the anniversary.'

'I know, I'm sorry.'

'No, you don't have to be sorry, it's not you, it's just that I had a call from the police this week.'

I sit up straighter in my seat. 'What did they want?'

'They want to do a ten-year anniversary appeal for Elle.' The weight of her words hangs over us like a storm cloud.

'An appeal?' My mind races with what this might mean. All the buried emotions that are going to resurface. 'Do they think it might throw up anything?'

Jo shrugs. 'Obviously I've got to do it, because there's the possibility of new evidence and whatever, but I'm bloody terrified.' She takes a huge swig of her drink and stares at me.

I don't know what to say because she's right. It's going to be stressful for all of us, even though it could be another opportunity to get answers. 'What does the appeal involve exactly?'

Jo sits up straighter. 'I spoke to Lucy – she's an inspector now – and she said they're going to do a reconstruction of what she might look like now. They're also going to offer a cash reward incentive.'

'What? You mean they'll pay for information? How much?'

'I don't know. And they said that media interest will probably be almost as huge as it was when it happened. They're even talking about it being on *Crimewatch* nearer the time.'

'Shit.'

'I know.' Jo shakes her head. 'I should be grateful they're doing this. I *am* grateful, but . . .'

'. . . but it's scary,' I finish her sentence. 'I get it. We just have to hope that it will work. I mean, they might just find her. You never know.'

Jo presses the heel of her hand against her breastbone and exhales slowly. 'I don't even want to let myself hope.'

'Yeah.' I nod. The question that always goes unspoken is whether we'll find her alive.

We sip our drinks in silence for a moment and I think about what this appeal will mean for the rest of my family. For Theo. For Georgia. Will there be journos knocking on our door again? Angling for interviews? There's also another thing I'm going to have to mention to my sister. I can't put it off.

'There is something I wanted to tell you,' I say. 'It's nothing bad, but it's a bit sensitive.'

Jo's expression snaps back to wary again.

'The thing is,' I continue, 'the anniversary is also Georgia's eighteenth and so . . .' I tail off.

'You need to be able to celebrate that,' Jo finishes. 'Of course you do. I get that. She shouldn't suffer because of what happened. I love little Gee-Gee. Course she should be able to celebrate without worrying about . . . the past.'

'Thank you. I'm sorry, I know it's insensitive, but she's having a party and I would love it if you came. She would love it. We all would.'

It's an impossible situation with Georgia's birthday falling on the day Elle went missing. Jo has always avoided it, taking herself off whenever we have a family gathering to celebrate. But as it's Georgia's eighteenth this year, I really want her Aunty Jo to be there. To celebrate with everyone. But I get that it's hard because every year takes Jo back to that terrible day at the ice rink.

For the most part, Jo has been good with Georgia. She falls somewhere between aunt and big sister and I love that they have such a nice relationship. It can't have been easy for Jo over the past decade, living with her niece while Elle is missing, and I've always wondered if she resents me having my daughter while I lost hers. If she's jealous of the life I have while she was denied hers. That's why I've always tried to be understanding and accommodating whenever she gets angry or quiet or does something that I don't agree with. Because she was the one who lost out. And it was my fault.

'It's great that she's having a party,' Jo says earnestly. 'I'm honestly happy for her. But I'm not sure if I'll be able to be there. If I'll be good company or if I'll just bring everyone down.'

'You won't bring everyone down.' Despite knowing Jo might flinch away I chance it and reach out, laying a hand on hers. 'Please say you'll come.'

'Can I think about it?' Jo asks.

'Of course you can,' I reply, realising that it's doubtful she'll attend. 'And just know that if you do come, we'll be there as much for you as we are for Georgia.'

My sister nods, but I can tell that her heart is quietly breaking all over again.

Chapter Ten

You knew it would be difficult. You knew it would be nerve-wracking. But you underestimated how much you would sweat. How fast your heart would beat. How many times you would tell yourself to just abandon this crazy idea, turn around and take her back to the ice rink. And yet you don't turn around. You don't take her back. You keep going. Jogging to the car park with the crying child in your arms. Telling her that it will all be okay. But your words don't soothe her. The excitement of winning a prize has faded.

Weaving through the crowds, no one looks twice at a crying, overtired little girl being carried home. You're not alone in that respect. You've passed more than a few bawling children this evening. But at least she's not screaming and shouting. Just rubbing at her eyes and sobbing softly.

It's a good job she drank the cola you gave her. Its effects are slowly working. Her eyes are growing heavier. Soon she'll be asleep, thank goodness, and things will be easier.

Chapter Eleven

NOW

Bridget returns from the back room with her iPad, her olive-green suit perfectly tailored, her shiny black heels clacking across the wooden floor. She sits next to me at the bar, and as she sweeps her glossy hair back over her shoulder, I get a waft of expensive perfume. Her make-up is flawless and I wonder if she does it herself. I'm pretty sure my make-up melted away some time around 3 p.m. I must look an absolute state. Georgia's always telling me to use a fixing spray. It sounds like another layer of work that I could do without. But maybe she has a point. I pull a hand through my windswept hair and wish I'd had time to run a comb through it after work.

'Is that okay, Natalie?' Bridget asks, her wide blue eyes looking at me with a tinge of concern.

'Sorry, what was that?'

'I was just saying that we can offer your guests a cocktail or mocktail as they come in. I'll let you take a drinks menu to look through and then you can decide which ones you'd like to select.'

'Yes, that sounds great.'

'Wonderful!' Her features relax and she gives me a beaming smile with beautiful white teeth. 'Of course, as it's an eighteenth birthday, we may have to card some of the guests if they ask for alcohol, so do make sure they bring their ID.'

I'm at the Hearts Club in town where Georgia's having her birthday party next month. The venue is on two floors. Downstairs is a restaurant, and up here is a cocktail bar with a dance floor and an outside terrace. We'll be hiring the whole of the upstairs area for a private function. I've never been here before, but it's popular – only a year old – and I'm always hearing people talk about it at work so I know it's going to be good. I want Georgia to have the best night.

Theo was supposed to join me, but as he's held up in a sales meeting I said I'd fill him in when I came home. It's not ideal as I wanted us to do this together, and maybe have a drink afterwards, but I don't mind too much. Theo's happy to defer to me on this as it's my forte.

Bridget moves on to the canapé menu, firing through all the packages – imaginatively named Bronze, Silver, Gold and Platinum – and it all feels very reminiscent of what I do at work, although I'm more of an overseer these days rather than getting involved with the nitty-gritty. I miss the personal connection with clients though – hearing about all the hopes and dreams for their special events and then witnessing their satisfaction when we make it happen. I hope Georgia's party turns out to be everything we hope for her.

'So, I shouldn't say this,' Bridget says conspiratorially, 'but I personally recommend the Gold Hearts package as it's not as expensive as Platinum Hearts, but you get almost all the same things.'

I recognise a sales ploy when I see one but I go along with it anyway, having already earmarked the Gold package online with Theo earlier. 'That sounds great. Let's go for the Gold one then.'

She seems a little taken aback by my easy capitulation. 'But, of course,' she adds, recovering, 'the Platinum Hearts package is absolutely top tier if you wanted to go all out.'

'No, I think Gold will be perfect.'

'Of course, no problem,' Bridget says, professional smile back in place as she scrolls to another page. 'Great choice. There are various combinations within the Gold package so could you get back to me with your cocktail and canapé selections within two weeks of the event? That's also when we'll need the balance paid, if that's okay? Oh, also, would you like a drink? I forgot to offer you one when you came in. I'm so sorry.'

'An apple juice would be lovely, thanks.'

She signals to the barman, who gives her a wink and nods. She blushes and I warm to her. She can't be that much older than my daughter. Her enthusiasm reminds me a little of how I used to be when I started out.

My phone buzzes in my bag, but I ignore it as we move on to talking about decoration. Bridget confirms that I can come in early on the night with balloons, banners and party favours. She also agrees that they'll store the birthday cake and bring it out, with the candles lit, at a pre-arranged time.

'Is there anything else you'd like to discuss?' she asks.

'I don't think so, no. You've got the name of the DJ we're using, right?'

'Yes, I've got all his details. He can set up any time from five thirty p.m.'

'Perfect.' I finish the rest of my drink and we stand and shake hands. 'Thanks so much. I'll get back to you with our cocktail and canapé choices.'

'Lovely. Have a great evening,' Bridget chirps, giving me a final megawatt smile.

I turn to leave and am surprised by how busy the place has become since I arrived. It's only 6.30 p.m. on a Thursday, but already the place is filling up with the after-work crowd. Some are in suits, but most are dressed casually. I can't remember the last time I went out for a drink with work colleagues. I suddenly realise that for the past decade, it hasn't really felt like I'm living properly. It's as though I'm in limbo, waiting for something. Waiting for permission to start enjoying my life again. I wonder if that will ever happen?

I'd thought to myself that organising Georgia's party might kick-start something. Might help us all to move past the tragedy, but, so far, it hasn't been as successful as I'd anticipated. Georgia's response was lukewarm, and Jo's was heartbreaking. I just have to hope that when the night finally arrives, it will be fun. A chance for all of us to let our hair down and start a new chapter of our lives. Or am I perhaps making a mistake? Pushing too hard for us all to celebrate?

Outside, the air is damp and cold with a tinge of wood smoke. Yesterday was bonfire night, and the festivities always trail into the weekend. Memories flash into my mind of fireworks nights when the girls were younger, of us waving sparklers in the garden and hiding foil-wrapped pound coins in hot apple pies. Those kinds of fun events tailed off after Elle went missing. As I shiver and stride up the road towards my car, a seemingly never-ending stream of fireworks whistle and bang in the distance.

With all this birthday-party planning, it's hard not to think back to this time ten years ago when I was organising Georgia's ice-skating party. When all she wanted was to go skating with her friends, followed by pizza. Only for it to end in such a bitter tragedy. That day, almost ten years ago, has marked all of us and we have never been able to get past it. To move on.

Even though Georgia's still with me, I feel Jo's loss almost as keenly as if it were my own daughter who never came home. Since coming up with the idea, I keep having the circular thoughts that maybe we shouldn't be having this party at all, but then I come back to the thought that it's important to celebrate our daughter's birthday.

It doesn't help that Georgia is so withdrawn at the moment; she has been for the past few months, even before any mention of the party. I wonder if there's anything else I should be worried about, or if it's simply the resurgence of old memories. I've asked her about her friends, sixth form doesn't seem to be giving her too much trouble, and she's not in any relationship – not that I know about anyway, despite dropping unsubtle questions about boys. I wrap my coat a little tighter around me to protect myself from the chill. This isn't helping, I need to get out of my own head. I think I need to do something nice. Something fun. Something that isn't just sitting on the couch or working. Maybe a night out with Theo at the weekend. Just the two of us. Yes. I'll suggest it.

Finally, I reach my car. Once inside, I turn on the engine and whack up the heating just as my phone starts ringing. I'm surprised to see my sister's name flash up on the screen. It's rare for her to call me.

'Hey, Jo, everything okay?'

'Where have you been? I've been trying to get hold of you for ages!' Her tone puts me on instant alert.

'I'm just on my way back. What's wrong?'

'Can you hurry?' She sounds out of breath, stressed.

'Jo, you're scaring me.'

'Just get home, okay?' She ends the call and my heart rate goes into overdrive.

Chapter Twelve

THEN

I'm racing through cold, dark streets, searching for my niece, trying to call out her name, but my voice has disappeared. Cold permeates my bones while sweat drips down my back. The roads all look the same, silent, except for my footsteps pounding the icy pavement and my heartbeats pounding in my ears. I run and run until I no longer know where I am. My eyes fly open and I sit up with a start, my heart thrumming, fingers tingling. Something woke me. A noise from downstairs. The front door banging.

'Ugh,' Theo groans next to me. 'I can't cope with this.'

As he speaks, I try to catch my breath. My feet are freezing, yet perspiration coats my skin. I think I had a nightmare, but I can't catch the threads of it. Theo's words anchor me in consciousness and I realise my sister has come in late again. I scrabble about in the darkness for my phone on the bedside table to see it's just after 3 a.m.

'I know she's going through hell,' Theo says groggily, 'but waking us up like this every night is exhausting. And what about Georgia? Her room's next to Jo's. There's no way she can be sleeping through all this.'

'What do you want me to do?' I ask thickly, not fully awake, trying to shake the remnants of my nightmare. 'Jo's not in any state to go back to her place alone and my parents can't deal with her.' I wince at a clattering of crockery and cutlery from the kitchen, followed by low voices.

'Who the hell is that?' Theo hisses, wide awake now. 'Has she brought someone back with her?'

'It's probably just Ollie.'

'Ollie wouldn't make that kind of racket. He'd tell her to be quiet.'

I squint as Theo turns on his bedside light.

'I'm going to see who it is.' He throws off his side of the duvet, his face creased with exhaustion and annoyance.

I reach out to grab his wrist. 'Please don't. Just leave her be tonight. We can talk to her tomorrow.'

'That's if she gets out of bed,' Theo mutters, sinking back into the pillows.

It's been five days since Elle went missing, but it feels like forever. Jo has been driving us crazy with worry. She sleeps most of the day, apart from the times our liaison officer is round. Then she drags herself out of bed around 6 p.m., which is when Ollie pops round to see her after work.

They've known each other since school. Jo was always a bit of a loner, but she liked Ollie's company and he always had a massive crush on her. He had lots of other friends and tried to encourage Jo to mix in his circles, but she always resisted. It probably came across as her having disdain for other people but, looking back, I think it was more a fear of rejection. I don't know why, because she could have made some good friends if she'd wanted. She was pretty and funny, but she always had this aloofness about her that said 'Don't touch'. I think that's another reason I'm so overprotective. Because she's never had a big friendship support network. All her friends are really Ollie's friends.

His job at the dry cleaners is only down the road in Pokesdown so it's convenient for him to come to ours after work. I'm glad Ollie visits so often. Jo seems to perk up while he's here and they usually spend a couple of hours together holed up in her room, where I take dinner in for them. After he leaves, instead of letting me talk to her or comfort her, or just *be* with her, Jo falls back into her withdrawn, subdued self and goes out. She says she's searching for Elle, but she won't let Theo or me go with her, and she doesn't get back until the early hours of the morning, making an absolute racket, like right now.

I plead with her in my head to not make any more noise, to creep upstairs to bed so that Theo will calm down and we can all get some sleep. But my wish isn't granted as the TV comes on, and it's loud. I hear her swear and giggle. The TV volume goes up further and then reduces slightly, but not enough.

'Sorry, Nat. I'm going down there.'

'Theo, wait.' I pat my face to wake myself up, and I get out of bed. 'Let me go. I'll make sure she goes to bed, and I'll tell whoever it is to leave.'

'It better not be some random bloke.'

'It won't be,' I reply, keeping my fingers crossed.

'I'll come with you.' Theo gets out of bed, bristling with irritation.

'Please, just let me go on my own, I don't want a confrontation with all of us getting upset. I just want to get her to bed with the minimum fuss.'

'Fine. But come and get me if you need me.'

I pull a cardigan on over my pyjamas and leave the bedroom, tiptoeing across the landing and creeping down the stairs.

I'm thankful Theo didn't come down with me because the front door is open, letting in a stream of chilly night air. The latch is on, so it's banging against the frame. I release the snib and close the door as quietly as I can before heading into the kitchen. Every single light is on down here. The hall, the lounge, the living room, the kitchen-diner, even the garden lights. The kitchen island is littered with kebab cartons, beer cans and an almost empty vodka bottle. A lit cigarette is smouldering on one of my Emma Bridgewater plates and another has been extinguished on the quartz countertop. The TV is blaring out some dance tune and my sister is on the sofa, half undressed, on top of a young dark-haired guy, who's trying to take off his jeans while still wearing his trainers.

I locate the remote and turn off the TV, feeling like my mother. The silence hasn't interrupted them so I clear my throat, but that doesn't work either.

'Jo,' I say.

No response. His jeans are around his knees now and Jo is undoing hers and pulling at them ineffectively.

'Josephine.' My voice is louder this time and they freeze. She hates her full name, but I like it. She banned me from using it when we were kids, but sometimes the occasion warrants it.

She turns around, surprised for a moment, and then she sneers. 'Oh, look, it's my sister come to tell us off for having sex on the sofa. Oops.'

The man – who I've never seen before – has the grace to look embarrassed. He tries and fails to pull up his jeans.

'This is my house,' I tell him. 'Can you leave, please.'

'Uh, yeah, sure. Sorry.' He looks up at my sister, who's still straddling him. 'We'll do this again sometime, yeah?'

She shrugs and slides off him, sinking into the sofa. I escort the man out of the kitchen after he's scooped up his lighter, vodka and pack of cigarettes from the island. I watch him walk out the door, across the drive and away down the road. Only once he's out of sight do I allow myself a sigh, lock the front door and return to the kitchen.

Jo is asleep on the sofa, curled into the arm with her thumb in her mouth. I'm relieved. At least this means we're not going to have an argument.

She's always had this wild, impulsive side. A side that doesn't like to think about things. That blocks out consequences and lives purely in the moment. I used to envy it. I used to wish I didn't think so hard about every single thing I do. The difference is that she always has people to pick up after her. To sort out the messes when the consequences come back to bite her. I don't have enough trust that people would do the same for me. And, even if they were willing, I wouldn't want them to.

Before Jo had Elle, it wasn't exactly strange to see her with a new man, but she hasn't been that way for years. Not since she got pregnant. Before then, she slept with so many guys that she didn't even know who Elle's father was. According to my sister, she didn't have an inkling. She had no steady boyfriend; it was all just random hook-ups. She was nonchalant about it, saying that even if she knew who the father was, she wouldn't want them involved as she didn't know any of them well enough to start a relationship. That's when my parents decided they couldn't cope with her anymore, and they kicked her out of the family home. It was Dad's decision more than Mum's. But Dad's word was law. He said that her being at home was making them ill with worry. He said they would help out with her child, but they weren't going to raise her baby while Jo continued partying.

They weren't completely heartless. Mum talked Dad into giving Jo a deposit and a few months' rent for her one-bedroom flat in Boscombe, but Dad said after that she had to be independent. I thought they were harsh at the time, but now I can see how difficult it was for them. Jo has never been an easy person to live with.

The problem is that their abandonment of Jo meant I was the one who picked up the slack. I guess I didn't have to. I could have left her to work things out for herself, but I couldn't do it. Especially when Elle came along.

Ironically, having Elle was the best thing that could have happened to my sister. She stepped up and has been a good mum, despite leaning heavily on me and Theo. She didn't let not having much money hold them back, she would never let Elle go without, working extra shifts so her daughter could learn to swim and have dance lessons. Sure, it was hard, and Jo missed her old, carefree life, but we've always been there to help her.

After Elle went missing, the police wondered if Elle's father was involved in the abduction until Jo confessed that she didn't know who the father was, and she'd never tried to find out. So the police took some of Elle's DNA and ran it through their database.

When Lucy asked to speak to Jo privately the other day, it was to give her the result of the DNA test, that they hadn't been able to find a match. Jo was irritated that the police spent so much time on a dead end.

I keep thinking back to the evening of the party and what I could have done differently, but my memories are a jumble. It was all great until Sasha fell over on the ice and I lost sight of Elle. That's when it all went wrong. I wish I could rewind time and do things differently, but wishing won't bring my niece back.

If only I could know what happened to her. And whether we'll ever get her back. Living in limbo like this is torture, but I can't lose hope. Every day I have to remind myself that the police are doing everything they can to find her. I even did a press conference yesterday, appealing to the public for any witnesses, which was terrifying and extremely emotional, but Lucy said I did a good job and they're already getting leads from it. So maybe we'll catch a break and someone will know where Elle is.

I gaze down at my sleeping sister, a wave of guilt washing over me. I can't even imagine what's going through Jo's head right now. Is she reverting to her old ways to block out the pain of the present? If anything happened to Georgia, I don't know how I'd cope. I'd love to cover her with a blanket and leave her sleeping on the sofa, but I don't want Georgia to see her like this when she comes down for breakfast. So, reluctantly, I wake her up. She's groggy and pliable, so I'm able to get her to drink some water. Then I soothe her up the stairs and into her room, which is an absolute mess and smells like a beer-garden ashtray. I make a note to give it a deep clean next time she's out, while I help strip off her clothes and manage to locate a semi-clean T-shirt from the floor, which I pull over her head.

She snuggles under the covers and I look down at her. My little sister who's going through absolute hell. Because of me.

Chapter Thirteen

NOW

I call Jo back straightaway, worried that something might have happened to Georgia or Theo, but she doesn't pick up, so I call Georgia's mobile. It goes straight to voicemail.

'Georgia, are you okay? Can you call me back as soon as you get this?'

I check the Find My Phone app to pinpoint Theo and Georgia's locations, but it's not connecting. After Elle went missing, Theo and I bought Georgia a phone and made sure she had the tracker app. She was one of the youngest of her friends to have a phone at the time, but we didn't let her download any of the social media apps. She just had it for getting in touch, and the camera was a bonus.

Next I call Theo, whose phone also maddeningly goes to voicemail, and then I remember he's in a meeting so I don't bother to leave a message. The best thing I can do is to get home as quickly as possible. My hands are shaking so I clench them and take a few deep breaths to try to calm down before pulling out into the evening traffic.

I barely register the drive home. All I can think about is whether Georgia is okay. She messaged me earlier to say she was going to a friend's house after school, but she didn't say who. Why the hell did Jo end the call so suddenly? Is she in danger? All kinds of worrying scenarios flash through my mind – Georgia's been in an accident, Jo has news about Elle, the house has burned down, Theo's had a heart attack . . . Is this some kind of karmic punishment for what happened all those years ago?

I'm startled by a horn beeping and I realise the red light I was waiting at has now turned green. I wave an apology and get the car moving again.

Finally, I arrive home and hurry into the house. The place is in darkness.

'Jo!' My voice is stark.

There's no reply.

'Georgia?'

Nothing.

I head to the kitchen, turn on the garden lights and unlock the back door. As I walk through the side gate that leads to Jo's little garden-room apartment, my phone starts ringing. Before I have a chance to answer Jo, she flings open the bifold door, wide-eyed, hair pulled back in a scrunchie, phone in her hand. 'You're home!' she cries.

'What's happened? Is Georgia okay? Are you okay?'

'As far as I know, Georgia's fine,' she replies, pulling me into her flat and closing the doors.

'I wish you'd told me that on the phone.' I pull out my mobile now that we're on Wi-Fi and open the Find My app, relieved to see that Georgia is at her friend's house.

'Sorry,' Jo says. 'I was running home and I lost signal, you know what it's like round here. I just got in and managed to call you back. Did you see anyone outside?'

'What? No. Like who?'

She crosses her arms and bends forward, breathing shallowly.

'Jo, what's wrong? You're scaring me. It's dark in here, let me put the light on.' I reach for one of the table lamps, but she wrenches my arm away.

'No!'

'Why not?'

'In case she can see in through the bifolds. I'm going to get some curtains.'

'In case who can see in? No one can see through the gate.'

'No, but they can see over it if they get up on tiptoe.'

I worry that my sister might be having some kind of breakdown. I leave the lamp and guide her to the sofa, where I sit and rub her back. At least the garden lights are bright enough for us to see each other. 'Now, take a deep breath and tell me slowly what's happened.'

She tries to take a breath, but she's still panting, her words tumbling out. 'I was walking back from work and there was this, this weird woman following me.'

'A woman?'

'Yes.'

'Are you sure she was following you?'

'Yes!' she cries, standing up and pacing, her hands on her hips.

'Is she out there now?' I turn to look out of the doors, but all I can see is the gate lit up by the security lighting.

'I think I lost her, but I can't be sure.' Jo turns to me with a panicked look in her eyes.

'Maybe she wasn't following you,' I suggest. 'Maybe she was just walking in the same direction.'

Jo gives me an exasperated glare. 'I *know* she was following me. Can we go in the house and look out of one of the upstairs windows? See if she's out there.'

'Um, sure, okay.'

'Good.' She opens the door and closes it behind us, glancing at the front gate as she hurries through the garden into the house.

As I follow her in, I wonder what to do for the best. Is she having some kind of episode? Jo can be a bit flaky, but to my knowledge she's never imagined things before. Is that what's happening now? Or was she really being followed? We go up to Theo's and my bedroom and, once again, Jo stops me from turning on any lights. I'm glad Theo isn't here because he would not be happy about creeping around the house in the dark with my sister. All he wants to do when he gets in from work is flop in front of the TV with a beer.

Jo and I stand by the bedroom window, peering through the half-closed shutters. I feel faintly ridiculous, but Jo is still clearly terrified so I go along with however she wants to play this.

'Can you see anyone?' she hisses.

I look down at our empty driveway and the quiet street beyond. 'Is that Ollie's van?' I ask, spying a grey VW Transporter parked a little way down the road.

We both jump as Jo's phone rings, its harsh tone unnaturally loud in the dark, quiet bedroom.

'Ollie,' she says breathlessly.

'I'm standing outside your flat.' His voice sounds tinny on the speaker. 'You said to come round, so I'm here. Are you okay?'

'Don't worry, Nat's home,' she replies.

'So you want me to leave?'

'No, course not. We're in the house. Come round the back to the kitchen.'

I follow my sister down the stairs, still confused as to what she saw and why she's so freaked out.

'Hey,' Ollie says, pulling her into his arms as we walk into the kitchen. 'What's happened? Is there a power cut? Can we turn a light on?'

He and Jo make an unlikely couple, but I thank God for him every day. Without Ollie, I dread to think what state my sister would be in. After the skating party, Ollie became her rock. She rarely let Theo or I in, but she would speak to Ollie for hours. I guess it was only a matter of time before they ended up getting together. It took over two years for her to accept that he was more than just a good friend, but they've been a couple now for almost eight.

I know Ollie wants more – a home together, marriage, kids, the works – but Jo has told him that she needs her space. That he either takes her as she is or he moves on to someone who will give him all the trimmings. I only know this because Ollie has confided in me a few times. But I couldn't give him any false hope. My sister is her own person. She's self-contained. I wish she would let herself be happy instead of holding everyone at arm's length, but I understand it.

Part of me wonders if she's simply with him for convenience. If I were looking out for Ollie more than Jo, I might even tell him to find someone else to love. To be with someone who could truly commit to him. But even thinking that makes me feel disloyal. Maybe I'm wrong about Jo needing him. Maybe losing Ollie would give her the push she needs to go out and start living properly again. Maybe it would be good for both of them.

She extricates herself from Ollie's hug and sits down heavily on the sofa while I turn on a couple of light switches, wincing at the overwhelming brightness.

'I was walking home from work,' Jo says, 'and I heard these soft footsteps behind me, quite a way back. I didn't think too much of it, but I didn't want to turn around, so I crossed over the road. A minute or so later, I could still hear them, so I quickly glanced back and saw a woman – a bit older than me, in a dark coat – walking on the opposite pavement. I relaxed a bit, because it was a woman. But when she saw me turn around, she stopped and dropped to tie her shoelace. Only she was wearing boots without laces, so that's when I thought she might be following me.'

'Maybe she dropped something?' Ollie suggests.

'Maybe,' Jo replies. 'But she had a dodgy vibe. She looked rough.'

'What did you do?' Ollie and I ask simultaneously.

Jo stands up and starts pacing again. 'I walked a bit faster, trying to come up with a plan. Like, should I run, or something? But I'm not exactly the fittest person. So I went into a newsagent, hung out there for a few minutes and bought some cigs. I thought she might come in, and I decided that if she did, I'd say something to her. At least I'd have witnesses if she did something. But she never came in. When I plucked up the nerve to leave, it looked like she was gone, so I relaxed. But then, a couple of minutes later, she was back again, walking behind me, and that's when I got really scared.'

'Shit,' Ollie says, echoing my thoughts.

'That's so scary, Jo.' My skin grows cold at the thought of how my sister must have felt at hearing those footsteps behind her again.

Ollie goes over to her and leads her back to the sofa.

Jo's hands are shaking now, and her voice is quavering. 'That's when I called you guys and asked you to meet me at home. I didn't want to come back to an empty house. Although I don't even know how I managed to work my phone. I was so scared, my fingers felt numb.'

'So she followed you home?' I ask, worried about a potential stalker knowing where we live.

'I hope not, but I don't know. After I called you, I legged it. I turned down a side street and hid behind a bush in someone's front garden. And then I saw the woman come down the road looking for me. It was the scariest, creepiest thing, Nat. Honestly, I thought she was going to kill me or something.'

'Did she see you?' Ollie asks.

'No,' Jo replies. 'She stood there, fuming, shaking her head like she was pissed off, and then she came down the road, looking for me. When she walked past the house where I was hiding, I thought

I was going to wet myself, or scream or something. But I clamped my hand over my mouth and managed to keep it together.'

'Jo, that sounds terrifying,' I say. 'No wonder you were freaking out. What did the woman look like?'

'Dark hair in a ponytail, pale skin, big build. She looked like she could handle herself, if you know what I mean? Black puffer-style jacket and black leggings with black Ugg-type boots.'

'We should call the police,' Ollie says, pulling out his mobile.

Jo shakes her head. 'No. I will if I see her again, but I can't cope with the police. I'm in too much of a state right now.'

'But—'

'Please, Ollie. Not now.'

He nods reluctantly and slides his phone back into his pocket.

'Who do you think she was?' I ask. 'I mean, it's a bit weird that someone's following you.'

'What if it's to do with Elle?' Jo whispers, her eyes glistening.

'In what way?' I add.

'I don't know, but . . . what if it's one of those cranks from back then?' Jo comes to a halt by the kitchen island, facing us both. 'You know, with the anniversary coming up they'll all be crawling out of the woodwork. And I'm willingly going along with this police appeal, which is only going to make things worse.'

My stomach clenches at the thought of it. 'We have to try to ignore the cranks and focus on the possibility that someone out there somewhere knows something. And they might get in touch,' I say, trying to put a positive spin on things.

'I know, but I just don't think I can handle going through it all again,' she says, shaking her head slowly. 'Why is this happening? Haven't I put up with enough?'

Chapter Fourteen

THEN

'It's good of you to do lunch today, Natalie,' Mum says as she and Dad rush in out of the rain.

I kiss their damp cheeks. 'It's only soup, sandwiches and crisps from Tesco. We didn't have time to cook.'

'Well, that's all we need, isn't it,' Mum replies kindly, shaking her golfing umbrella and leaving it on the porch step. 'No one wants a heavy lunch to make us all sleepy when there's so much to do.'

'Don't suppose you got BLTs, did you?' Dad asks.

'I did, especially for you.'

Dad gives me a wink and I feel a warm glow from that little gesture. I hadn't realised how much I needed my parents here. After so much pain, it's a relief to have some extra support. I sag a little, looking forward to letting them take over for a bit.

'I hope the weather's not going to stay like this,' Mum adds. 'Will people still come, do you think?'

'I hope so. Theo checked the forecast and said it's supposed to clear up by one,' I reply, taking their coats.

'Hmm.' Dad frowns. 'Did he check the Met Office site, because the others are useless.'

'I'm sure he did, Dad. Come through. Everyone's in the kitchen.'

Mum holds me back for a moment and lowers her voice. 'How is she?'

I shake my head. 'Not great.'

She blinks, her eyes bright with tears. 'I just can't believe it. Our darling little Elle. The sweetest girl.' Mum's voice breaks and she rummages in her bag for a tissue.

'Come on now, Barbara.' Dad pats her arm. 'We need to stay strong for Josephine. Let's hope that someone's going to find our little granddaughter this afternoon.'

Today marks one week since Elle disappeared, and I've organised a search party. We're not expecting to find her out there, but the plan is to go into town and speak to people. To hand out flyers and show Elle's photo to shoppers and visitors, to stallholders and shop workers. We also managed to get hold of some video footage of the person in the dog costume. Someone forwarded it to the police after their request on social media. Unfortunately, it's just a snippet of video and the dog isn't skating with Elle. But we took a still image so at least we have a photo to show people. Maybe it will jog someone's memory.

Unfortunately, the downside of getting the public involved is that we've had quite a few nasty comments from people on social media. Trolls saying things like Jo doesn't deserve to have a child, or that she's staged the whole thing for attention. It's been sickening. We block those accounts, but it's like being punched in the ribcage every time another one pops up. I don't understand how people think they have a right to pass judgement on someone else's life. On someone else's misfortune. How can people be so cruel? It's made Jo retreat into her shell even more.

I've even seen some locals on Facebook make comments about Jo's character. A lot of, *I told you so*, and, *it was only a matter of time*, and, *that poor child having a mother like that*. Sure, Jo had a bit of a wild past and probably didn't endear herself to everyone she met, but since having Elle she's calmed down a lot and has been a great mum. So for people to turn around and claim she's an unfit mother is nothing but malicious gossip. I guess some people don't have anything better to do.

Worse, there have also been a couple of anonymous online threats made to Jo's life. And one instance where a woman parked outside the house waiting for her to come out before yelling that she was an unfit mother. She drove off before my sister could get her number plate. Jo didn't recognise her, but we wondered how she knew our address, and how she knew Jo was staying with us. We reported everything to the police, and they're investigating. But they told us that unfortunately this is a common occurrence and there's not a lot that can be done.

Jo isn't coming with us on the search today. She said there's no chance of finding Elle in town and she can't face asking strangers if they've seen her daughter. She's nervous of people's reactions, worried in case they're abusive. I tried to reassure her that those sorts of idiots aren't brave enough to say things to her face, that the people we meet today will all be kind and sympathetic. She replied that sympathy is almost worse. That it will finish her off. I know what she means. It's going to be emotionally draining.

But I can't stop myself doing everything in my power to find Elle. What if talking to one person today is the difference between finding her and not? Maybe someone was away or on holiday and now they're back. I can't leave any stone unturned. The other reason I'm pushing myself to do this is that I know once I stop, I'll fall to pieces, and I need to stay strong for Jo, and for the rest of my family.

I let Jo know that I understood her reasons. Ollie has offered to stay home with her today. I also didn't want Georgia coming with us because I felt it might be too traumatising. She begged to be allowed to hand out flyers with her friends, but the last thing I want is to be worrying about her and her friends' safety, on top of everything else. So my parents are going to take her to the cinema in town and meet up with us afterwards.

Mum and Dad go cautiously through to the kitchen, where Georgia is opening the sandwich packs and arranging them on plates and Theo is standing at the range stirring the Moroccan vegetable soup.

Mum bypasses them and hugs Jo, choking back a sob. I can tell that Dad is trying to hold it together too. I've never seen him this emotional. Since they returned from their holiday in Austria, they've been round each day, but Jo has been in bed and unwilling to talk to them, or us, for more than a minute or two. Today is the first day they've seen her up and dressed.

I've made Theo promise not to mention Jo bringing a guy home the other night. Not to her and absolutely not to my parents. He said that was fine, as long as it didn't happen again. I agreed with Theo, but I'm nervous that my sister will go on another bender. I'll have to tread carefully around both of them and work out the best way to deal with things.

'Right,' Mum says with a sniff, clapping her hands together. 'Shall I help you with those sandwiches, Georgia? Maybe we can cut them into quarters?'

The doorbell rings and Jo heads for the door. 'That'll be Ollie.'

'Ollie's here?' Mum says. 'That's nice.'

'He comes round every evening to see Jo.'

'Nice chap,' Dad says, which is high praise from him.

'Hi, everyone.' Ollie comes into the kitchen with his usual golden-retriever energy. All blond hair, brown puppy-dog eyes and smiles.

'Ollie,' Mum says. 'It's so lovely to see you. We've just heard how you've been a real rock for Josephine.'

He gives her a hug. 'Hi, Barbara.'

'Oliver.' Dad shakes his hand. 'Good to see you.'

'Nice to see you too, Derek.'

'Shall we sit?' I help Theo dish up the soup and bring the bowls to the table, where we all tuck in. I don't feel hungry, but I know I'll need the fuel for later.

'This is delicious,' Mum says after a bit of an awkward silence, the sound of soup spoons clanging against bowls setting my teeth on edge. 'So, Ollie, what are you up to these days?'

'I'm managing a dry cleaners,' he replies. 'Living the high life.' He smiles and gives a little laugh.

'That's a decent job,' Mum says, a little patronisingly. 'Whereabouts?'

'It's called Dry Your Eyes. The one at the Pokesdown end.'

'Oh, I know it. We use the one up near us, but I'll come to yours next time.'

'I'll give you the family discount.' Ollie blinks rapidly, the only clue that he's finding this forced jollity as painful as I am.

'Well, you do feel like family,' Mum says.

'I always said you and Josephine should have got married,' Dad says, heaping his side plate with BLT sandwiches.

'Dad!' Jo and I both shut him down, catching each other's eye with a brief look that catapults me back to lighter times when we'd despair of Dad's tactlessness.

'I'm only saying, you two are a good match,' he replies grumpily.

'Please, Dad.' Jo shakes her head, her demeanour sinking back to heaviness once again.

Ollie grins. 'She knows I'd marry her in a heartbeat. But she likes to see me suffer.'

Jo scowls and Mum tuts, whispering under her breath to Dad, 'Derek, leave the poor girl alone. She's got enough to worry about.'

'Sorry,' Dad says uncharacteristically. 'I just thought—'

'Paul sends his love to you, Jo.' Mum interrupts Dad before he puts his foot in it again.

'Paul sends his love?' Jo retorts. 'Well, that's nice of him. Does Susie send her love too?'

'Oh, Josephine,' Mum replies. 'It's difficult. They live in another country. Paul would be here lending his support if he could. He's devastated for you.'

'If he was so concerned,' Jo says, 'he would have called me. Shit, he could have even texted.'

'Don't swear in front of Georgia,' Mum says.

'Don't take it out on your mother,' Dad adds. 'She's just passing on a message from your brother.'

Theo shakes his head and stands up. 'Georgia, shall we take our sandwiches into the lounge while the rest of the grown-ups talk?'

'Why?' Georgia asks, staring around the table. 'Are they going to have an argument?'

The table goes silent for a moment.

Jo deflates. 'No. No, we're not. Sorry. I didn't mean to get annoyed. Sorry, Georgia. Sorry, Mum.'

'It's fine, love.' Mum pats her hand. 'Nothing to apologise for.'

'I don't mind if you argue,' Georgia says. 'Me and my friends have arguments all the time, but we usually make friends again.'

Her words lighten the mood a fraction.

As Theo sits back down, I throw him a quick smile, grateful to have him looking out for Georgia while I manage the rest of my family. Everyone's nerves are frayed, but thankfully the rest of lunch goes smoothly with Ollie and Mum carrying most of the conversation, talking about mundane things.

But I can tell that Jo is simmering under the surface, hating every moment. The truth is that if we all showed how we really felt – the fear, the helplessness, the cold, sucking terror – we wouldn't be able to function properly. There would be no lunch, no conversation, no search party, no nothing. I comfort myself with the fact that Jo and Ollie will have the house to themselves soon, and then she'll be able to relax, or sleep, or cry in peace.

Chapter Fifteen

NOW

'Whose idea was it to come to an outdoor bar in November?' I ask Theo, smiling as I tug my coat tighter around me.

'I think that would be yours,' he replies, grinning back and poking me in the ribs, only I can't feel it because I'm so cold.

We're having drinks at the Beach Shack, a pop-up restaurant and bar on our local beach built from painted shipping containers. The place is buzzing with people enjoying the food, the drink and the live music. The Shack is usually only here in the summer, but the owner, Madeline, who's a friend of ours, is trialling weekends in the run-up to Christmas, putting on themed evenings with speciality food and music. Tonight is Caribbean night. She asked me to spread the word a while back and so I thought it might be fun to pop along, especially as Theo and I need to spend some quality time together. His comments about what we're going to do once Georgia leaves home have made me realise that I need to put more effort into our relationship. We both do. I'm happy we're here, only I wish it wasn't quite so cold. The covered outdoor area has heaters, and plenty of throws and blankets, but the temperatures are arctic and don't quite match the theme of the night.

'Natalie, Theo, you came!' We look up from our table to see Madeline bearing a tray of drinks. 'I'm bringing everyone a hot spiced rum punch, compliments of the house.' She sets our drinks on the table. 'That'll warm the cockles of your heart,' she adds.

'Thanks, Madeline,' I say, enjoying the warmth of the glass against my icy fingers. 'These look amazing.'

'Great turnout.' Theo gestures to the packed bar.

'It's not bad, is it?' she replies. 'I only wish our indoor area was bigger. We'll have to remedy that next year.'

'A few more of these rum punches and we won't notice the cold,' Theo says.

'Or you could be the first to get on the dance floor,' she wheedles, gesturing to the empty space in front of the live band. 'That'll get the blood pumping.'

'Maybe later.'

'I'll hold you to that,' she says before sashaying off to the next table.

'I can't believe it's so busy down here,' Theo says. 'It's great though. Feels like we're in our twenties again.'

'I wish,' I reply with a grin. 'Can you believe that Georgia will be in her twenties in a couple of years?'

'Shut up, that's impossible.' Theo takes a sip of his drink. 'Jeez, that's strong.'

I sip mine carefully. 'Wow, that'll strip the roof of your mouth.'

We grin at each other and I feel like maybe things will be okay.

'She's eighteen next month,' he says. 'Our little Gee-Gee.'

'I know. How did it all go by so quickly?' I muse.

We've all been quite shaken by Jo's traumatic event a couple of days ago and so it's nice for me and Theo to get out and have some time alone together. To reconnect and have a bit of fun. To talk about anything other than my sister's drama. We chat about mundane things for a while. Work, friends, what we're doing for Christmas this year. I'm nicely drunk. That stage where you're warm inside and everything is mildly fuzzy. I'm still cold, but it's not so noticeable now. For a short moment, I feel deliciously unworried about everything. I'd almost forgotten what that felt like.

'It's nice, just the two of us,' I say.

He starts singing that song and swaying in his seat. I laugh at his goofiness and feel a bubble of joy in my chest. This feels good.

We ate before we came out, but the cold is making us hungry, so we order a couple of plates – some barbecued sweetcorn ribs with plantain hummus, and a portion of sweet potato and lime curry with roti bread. It comes out piping hot and Theo and I devour the lot, letting it soak up some of the alcohol.

'Is Georgia out tonight?' Theo asks.

'They've all gone to Naomi's, I think her parents are away.'

'They're a good group of kids.'

'They are. She's a bit gloomy at the moment though,' I say, thinking out loud.

'Who, Georgia?' Theo squints across the table at me and I can tell he's pretty drunk.

'Yeah. She's not herself.'

'I've noticed that too,' he replies thoughtfully. 'Maybe we need some time away together as a family.'

'A holiday in the sun?' I ask, perking up. When was the last time we had a holiday abroad?

'Not sure we can stretch to that. Maybe a short break.'

'That would be nice.'

'I worry about Gee-Gee,' Theo says. 'She's had it tough after Elle, and now she's going to be an adult . . .' His eyes glisten with emotion.

'Going off to uni,' I add.

'Don't remind me.' Theo's face falls. He's always been a hands-on dad, but after Elle disappeared he became even more protective of Georgia. I don't know how he's going to handle her leaving home.

I need to change the subject before things turn maudlin. 'We could have asked Ollie and Jo to come along tonight, they'd have loved it.'

'No, it's good to have time away.' Theo reaches out and squeezes my hand. 'We see them every day.'

'Not *every* day.' I frown, trying to keep my voice level.

'Most days,' he amends.

I realise things can get a little claustrophobic with us all virtually living together, but I tend to get defensive when Theo mentions it. Even though Jo is technically in the garage and Ollie has his own place, they do spend an awful lot of time in our kitchen. I don't like to admit it, but Jo living with us does put a bit of a strain on our marriage.

'I think we need more time apart from them,' Theo says tentatively.

'They're fine,' I reply, not wanting to get into this now. Not while I'm feeling so buzzed.

'We need to talk about it, Nat. But every time I try, you get upset or deflect. We need to stop treading on eggshells around her.' He pauses as if choosing his words carefully. 'I don't like the fact that it's impossible to relax in our own home.'

'You're exaggerating,' I huff. 'It's not that bad.'

'You're in denial,' he replies. 'And anyway, you're her sister so of course you feel more at ease around her. But for me it's less . . . relaxing. Your sister's always been flaky, but now she's totally dependent on you. She's always guilt-tripping you, and you always fall for it.'

'She isn't.' I frown. 'And I don't!' Although his words have hit a nerve. This isn't what I wanted to be talking about tonight. I wanted us to have a bit of fun. To escape our worries. Why is he bringing all this up?

Theo raises his hands in surrender. 'Okay, but we do need to talk about this. Look at what happened the day before yesterday when she was being followed. It's always you who has to calm her down. It's not good for you, or her. And then I get in from work after a long day of meetings and the place is like a madhouse with Jo crying and you stressed, and Ollie just hanging around like he always is. What about your parents? Can't they help out more? They're rattling around in that big old house of theirs. Surely they can convert part of it into a wing for Jo.'

I sigh, realising he's not going to let this drop. 'Mum and Dad do what they can,' I reply, sticking up for them even though they actually don't do that much at all. 'But they're getting on a bit and they definitely don't have the money to remodel their house.'

I guess they thought their days of active parenting would have eased off by now. I'm beginning to realise that parenting never stops. The older your kids get, the more complicated the problems. If I allowed myself to think more deeply about it, I think I'd feel some resentment towards them for allowing me to take over my sister's emotional and financial support. They must see that it's taken a toll on me and on Theo, especially after Elle went missing.

I tried to talk to Mum about it a few years ago, but she shut me down quite quickly and so I don't dare let myself open that can of worms again. I have too many precarious relationships to juggle right now and I don't want to tip any of them over the edge. I just don't have the mental energy for it. And if Theo knew I resented Mum and Dad for their abandonment of Jo, he would push me even more to have it out with them.

'Anyway,' I continue, casting about for any way to defuse this situation but at the same time wanting him to understand, 'being followed was a scary thing for Jo to go through so of course I comforted her, what else should I have done? We reported it to the police, but they haven't come up with anything.'

Back when Elle went missing, Jo was targeted by a few anonymous trolls online issuing death threats and saying other awful things. As well as the person who parked outside our house and shouted at Jo, there was a local woman who was given a restraining order after she threw a milkshake at my sister and told her she was going to burn in hell. Unsurprisingly, it left Jo really shaken. And now she's worried that, with it coming up to the ten-year anniversary of Elle's disappearance, it might be starting up all over again.

'I love Jo,' Theo continues, 'but I think she needs professional help to get her back on her feet properly. We should have insisted she get help years ago.'

'Short of dragging her into a counsellor's chair, I'm not sure how we could have done it,' I retort. 'And this week was an exceptional circumstance. She was being followed. I'd have been just as scared if it happened to me.'

'That's my point,' Theo says frustratedly, leaning back in his chair and looking up at the pitch-black starless sky. 'It didn't happen to you. These things always happen to *Jo*. It's always Jo pulling you into her dramas.'

'But it wasn't her fault.'

'Maybe not, but it's still bloody exhausting. I know she's had it rough,' Theo continues, 'and, God knows, I feel for her, but maybe . . . No, never mind, forget it.'

'Maybe *what*?' I push, even though I know that it's better if I allow him to leave the words unsaid. Our fun evening is unravelling faster than a kitten's ball of wool.

Theo takes a breath. 'I was just going to say that it's been ten years. Do we have to keep doing this for another ten? And then another ten?'

My face heats up. 'What do you want me to do? Kick her out? Tell her that her time's up? You know she won't make it on her own. She'll end up on the streets.'

'No she won't. She'll move in with Ollie and they'll live happily ever after. Even before Elle went missing, we were propping Jo up. We were like Elle's surrogate parents. I know it was hard for Jo as a single parent, but we really did pick up the slack. I felt like Elle was my daughter as much as Georgia, she was round our place so much. But that was fine because I loved that girl.' Theo swallows and blinks back his emotions. 'And it was manageable because she and Jo had their own place to go back to. But now . . . it's just . . .' He clicks his teeth and sighs. 'At the moment, don't you think we're just enabling Jo? Giving in to all her whims and letting her walk all over us.'

'I can't believe you said that! We're not enabling her. We're looking out for her. We're responsible!'

'Responsible? She's a grown woman.'

'I mean . . .' I take a breath and feel tears smarting behind my eyes. 'I mean, we're responsible for what happened. Elle went missing on our watch. We owe Jo her life back. We can never make things right, but we can at least smooth the way a little. It's the least we can do.'

Theo shakes his head, still annoyed. 'We're not responsible for that, Natalie. Someone obviously took Elle. They're the one responsible. Not us. We were at a birthday party with six little girls. It was impossible to watch all of them at once every single second while they're skating around. You can't blame yourself.'

'I was looking after Sasha at the time,' I say, lost in the memories. 'I wasn't with the rest of the girls.' As soon as the words leave my lips, I wish I could take them back.

Theo grows still and sets his glass down carefully on the table. 'So you're saying you blame me, is that it?'

'No!' I cry. 'Of course not. I would never say that.'

'You've never said it before, but you think it, right?' Hurt spreads across his features, followed by a tight-lipped anger. 'You think I should have kept a closer eye on Elle.'

'You've misunderstood me, Theo.'

'The thing is, Natalie, I don't think I have. You were very clear.' He gets up and walks away while my fuzzy brain scrambles to catch up with what just happened.

Chapter Sixteen

THEN

There are over two hundred of us gathered on Bournemouth Beach to the left of the pier, drawing curious looks from day trippers and dog walkers. The rain has eased and the wind has dropped, but the sky is a thick steel blanket. It's early afternoon in December, but the muted grey light makes it feel like evening. Behind us, surfers bob in the iron-dark sea like black seals, while overhead white seagulls wheel and dive, calling out bleakly to one another.

I check my watch and see that it's a few minutes after 1 p.m. I asked volunteers to be here by one, so I take a couple of steps away from the gathered crowd and turn to face them.

'Hi, everyone,' I call out, hoping my voice is loud enough to carry. 'Can I get your attention, please?' It takes a few moments for the crowd to settle down and realise I'm addressing them. Eventually, after several nudges and shushes, they all turn my way. A few stragglers are joining them. I recognise a lot of school mums, neighbours and work colleagues, which is heartening to see.

'In case some of you don't know, my name's Natalie Edwards. I'm Elle's aunt. Her mum, Jo, and I honestly can't thank you enough for joining the WhatsApp group and for showing up today. We really appreciate it from the bottom of our hearts.

'This time last week, Elle was with us safe and sound, but now . . .' I swallow and take a breath. 'Now, she's missing, and we desperately want to find her. The aim of today is to speak to as many people as possible and to ask people in town to put up flyers. To share on social media. To ask their friends and families if they've seen Elle. Remember to speak to teenagers who have Saturday jobs because chances are they'll probably have been here last Saturday too. They could be our best chance at getting a lead. Also ask older people who might not have seen the posts on social media.'

As I talk about leads, flyers and posts, I try not to give in to the crushing disappointment that here we are a week later and there's still no news. Even the ice-skate prints found outside the rink, which I'd felt sure would lead to something, have turned out to be inconclusive evidence. I give myself an internal shake and continue talking:

'I've put each of you into zones. Some at the beach, some in town and some at the gardens. Keep to your zones as there will be a high turnover of people and we don't want to miss anyone or double up asking the same people. It's only thirteen days until Christmas so everywhere will be really busy.

'You've been added to two new WhatsApp groups. The one entitled *Elle – Questions and Information* is for – you guessed it – any questions you might have and answers you can give. The second WhatsApp group, called *Elle – Sightings*, is for that specific information only. Please only post in that group if you come across someone who thinks they might have seen either Elle or the person in the dog costume. In that case, please post their name and contact information so we can pass it along to the police to follow up.

'I have bundles of flyers here in these cartons. So please don't forget to take plenty before you head out. Any questions before we get going?'

An older gentleman raises his hand. 'Are we meeting back here afterwards?'

I glance across at Theo, who shrugs and then shakes his head. 'Umm, probably not,' I reply, 'because people will want to leave at different times. But we can keep in touch via the main WhatsApp group.'

Along with all the volunteers there are a couple of plain-clothes police officers, who are here to mingle with everyone, to see if anyone here knows anything or seems suspicious. Shockingly, the police informed us that it has been known for perpetrators to ingratiate themselves with the family or friends. To join in the searches and try to glean information about the investigation. That whole scenario gives me the creeps, but I'm trying not to dwell on it. Not to look at any of these kind people through suspicious eyes.

'Any more questions?' I ask. 'No? Okay, good luck and thank you all so much again. Keep hydrated and keep warm. At least it's stopped raining now!'

I watch everyone collect their flyers and head off to various parts of the town. Despite what I heard about one of these volunteers potentially being the perpetrator, the sight of this little makeshift army of friends and Good Samaritans lifts my spirits. Maybe we really do have a chance of getting a decent lead today. Maybe there will be something that draws us back to Elle. For a second, I let myself imagine that we find her safe and well. That we bring her home to Jo. That there's an end to this nightmare . . .

As I get chatting to the public and the shopkeepers, handing out flyers and talking about Elle, it's clear that a lot of people have already heard about what happened and are pretty emotional about it. Letting me know that they'll do everything they can to look out for her, and promising to spread the word. I think Jo was right not to come today. It would have been too overwhelming for her. I've already had to fight back tears on numerous occasions because of people's concern and kindness.

As I'm coming out of The Arcade into Old Christchurch Road, I overhear Elle's name being spoken by a woman.

'Poor little Elle,' the woman says. 'It's such a tragedy.'

I turn around with a smile, but pause when a dark-haired woman responds:

'I know, especially having a mother like that. Apparently, she was out clubbing when it happened. And she didn't join in the search for hours because she was too busy having fun.'

Both women are around my age, expensively dressed, with sleek hair and immaculate make-up.

'Mm,' the blonde woman replies. 'Who goes clubbing while your daughter's missing? My two are my first priority. If anything happened to them, Grant and I would be tearing across the whole town to find them.'

'I know. My friend's daughter's in Elle's class at school and she said that Jo hardly ever does pick-ups or drop-offs, apparently she—'

'Excuse me,' I say, closing in on them, hot with rage at their mean-spirited words.

They both turn and give me a disdainful look before realising who I am.

The blonde-haired woman smiles and waves some flyers at me. 'Hi, I'm Abi. We're part of the search party. You're Natalie, right? We're so sorry about Elle.'

'So sorry that you don't mind slagging off my sister when she's suffering one of the worst fates imaginable?'

The blonde woman flushes at being caught out, but the other woman scowls.

'Because if that's how sorry you are,' I continue, 'then we don't need your condolences or your help, thanks anyway.'

I snatch the flyers from her hand, turn and stride away from them, shaking with rage and disappointment. Why do some people have to be so nasty? Why can't they have some grace and be kind? But I have to calm down. I can't let a couple of bitchy mums distract from why I'm here today. And that is to find my niece. I slow my walk and slow my breathing, telling myself to forget what I heard and concentrate on Elle. I'm determined that this afternoon's efforts will lead us to finding her.

But today turns out to be the first of many, many search parties and campaigns spearheaded by me over the next few weeks. Each one organised with less and less optimism, and none of which is ultimately successful.

Chapter Seventeen

NOW

I'll kill her when she gets home. I'll absolutely kill her.

I look out of the bedroom window, peering up and down the road for any sign of a taxi or a car. But the road is silent. Just a brown fox trotting along the middle of the street.

This time it isn't Jo I'm angry at, it's Georgia. She's out clubbing in town with her friends and she's late home. She told me she'd be back by 1 a.m. and she promised she'd call if she somehow got delayed. But it's almost one thirty and there's no sign of her. She already bargained me up from midnight to one o'clock. According to my daughter, things don't even get going until twelve, which is different from back in my day when the licensing laws were stricter and things shut down earlier.

Georgia's never been to a nightclub before – well, not as far as I'm aware – and so I made her promise to keep me in the loop. As she's not quite eighteen, she's using a friend's ID to get into the venue, which I'm not exactly happy about, but apparently all the kids do it, or they have fake IDs. So I either have to be a liberal parent and turn a blind eye or make her a social pariah. Neither of which is an appealing option.

Liz and I have had numerous conversations about these types of things over Georgia and Sasha's teenage years. She knows how hard it is for me to loosen Georgia's reins after what happened to Elle, but she agrees that these milestones give her sleepless nights too, although Sasha has an older brother, Finlay, at uni, so at least Liz has had some experience of letting go.

Infuriatingly, Georgia has taken herself off the Find My app, which was a condition of her being allowed to go clubbing in the first place. Mingled with my fury is a crippling fear that something bad could have happened to her. Is that why she deleted the app? As some kind of coded message that she's in danger? No, that's too obscure. My sleep-deprived brain is spiralling.

Should I go out trawling the streets, looking for her? Should I call her friends? Only I don't have their numbers so I'd have to get in touch with their parents or via social media, and then Georgia will be furious with me for being overprotective. Not that I'm worried about that right now. I'd rather have a cross daughter than a missing one.

Georgia has always been sociable, but she's never pushed the boundaries like some of her friends. I've always felt quite lucky that we have such an open and honest relationship. I think losing her cousin has made her more wary, and more attuned to Theo's and my feelings. That's why tonight is so out of character. Although, she's been acting out of character a lot lately, being snappy and rude, not helping out with chores or letting us know her plans, and she seems to be getting worse. I think it might be something to do with her eighteenth coming up. I'll have to sit down with her sometime this week; see if she'll open up about what might be troubling her.

I check my phone for any missed messages, but there's nothing. And my texts and WhatsApps to her are sitting on the screen unread.

Tonight is doubly hard as Theo is away for a couple of days. He said that his works event in Milton Keynes today was going to be a late one, so he would probably stay over. Theo never stays over when he has work events or meetings – not if he can help it. He always said he prefers to come home and sleep in his own bed rather than in some lonely hotel. So it hurts that he's decided to stay over. After our disastrous night at the Beach Shack last weekend, we both apologised to each other for letting the conversation get out of control, but things have been awkward between us ever since.

I think Theo might have thought that a night away would do us good. But, in my opinion, it's the opposite. It feels like we're drifting further apart. All those things he said about my sister were nothing compared to what I said about Elle's disappearance. *Blaming him.* How could I have insinuated that it was his fault? I'd like to think it was the fault of the rum punch, but the truth is that I've had those thoughts swirling around my brain for years. I've just never voiced them until now.

I don't know how to fix this. Will he ever forgive me? I can't wait for him to come back so that I can try to make things right again. How can the fallout from Elle's disappearance still be rippling down through the years? Will it never end? Will Theo and I keep circling around the same frustrating, guilt-laden conversations forever?

And now, here I am, home alone on a Friday night, worried out of my mind about every person I love. It's not what I signed up for when I was young and dreaming of having a family. This fear and anxiety over their well-being and our relationships with one another. It's exhausting and terrifying.

I give myself a shake and tell myself to stop being so bloody miserable. I'm just tired, that's all. Everything will be fine. Georgia's being a typical teenager and having too good a time to worry about her mum. And Theo and I have had worse arguments. When he gets home, I'll let him know how much he means to me and we'll get through it, somehow. Try to come up with a solution that is good for all of us. If I didn't have him by my side, I don't know what I'd do.

My heart skips as I see headlights sweeping down the road. A car! Please say it's my daughter. A yellow taxi pulls up outside next door's and idles for a moment. Could it be her? I keep watching out the window, ready to go downstairs if it's Georgia. The driver, a woman, gets out and glances at the neighbour's place, then heads towards our house. I tie my dressing gown tightly and rush down the stairs before flinging open the front door, where a blast of cold, damp air makes me catch my breath.

'Hello.' I wave at the woman.

'I think I've got your daughter in the car,' the driver says. 'She's passed out. Can you give me a hand?'

'Is she okay?' My relief is swiftly being replaced by anxiety again. I wonder if I'm going to have to take her to the hospital to get her stomach pumped like Naomi's mum had to do last year.

'She's fine, but totally sparko.'

I slip my trainers on and follow the woman to her cab, where she opens the back door.

'Sweet girl,' the woman says kindly. 'She was so chatty for the first part of the journey, but then she just fell asleep and I couldn't wake her. Thought I'd see if anyone could give me a hand getting her out. I didn't want to yank her out of there. Thought I'd let her mum or dad do that. At least she didn't throw up in my cab.'

I peer in and see Georgia sprawled across the back seat, fast asleep. Relief floods my body. She's finally home. She's okay, just a bit drunk. I reach out and give her bare leg a shake. 'Georgia, Georgia, wake up. You're home.'

She mumbles and turns over, trying to make herself more comfortable.

'Up you get, Georgia. Come on, up!' I reach in and try to hoist her up by her arm.

After a few seconds, she opens her eyes and then closes them again. 'Sleeping,' she mumbles.

'Time to get up!' I say loudly, tugging her upright. 'Come on, open your eyes, Gee.'

'What?' This time she opens her eyes properly and focuses them on me. 'Mum, what are you doing?'

'You need to get out of this lady's taxi.'

'Oh.' She looks around. 'I fell asleep.'

'No shit, Sherlock,' the woman says, giving a little laugh.

Finally, I get my daughter out of the cab and link arms with her in case she's wobbly. I turn to the driver. 'Do I owe you anything?'

'No. It's all done through the app. You good?'

'Yes. Thanks so much for looking after her.' I open Georgia's bag and root through for some cash, locating a tenner, which I hand the driver.

'Very kind of you,' she replies, getting back into her cab.

'Let's get you inside,' I say, leading my daughter back into the house and wondering how many neighbours are watching out of their windows, cursing us for waking them up.

'Gonna be sick,' Georgia says, rushing to the downstairs loo and chucking her guts up into the toilet.

I'm half relieved. She'll feel much better after throwing up. I follow her in and rub her back, holding her hair away for round two. I'll have to get her in the shower before she goes to bed.

'I feel horrible, Mum,' she sobs.

'I'm sure you do. You'll be fine after a good night's sleep.'

I don't quiz her about why she's late. It's not the time. Instead, I pour her a glass of water and take her up to her room.

'I need to sleep,' she mumbles.

'Quick shower first,' I say.

'Ugh, do I have to?'

'Yes.'

She takes off her dress and I freeze at the sight of a multitude of thin white lines running across her upper thighs. I feel as though I might be sick myself. Are those what I think they are? I think so.

My daughter follows my line of sight and grabs her dress to cover them up, her expression instantly alert.

'Georgia,' I say slowly, carefully. 'Georgia, what are those marks?'

'They're nothing, Mum. They're old. I did it a while ago, like an experiment to see. But I won't do it again, I promise.' She flops on to the bed, tears welling. 'I'm sorry, Mum. I'm really sorry.'

'You don't have to be sorry, my darling. You just need to talk to me. Tell me why you did it.'

'I don't know. Can we not talk about it, please?'

I sit next to her and take her hand. It's cold and feels so fragile. 'Don't you think it might be better if we did talk about it? Try to work through whatever it is that's making you feel like you have to do it?'

'I told you I don't do it anymore! Just let me have my shower and go to bed, please.' She's sobbing now, tears and snot running down her face. She uses her dress to wipe it away. She looks so young, so frail. And I can't stop thinking about those marks. About the fact that she cut herself so many times. It makes me feel so sad. Like I've failed her as a parent.

Chapter Eighteen

THEN

'Knock, knock!'

I peer around the fridge to see Mum coming into the kitchen.

'You know your front door's wide open, Natalie. Anyone could walk in.'

'I've just been unloading the shopping from the car,' I reply, stashing a carton of oat milk in the fridge. 'Must've forgotten to close it.'

'Do you want a hand?'

'No, it's okay, I've finished now. Did you close the front door behind you?'

'I did.'

'Thanks,' I reply. 'Where's Dad?'

'He'll be here soon, he's—'

'Actually, Mum, I wanted to talk to you about something.'

'Oh yes?' Mum looks worried. 'Is there news?'

'Not about Elle, no.'

'Not even after last week's big search?' Mum asks. 'I can't believe how many people showed up. Over two hundred, you said? It's heartwarming there's so much love for our little Elle.'

'The police said they had lots of leads and phone calls to chase up,' I say, 'but nothing positive.'

'Nothing positive *yet*,' Mum amends. 'We will get her back, Natalie. I just know it. We can't let ourselves think otherwise. Where's Josephine? How's she holding up?'

'That's what I wanted to talk to you about.' I walk over to the kitchen door and peer out to make sure no one else is around, but it's all clear so I close the door and then head to the kitchen table.

Mum sits opposite me. 'This is all very mysterious, Natalie.'

'I just, I wanted to ask if maybe you should offer for Jo to move in with you for a while.' I exhale. I hadn't planned on asking that at all, but when I saw Mum, I realised that I needed to say it. 'Of course,' I continue, 'she's welcome to be here, but I don't know how great it is for her to be around Georgia while Elle's missing. It's like this constant reminder that my daughter is here while hers . . . isn't.'

'Oh, she wouldn't think like that at all,' Mum protests.

'And also, it's not great for Georgia,' I add. Jo has been picking fights with me this week, and I've let them go because I know she's in a bad way, but I worry for my daughter being exposed to all this stress.

Mum is quiet for a moment, and I'm mindful that Theo, Jo or Georgia could come in at any second. I should have picked a better time to talk about this.

'Mum, what do you think? I know Jo would be grateful if you asked her to come back home for a while. A bit of TLC and some of your home-made soup.'

Mum gives a weak smile. 'She's settled with you though, isn't she, Natalie? You and Theo are more relaxed with her. You know what your father's like. Those two always rub each other up the wrong way. Anyway, it's only until they find Elle again, and then they'll both be back in their little flat.'

I'm just about to push it some more when the kitchen door opens.

'Is that Mum's car out front?' Jo walks into the kitchen in her dressing gown.

I can sense Mum's relief that the conversation's over and she thinks the matter's settled. She stands up and walks over to Jo. 'Hello, darling.' Mum kisses her cheek.

A few seconds later Theo comes down the stairs to join us, his hair damp from the shower.

'Hi, Theo.'

'Hi, Barbara,' Theo says. 'Derek not with you?'

'I dropped him off at Sainsbury's with orders to pick up some Danish pastries. He'll be here any minute. Natalie was just telling me that there's no news yet.'

'There's nothing,' Jo replies, leaning against the island.

'Shall I make coffee?' Theo asks.

'Lovely,' Mum says. 'Where's Georgia?'

'In her room,' I reply. 'I'll leave her for now. She's not been sleeping well. We'll call her down to say hi when her grandpa arrives.'

'Oh, I almost forgot.' Mum rummages around in her bag. 'The reason we popped over so early is because Paul and Susie sent us a little Christmas parcel – so thoughtful of them. They sent me a bar of that delicious nougat, turron I think it's called. I love it, but your father can't eat it – too chewy. Anyway, I'm rambling.' Mum sits back down and sets her handbag on the kitchen table. 'Where are the blasted things?' She opens her bag wider and by now we're all interested in what she's looking for. 'Oh, here we go.' She pulls out two white envelopes. 'Two cards. One for you, Natalie, and one for you, Josephine.' Mum holds them out for us to take.

I take mine, but Jo is reluctant, looking at hers like it's an unexploded bomb. 'What is it?' she asks.

'I presume they're Christmas cards,' Mum replies. 'From Paul and Susie. They were in the parcel with our goodies.'

'They never send us Christmas cards,' Jo says.

'Well, yes, but maybe they felt they wanted to this year,' Mum says, her eyes misting.

Jo takes an annoyed breath.

A cynical voice in my brain wonders if this is in response to Jo's outburst last week about Paul's lack of concern. I'm wondering if Mum insisted they get in touch. Christmas cards are definitely the easy option. Easier than picking up the phone anyway.

'Here, Josephine.' Mum waggles the card in my sister's direction and she eventually comes over to take it.

I open mine. It's a glitzy, expensive-looking image of a dove with an olive branch. I try not to roll my eyes at the symbolism and show it to Jo, who isn't so restrained. She swears under her breath. I open the card and read Susie's swirling script:

Dearest Natalie, Theo and Georgia,

We're thinking of you during this terrible time

and praying our beautiful niece is returned to us before Christmas.

Much love

Susie and Paul

I grit my teeth at the phrase 'our beautiful niece' when the woman hasn't even seen Elle since she was two. And then on the opposite page, Paul has scribbled a note:

Hey Nat,

I can't believe what's happened. I'm so sorry for what you must be going through. I'm sure you'll find her.

Give Jo a hug from me.

Sending all our love,

Paul x

It's a shock to see Paul's words written so casually as though we only spoke a few days ago when in fact it's been years. As I read the words, I can hear his voice in my head, and it makes me so angry all over again that he's wilfully chosen to be swayed by his wife and cut us out of his life.

Jo takes hers over to the other end of the kitchen and sits on the sofa to open it. I catch a glimpse of a card with a childlike angel on the front and I gasp at the insensitivity. Surely Susie can't have picked that card purposely, can she?

'Blah, blah, blah, thinking of you, if there's anything we can do, blah, blah, pointless platitude, blah, blah.' Jo tosses the card on to the coffee table and I get the feeling that if Mum wasn't here she'd have ripped it up, chucked it in the bin, and stormed back upstairs.

Mum catches my eye but thankfully she doesn't say anything. I'm grateful Dad's not arrived yet because he would certainly be putting his foot in it right about now. He and Jo are like oil and water. And while sparks are flying, she's dangerous to be around.

I look around for Theo, finding him with his back to the room busying himself with making everyone's coffees. He definitely has the right idea; I wish I could avoid it too.

On the one hand, I wanted Paul to get in touch to express his grief and sympathy at his niece's disappearance. But I also find it really insensitive that he's waited two weeks to do anything. He should have called Jo the minute he heard. If he'd spoken directly to her, apologised for being so absent, then maybe we could have believed in his sincerity. But the cards feel like they were Mum's suggestion, not his. And Susie's words make me want to vomit.

Jo looks at me and I just know we're going to have a long conversation about these cards later. Where Paul used to be the bridge linking me and Jo, now it's Paul and Susie's breathtaking insensitivity that's bringing us closer.

The doorbell rings and Mum gets up. 'That'll be your father with the pastries.'

As she leaves the kitchen, Jo comes over to read my card. 'I don't even have the words,' she says. 'Hello, I'm Susie, let's make it all about me. You just know she's playing the victim with all her friends and family.'

'Don't think about it,' I reply. 'She's an insensitive cow.'

Jo nods. 'You're right.'

I look up as the door opens, ready to say hello to my dad, but Mum is followed into the kitchen by DS Lucy Gilligan and a uniformed male officer. 'It's not your father,' Mum says quietly, going to stand by Jo.

'Hi, all,' Lucy says, a serious note to her voice that sends a fizz of fear down my spine.

'Did you hear something?' Jo asks, her face taut with worry.

'Nothing yet, I'm afraid.'

I'm disappointed that there's no update on Elle, but relieved she isn't giving us bad news. I can tell that everyone else feels the same. I'm nervous as to why she's here with another officer though. She comes to the house most days, and every time, she's been alone.

Lucy looks over at my husband, who's spooning sugar into Mum's cup. 'Hi, Theo,' Lucy says. 'I'm here to ask you to accompany me to the station to answer some questions.'

My stomach drops. Why does she need to speak to Theo again? We've already been interviewed multiple times. And why has she come here with a second officer? It's almost as though she's brought backup.

'Am I under arrest?' Theo asks, still frozen in place, the spoon of sugar poised over the cup.

'No,' Lucy replies, her tone more professional than the usual warmth we're used to. 'We just have further questions that we'd prefer to ask down at the station. We can drive you or you can follow in your vehicle, if you prefer?'

'Can't we talk here?' he asks, a hint of panic creeping into his voice.

'We can give you some privacy in the living room, if you like?' I add, worrying about Theo having to go with them. I can see the stress radiating off him.

'We'd rather go to the station,' Lucy says firmly.

'What's this about?' Mum asks, her mama-bear hackles rising on behalf of Theo.

Jo gives Theo a penetrating look and I'm suddenly sick with worry.

'So I have to come with you?' Theo asks Lucy.

'We'd prefer it,' Lucy replies, her lips pressed in a firm line.

'Okay then.' He sets the teaspoon down on the counter carefully and wipes his hands on the side of his jeans, not catching anyone's eye. Not even mine. 'I'll follow in my car.'

'I'll come too,' I say.

'No, you stay with Georgia,' Theo snaps back, but I can tell his tone is down to his anxiety.

'I'm coming,' I insist. There's no way I'm letting him drive in this state.

'We'll stay with Georgia.'

'Thanks, Mum.' I exhale.

'Morning!' Dad walks into the kitchen, a bag of pastries in one hand and a newspaper in the other. He glances at our visitors. 'Everything all right, Officer?'

Lucy nods. 'Morning, Mr Warren. I'll let your wife fill you in.'

Dad looks from Lucy to Theo, trying to assess the situation. 'What's happening, Theo?'

'They want to talk to me down at the station,' my husband replies woodenly.

'You're questioning Theo?' Dad asks Lucy. 'Barking up the wrong tree there. I've known my son-in-law for, must be almost fifteen years. He's been like a father to Elle, isn't that right, Jo?'

Jo doesn't reply and neither does Lucy; she just gives my dad a tolerant smile before turning to Theo. 'Ready?'

My husband nods, but I can see genuine fear in his eyes. This whole situation has been hard on him, bringing up memories of the past we both thought were long behind us. I know he's paranoid that the same thing is going to happen to him again. That he's going to be accused of a crime he didn't commit. Only this time, the crime is a million times worse.

I want to comfort him, but it suddenly all feels too much. It's one thing to have this devastating thing happen to our family and hold it all together, but then for Theo to be treated like a suspect, no matter how subtly, is terrifying. I can't let my husband down. I need to be strong and positive.

'I'm definitely coming with you,' I say to Theo. The relief in his eyes makes me want to hug him. I turn to Mum. 'Tell Georgia that . . .' I tail off.

'Don't worry,' Mum says. 'We'll do something fun with her.'

I throw her a look of thanks and walk out of the house with my husband.

Chapter Nineteen

NOW

Outside, cold sleet is blanketing the town of Lymington, blurring the edges with a rough grey haze. But even the foul weather can't dampen the prettiness of the place with its cobbled streets and quaint boutiques and eateries. Theo and I have come here for Sunday lunch with Jo and Ollie in an attempt to build bridges and restore harmony. I don't know how successful it will be, but at least we'll get a nice meal out of it. Sometimes that's all you can hope for.

Georgia wanted to stay home as she has a ton of coursework to get through, and yesterday was a write-off as she had the mother of all hangovers after Friday night. I didn't question her about her self-harming because I want to read up about it some more. To know something about what I'm dealing with here. When I told Theo after he got home yesterday, he was as appalled as I was. The fear of her unhappiness put our own issues on the back burner yet again, and we agreed to set them aside. To support our daughter. We had a look at some websites that suggested strategies to help. For now, we're giving Georgia some space and hoping that she'll be receptive to a conversation later.

Right now, we're sitting in a gorgeous sixteenth-century inn with ship's beams, inglenook fireplaces and deep leaded windows that look out on to a quiet street. Our round wooden table is next to one of these impressive fireplaces, which is currently chucking out a small sun's worth of heat. It was lovely and toasty when we first got here after rushing through the icy rain from the car park at the other end of town, and we congratulated ourselves on bagging the best table in the pub. But now I realise why it was left vacant. Because its proximity to the fire means it's like sitting inside a volcano.

'It's boiling,' Jo says, pulling at the neck of her jumper.

'Should we move tables?' Ollie asks, glancing around.

'We'll be lucky,' Theo replies. 'Looks like it's standing room only.'

'It'll be fine, guys,' I interject, trying to keep everyone upbeat. 'Those logs will soon burn away, and then it will cool down.'

Everyone sips their drink and mutters their scepticism, but I ignore them, determined to change the subject. 'Hey, Jo, do you remember when Mum and Dad brought us to Lymington as kids, and Charley weed up that woman's leg?'

'Oh, yes, that was mortifying!' She snorts. 'Dad had to give her a tenner to get her trousers dry-cleaned.'

Charley was our little Jack Russell. He was a grumpy sod who kept us all on a tight leash, but we absolutely adored him.

'I've never heard that story,' Theo says.

'Jo, Paul and I couldn't stop laughing. But Dad was furious.'

'I remember,' Jo says. 'Dad and Charley had some kind of dominance thing going where Dad thought he was the boss, but Charley always had the final say.'

'He was Mum's dog,' I remind Theo, 'but Dad cried like a baby when he died.'

'Ahh, little Charley.' Jo sighs. 'We should get a dog.'

'No,' Theo and I say in unison.

Ollie laughs.

'Why not?' Jo takes a long slurp from her pint. 'It'd be great. Georgia would love a dog.'

'Because Theo and I would be the ones taking it for walks and cleaning up poos and vomit.'

'Fair enough,' Jo replies, with a disappointed sigh. 'It would be lovely though. Maybe we should ask Mum and Dad to get another one.'

'They won't,' I tell her.

'Paul and Susie have just got a Pomeranian,' Jo says. 'I saw pictures on Instagram. It's the cutest.'

'Really? Mum never said.'

'I think it was only like a few days ago.'

'I didn't know you followed her account,' I say, surprised.

'I don't, but I can't help hate-scrolling every so often.'

'Same,' I reply. Susie's Instagram is a perfectly curated snapshot of their lives, showing off their immaculate apartment, their glittering social life and now, apparently, their new dog. We don't follow each other, but from time to time I have a nose around on there to see what they're up to.

After their insensitivity around Elle's disappearance, Jo and I gave up trying to get Paul back in our lives. Susie is just too toxic to deal with and we have enough stress without courting more of it. The Christmas cards were the last we heard from them directly.

Mum only speaks to Paul every couple of weeks or so, if that. She's always the one to call him and they don't speak for long, but she's determined to keep their mother-son relationship alive. *After all*, Mum once said to me, *he might need to come back to us one day, if things don't work out.*

Lunch arrives and it's really good. The portions are massive and it's all cooked to perfection. We order another round of drinks and enjoy an hour of eating, drinking and chatting without any major incidents. Although Jo seems like she's a bit on edge. I'm not surprised. Over the last few weeks she's already had a couple of journalists asking her for an interview to coincide with the ten-year anniversary. She decided that she will give one, but she wants to think about which media outlet to go with and what she wants to say. The whole thing is pretty overwhelming.

One of the waitresses comes over and reaches into the basket to add another log to the fire, but we all plead heat-stroke and she backs off. Jo orders another pint. Before she drinks any more, I want to check Jo's okay after her upsetting experience with that stalker the other week. I've been so busy at work that we haven't had time for a proper catch-up and I worry that she might think I've forgotten about it. That I don't care.

'How are you feeling after the other night?'

'The other night?' Jo looks confused.

'With the woman who was following you. You haven't seen her again, have you?'

'Can we talk about something else?' Jo asks curtly, giving me a surreptitious glare.

'Oh. Sure.' I'm surprised by her tone. But maybe she just wants to forget about it for now. After all, today's about enjoyment. I probably shouldn't have brought it up.

'Don't worry,' Ollie reassures me. 'She hasn't seen her again.'

'Thanks, Ollie,' Jo snaps, 'but I can answer for myself.'

He flushes. 'I know, I was just—' He shrugs and seems to shrink a little.

I give him a look of what I hope is thanks and a bit of sympathy, but Jo catches us and immediately jumps on the defensive.

'You know, you two should be a couple,' she says, pointing between me and Ollie. I think she's trying to sound jokey, but it comes off as spiteful. 'You're always sticking up for each other. Singing each other's praises. You'd be perfect for each other.'

I catch Theo's irritated expression at Jo's antagonistic attitude.

'It's only because we care,' Ollie says quietly. 'Natalie's worried about you, that's all. I was putting her mind at rest that you hadn't seen the woman again. Nothing wrong with that.'

'Of course,' Jo snaps. 'Nothing wrong with that. It must be *so* nice being *so* perfect all the time.' She slams down her glass, her eyes blazing. 'Looking out for poor old Jo, the charity case who's always screwing up and freaking out. Honestly, it's so exhausting having to live up to the high-and-mighty standards of Saint Natalie and Saint Ollie.'

I shake my head, not even trying to answer. We had these types of conversations multiple times back when Elle first went missing, and it's disconcerting to hear her talking this way again. They were usually just between the two of us. And she always apologised afterwards. But this time she's treating Theo and Ollie to front-row seats and I'm cringing for her. Knowing that Theo, in particular, won't understand that she doesn't really mean what she's saying.

'Not like Theo,' Jo adds with a sly smile. 'Theo doesn't bother to hide how he feels about having his pain-in-the-arse sister-in-law living in the garage.'

My husband opens his mouth to reply, but she cuts him off, waggling a finger in his direction. 'No, no, no,' she says. 'Don't try to deny it. It's refreshing. It's honest.' She turns to look at me and then Ollie. 'You two should try it. Take a leaf out of Theo's book and tell me to piss off. You'll love it, I promise.'

I bite back the reply that comes to my lips. 'Time for the bill,' I say to Theo. 'I'll go and pay at the bar.'

Chapter Twenty

THEN

'This is just like a repeat performance of what happened at uni,' Theo says as he slumps into the passenger seat of my little Peugeot 208.

'It isn't,' I reply as long-buried memories from that time jostle to the front of my brain. Remembering how our new relationship was battered by his wrongful arrest and sentencing. I'd been head-over-heels for Theo from the moment we'd got together. It would have been easy to let the relationship slide once he'd gone to prison, but I'd already fallen so hard that I wasn't about to let go of him. Even though it had soured my university experience. I'd spent my time writing to him, visiting him and thinking about him instead of concentrating on my studies. All the while keeping him a secret from my family, until he was released.

Like Theo, I now can't help worrying that the police might try to pin Elle's disappearance on him, simply because he has a criminal record. But I can't let my husband know my worries. I have to give him confidence and hope. 'Just tell them the truth and you'll be fine,' I say, as the squad car pulls out into the road.

'Well, I did that last time, and that didn't exactly work out too well, did it?' He yanks at his seat belt too hard, but it won't come loose.

'That was then.' I click on my indicator and follow the police car. 'You were with me at the rink, so I don't even know why they want to talk to you?'

'Maybe they think I've got an accomplice.' He rubs his face and groans. 'I can't do this, Nat.'

'Listen to me, Theo. The past is in the past. You've done nothing wrong. Just don't get defensive with them, okay?'

He doesn't reply.

'Theo?'

'What?' he growls.

'I said, don't get defensive. You know what I mean. Just try to relax and talk to them like they're regular people asking you questions. Otherwise you're going to come across like you're guilty of something.'

'Mm,' he replies morosely.

I put a hand on his leg. 'It will be fine. Just a few questions and then we can go home and carry on with our Saturday, okay?'

'I just . . . I can't deal with this shit. I love Elle like she's my daughter. Just them thinking I might have something to do with her disappearance makes me want to throw up.'

'They don't think that. They're just crossing people off their list, that's all.'

'So why is it just me they want to talk to?'

'Well, it's you today. It might be me tomorrow.'

'Doubt it.'

The seat belt warning alarm comes on and Theo swears, trying again to get it to work. Eventually, he clicks it into place and the beeping stops.

It's horrible seeing my husband so upset. He's hardly ever negative and grumpy, but this situation has got him spooked. 'Just think of it like this,' I say. 'Once they've eliminated all of us from their enquiries, they can get on with catching the real culprit.'

He exhales. 'Where is she, Nat? I keep going over and over that evening at the skating rink and it really was like Elle vanished into thin air. There's nothing on CCTV and no one at the rink saw anything. It's just so weird.'

'I know. I keep thinking I'm going to wake up and it will all have been a bad dream.'

'Same. What do you think the police will ask me?' he says. 'I told them everything in the first round of interviews.'

'They probably just want to go over it again. To make sure this account matches up with the first one.'

Theo shifts in his seat. I glance over to see him lean back and close his eyes for a moment, breathing deeply. I feel so nervous for him. It sucks if the only reason they're pulling him back in is because of his previous record. But what if it's not that? What if it's because of some new evidence? Or because someone else saw something? I know Theo is innocent. But what if he's being set up somehow by the real perpetrator? If these thoughts are flitting through my mind, then goodness knows what Theo is thinking. I have to stay positive. I can't let my brain spin out like this.

We spend the rest of the twenty-minute journey to the police station lost in our thoughts. Desperately trying not to think about where we're going, my minds flits to Susie's insincere words in her Christmas card. Calling Elle 'our' beautiful niece like she has any kind of relationship with her. Paul's message was better, but it still hurts that this is the first time he's reached out to me and Jo in years.

I feel sorry for my parents. It must be so difficult to have children who don't get along. It's especially hard on Mum, who just wants to act like everything's okay. But then she's always been the peacemaker. I think that's where I get it from. If Paul reached out to me with an apology for his absence, I know I'd eventually forgive him. But I'm pretty sure Jo wouldn't. And if she did, it would take an awful lot of grovelling on Paul's part.

We're finally outside the police station and I manage to find a parking spot on the road, paying the parking fee through one of the only apps that's working today. Theo doesn't make any move to get out and so we sit in silence for a few moments.

'Right,' he says eventually. 'I suppose I'd better go in.'

'I'll stay in the waiting room.'

'Thanks, but go home if I'm more than a couple of hours. I don't want Gee to worry.'

'She'll be fine, she's with my mum and dad.'

We get out of the car and head to the station, an icy wind lifting my hair and chafing at my skin. I link arms with Theo until we reach the door, where I walk in first. We were here a lot those first few days after Elle disappeared, so the building and layout feel depressingly familiar.

Inside, the waiting room is almost full; lacklustre Christmas decorations hang from the walls and there's a sad fake tree behind the reception desk. It will be Christmas Day on Friday, normally a time that Theo, Georgia and I love, but I realise I haven't even thought about it since Elle went missing. There's a young couple arguing at one end of the long waiting room. I don't pay any attention to their words, but the sound of their angry voices adds to my anxiety. Having followed her to the station, we now see the DS standing by one of the doors that leads to the interview rooms. She nods at Theo and he turns to give me a brief peck on the lips.

'You'll be fine,' I murmur in his ear.

He nods and leaves the room with Lucy. As he disappears through the door, I exhale and blink back tears. This is all so horrible. The only spare seats in here are near the arguing couple so I decide to remain standing on this side of the room. Maybe I should have waited in the car, but I already told Theo I'd be here, so it would feel disloyal to leave the building.

Half an hour later, the arguing couple's number is called and they're shown into an interview room. After a minute or two, I walk over to one of the seats, along with an older woman who also chose to keep her distance. We catch each other's eye and manage a smile.

Despite the number of people, the room is eerily quiet now and I don't know which is worse – the arguing or the silence. I hate not knowing how long Theo's interview will last and my mind keeps imagining worst-case scenarios. What if he's kept in overnight, or they find some circumstantial evidence against him? My pulse is skittering and I feel queasy at the thought of what could lie ahead of us. Please don't let them think Theo had anything to do with this. I don't know how we would bear it.

Chapter Twenty-One

NOW

After Jo's verbal assault on us, Ollie mouths an apology at me, but he has nothing to apologise for so I just shrug and leave the table to pay the bill. Jo watches our exchange like a hawk about to dive on its prey. As I walk away, I hear her say something to him, but I try to tune it out. Jo hasn't been like this for years and I'd thought these outbursts were behind us. I think it must be the stress of the stalker the other week, coupled with the anniversary and the countdown to Georgia's birthday.

People might think I'm a doormat to put up with this sort of behaviour, but I know Jo's heart. She doesn't mean it. It's just sometimes she remembers that people can disappear and that it hurts really badly. So she pushes us away on purpose because she can't bear to be that close to anyone again. To risk going through that type of pain. People shouldn't judge if they haven't been in that situation.

I pay the bill and return to the table, where Jo is now subdued. She doesn't make any more cutting comments, but she doesn't apologise either. We leave the pub and head home. I'm driving and put the radio on so we don't have to talk. I'm disappointed that our lovely pub lunch has ended this way. But I'm also not surprised as the stress has been building recently in the lead-up to the ten-year anniversary.

Once we get home, Jo disappears into her flat and Ollie goes home. Theo and I enter the house wearily. I can hear Georgia upstairs in her room FaceTiming Sasha. At least she sounds happy. Theo looks at me and I'm dreading what he's going to say about Jo's behaviour.

'Shall I make us a cup of tea?' he asks.

I nod and follow him through to the kitchen, closing the door behind us.

I sit on one of the stools while Theo puts the kettle on and gets a couple of mugs out of the cupboard. He doesn't speak while he's making the tea, but I can feel the heaviness of what's on his mind and I'm not sure I have the energy for this conversation.

'I'm sorry about my sister,' I say as he pushes my tea across the island towards me.

'I know you are, Nat, but it's just the same old crap over and over again.'

'It is, but she's been pretty good over the past few years. It's just the prospect of the anniversary coming up that's tipped her over the edge.' I blow on my tea. 'She'll apologise later.'

'Will she? I'll tell you what it's like, Nat,' Theo says, looking at me. 'It's like I can't relax in my own house, with my own family. I'm always having to watch what I say. I can't express how I feel, because that would be insensitive, because I'm not the one whose child went missing. Every time we try to do something nice, either for Jo or for ourselves, there's always this elephant in the room. This reason why we shouldn't be enjoying ourselves. It's either our own guilt, or it's guilt being heaped on to us by your sister. And you won't acknowledge any of it. You always stick up for her because you're a loyal person, which is what I love about you. But what about your loyalty to me?'

He looks down into his mug as I absorb his words.

'I know what you're saying,' I reply carefully. 'But it's impossible for me. I was the one who lost her daughter. I can never make up for that. Ever. But I also know that it's not fair on you, having Jo live with us. The way that she is makes things so hard, but I literally don't know what to do about it. Every time I sit down and try to think of a solution, my mind runs round in circles.'

'It wasn't you who lost Elle,' Theo says quietly. 'As you pointed out the other night, it was *me*.'

My stomach lurches with more guilt. 'You know I didn't mean that. It was a stupid slip of the tongue. A sentence that came out wrong. Like you said, it wasn't our fault, it was the fault of whoever took her. Can we please agree on that now?'

But the thing is, there had always been this tiny, hateful part of me that *had* blamed Theo for taking his eye off Elle, that held him responsible for her disappearance. However, once I voiced it and felt how unfair it was, once I saw how much it hurt him, then that blame evaporated. I now feel ashamed that I ever felt that way. Of course it wasn't Theo's fault.

'I'm truly sorry I said that,' I add. 'Can you forgive me? Please.'

Theo nods. 'I know you didn't mean it. You only said what I'd been thinking too. That's why it hurt so much. If I could've rewound that night at the ice rink, I would've kept a better eye on her.'

'You and me both.'

'Guilt aside,' Theo continues, 'it doesn't solve the issue of Jo's behaviour. And it's not just today's outburst, or her behaviour since Elle disappeared. Jo has always relied on us way more than she needed to. Ever since your mum and dad washed their hands of her, she started to turn to you. You always dropped everything for her and Elle. She knows exactly how to flick the guilt switch.'

I shake my head. 'She's not that bad.'

'She is, Nat. It's like you're her surrogate mother. Maybe – even though it was your mum and dad who threw her out when she got pregnant – she's transferred her resentment on to you instead of them.'

'I don't think she resents me. I'm sure it's just a sister thing. If you had siblings, you'd do the same for them. Your parents live abroad so you don't have those ties here. I know my family can be a lot, but you knew what they were like before you married me. I'm never going to stop caring for them.'

'I don't expect you to, but why is it always at our expense?' Theo replies.

I cover my face with my hands and take a breath, trying to clear my mess of thoughts. After a moment I look at my husband again, at his tired eyes and greying hair. 'Can we please just wait until after all this ten-year-anniversary stuff is over?' I ask. 'I promise we'll talk about this again and we'll come up with a solution. But can we leave it until the new year?'

Theo blinks. 'Okay, that's fair. But this isn't going away, Nat.'

'I promise we'll talk again in January. Right now, I think we need to focus on Georgia.'

Theo picks up his mug and heads over to the sofa. I follow him and we both sit looking out at the darkening rain-drenched garden.

'I feel sick whenever I think about it,' Theo says.

'I don't think she's cutting herself anymore. The marks on her legs were old and she was upset about the scarring, which makes me think she won't do it again.' As I speak the words aloud, I wonder how much is wishful thinking. Georgia hasn't been herself for a few months now. She's been quieter, less open with us. I'd put it down to her getting older, becoming more of an adult, but there must be more to it than that.

'What do we do?' Theo asks. 'She said it was in the past. Do you believe her?'

'I don't know. We need to talk to her. Try to get her to open up.'

'I think you're right,' he replies.

Chapter Twenty-Two

THEN

It's another two hours before Theo is released via the same door he went in through. My heart lifts as I see his tired face come towards me. He takes my hand and we leave the station. He doesn't say anything, and I don't ask, giving him a few moments to decompress. Instead, I ask if he wants to go somewhere for a drink.

'I just want to go home,' he replies.

'Of course.' I start driving, desperate to find out what happened. 'You okay?'

'Glad that's over. It was like you said – they just wanted to hear my account of that evening again. Waste of time.'

'It's done now.'

'Thanks for coming with me,' he says.

'Of course.'

Back home, there's a note on the kitchen island to say that Mum and Dad have taken Georgia back to theirs. I'm relieved she's not at home to witness our stress. I worry how all this is affecting her, but it's all been so hectic and upsetting that I haven't had time to properly think about how she's doing. On the outside, our daughter seems like she's handling things pretty well. She's been helpful and sweet, and hasn't caused us a second's worry. Whenever I ask how she is, she says she's fine, and never brings up the subject of her cousin. I make a mental note to talk to Theo about her later this week.

Theo casts me a pissed-off look at the sound of footsteps coming down the stairs.

'She'll go back up in a minute,' I mouth to him just before Jo comes into the kitchen.

'How did you get on?' she asks.

'Fine,' Theo replies, heading over to the fridge and taking out the remains of a bottle of Riesling.

'What did they ask?' Jo's questions are blunt, and I wish she'd be a little gentler with him, but she has every right to be curious.

'Same as they did before.' Theo heads over to the sideboard to get a wine glass.

'*What*, that's it?' Jo frowns at his back and then looks in my direction.

I'm standing in the kitchen, wanting nothing more than to go upstairs and take a shower to wash the grotty waiting room off my body. But I need to stay here to ensure this conversation doesn't escalate because both my husband and my sister are bristling with negative energy right now.

Theo comes to the island and empties the wine bottle into his glass.

'They just asked him the same questions, Jo,' I say.

'Were you in there with him?' she asks.

'Just say you don't believe me, Jo,' Theo says, taking a large swig from the glass.

'She didn't mean it like that, did you, Jo? She just wanted to know if I was in there too.'

Theo glowers at me and Jo doesn't reply.

'Is anyone hungry?' I add. 'We missed lunch. I could do us some toasties.'

No one answers.

'Okay, well I'll make some anyway. You must be starving, Theo.'

'So how did the police leave things?' Jo asks him. 'Did Lucy say they want you back in again?'

Theo takes a breath and I can see he's about to go off. Why am I always caught in the middle of these two? It's so stressful and exhausting, but I don't have a choice because if I left them to get on with it, World War Three would break out.

'Jo, let's just leave it for a bit,' I say. 'It's been a rough morning.'

'We're talking about my daughter here. So forgive me if I don't want to leave it. I want to know what's going on.'

'I already told you,' Theo says through gritted teeth.

'Look, Jo. We're both on your side. We love Elle and we want her back with you, but snapping at Theo isn't going to help.'

'I'm not snapping,' she huffs. 'I'm asking what happened, which isn't exactly unreasonable.'

'You asked and I answered,' Theo replies. 'End of.'

'This is bullshit,' Jo replies. 'You're hiding something.'

'I'm going upstairs.' Theo leaves the room. At least he doesn't slam the door.

My first instinct is to go after him, but it's probably better if I let him cool down first. It's probably a good thing he's taken himself off because if he stays down here, he and Jo will definitely say things they'll regret. But I hate leaving things unresolved like this.

Theo and Jo have always rubbed each other up the wrong way. He's never said so, but I know it rankles that Jo never expressed any gratitude whenever Theo and I helped out with Elle. He loves Elle and has always been happy to have her on weekends and evenings when Jo's working or socialising, but Jo has taken it for granted.

I know she's appreciative, and I tell Theo this. She's just not the kind of person to gush about it all the time. I also know that Jo has picked up on Theo's feelings towards her. So there are all these frothing resentments below the surface that I'm terrified are about to erupt. Whenever I manage to tamp one down, another threatens to explode.

I get why Jo's unnerved that Theo was brought in by the police, but surely she doesn't think Theo has anything to do with Elle's disappearance. I think she's just grasping at anything that might lead her back to her daughter. And I can't blame her for that.

'So,' my sister says, sitting opposite me on one of the kitchen stools. 'They just randomly called Theo in to ask the same questions as before?'

Jo doesn't know about Theo's past conviction and I don't think telling her will help the situation. Anyway, it's not my story to tell. She's sharp though, and it's clear she's worked out that we're not quite being one hundred per cent with her.

'If there was anything wrong, they wouldn't have let him come home. Anyway, you know Theo. He loves you and Elle. Everyone's upset right now, but we can't go blaming each other. That's not going to help.'

'I can't cope with this,' she cries, standing up and pacing the kitchen. 'I feel like I'm losing it. Every time a new thing happens, it's like I'm being pushed off a cliff. First, bloody Susie with her fake concern, then the police pulling Theo in for questioning.' She takes a breath. 'There are journalists messaging me all the time, and I'm still getting a ton of online hate from people saying all kinds of messed-up shit that makes no sense. I'm literally suspecting everyone, and I have all these scary thoughts about where Elle is and what's happening to her, but I can't let myself think about it because it's too terrifying.'

'I know, I know. It's awful and I'm so sorry that it happened while she was with me and Theo. I'm so sorry.' Listening to my sister, my heart feels as though it's being squeezed to a pulp. I wish Theo could hear her pouring her heart out like this, but she's never this vulnerable in front of him. She only shows him her hard side.

Jo shakes her head. 'All I want is to get my daughter back.' She looks up at me, her face taut, her eyes almost black with fear. 'Where the hell is she, Nat? Where's Elle?'

I stare back at my sister. 'I wish I knew, Jo. I really do.'

Chapter Twenty-Three

NOW

'Mum! Mum! Are you still at work? Can you come home now? I'm really scared.'

An icy fear grips me as I listen to Georgia's distressed voicemail. She's crying and her voice is high-pitched, terrified. I'm in my office, about to go into a meeting, but I call Georgia back with shaky fingers. It goes to voicemail so I try the landline, but that goes to answerphone. I call her mobile again and leave a message:

'It's Mum. I'm leaving work now. Should be there in twenty minutes. Call me back if you get this. See if Aunty Jo's home.'

Shit. What's happened? It's three thirty so she must have just got in from sixth form. My brain is spooling through a hundred and one possibilities. None of them good. I start gathering up my stuff – my bag, my coat, my laptop. She said she's scared, not hurt. Scared of what? Of who? Is someone at the house? Should I call the police?

I call Jo, but she doesn't pick up. 'Jo, are you home? Can you go to the house and check on Georgia? I think something's happened!'

I hang up and then call Ollie, but he doesn't pick up either. He works close by so he could get there quicker than me. 'Ollie, can you please nip over to the house as soon as you get this message. Something's happened to Georgia. I'm on my way back now too.'

Theo works over in Poole, which is an hour away, so I'll call him as I'm driving. I leave my office and run into Liam, a new intern. 'Can you tell Fran that I've had a family emergency and had to go home?' I call to him as I hurry along the corridor. He stares at me like a rabbit in the headlights. 'Now, please! Thank you!'

Hopefully, he'll pass the message along, but I can't worry about it now. I almost collide with a couple of colleagues, who say something after I call out a breathless 'Sorry!' But I don't have time to stop as I make a beeline for the staff exit and head out to the chilly car park.

I drive home in a blur of panic and I don't remember any of it as I finally turn into our road and head towards the house. But as I approach, I can see a cluster of vehicles blocking the driveway and several people on the pavement outside.

What's going on?

And then I see the cameras, microphones and videos. It's the press. My heart sinks. I remember this from ten years ago, only it didn't seem as full-on as this. This is like something you'd see on the news. I realise today is the first of December. Four days until the tenth anniversary of Elle going missing. The police warned Jo that it might get a bit intrusive when they told her about the appeal, but I never expected all this.

At least this explains Georgia's phone call. No wonder she was freaking out. Goodness knows what this lot were asking her as she tried to get in the door. Fury heats up my blood. I know we need the media's help to spread the word, but why do they have to be so aggressive about it?

I park a few doors down and hoist my bag on to my shoulder, gripping the strap tightly like a shield or a weapon. I briefly consider driving to the next road and seeing if it's possible to skip over the neighbour's back fence, but quickly dismiss it – not in these heels. And why should I be forced to skulk around like a criminal? Head down, I march up to the house, trying to keep my breathing even. My main concern right now is Georgia. I'll deal with this lot later.

'Natalie, Natalie! Have you got a moment to chat?' I glance up to see a young blond-haired man jogging over to me, holding out his phone. Of course, he's done his research and already knows my name. 'We understand there's an anniversary appeal for your niece with a cash reward. Do you think someone out there knows what happened to Elle? How does Georgia feel about it, given that it happened at her birthday party?'

His mention of my daughter makes me want to spit venom in his face. It's not surprising Georgia was in tears if she had to put up with this lot. I shoulder my way past him, only to be flanked by a man and a woman who both start asking different questions simultaneously. Phones are pointed my way and news cameras follow my progress. A few neighbours and passers-by stare in my direction and Bob from over the road calls out, 'You okay, Natalie?'

I wave in his direction and mouth 'Fine', as some of the cameras swivel to catch a shot of him. I'm pretty sure they'll be approaching him for an interview too as he's been here longer than us and would remember what happened.

I'm almost surrounded now, but I keep walking at a steady pace.

'Natalie, could we do an interview? We're happy to spread the word about your niece.'

'Hi, Nat, we're from the *Herald* and would love to talk about Elle, ten years on. Hopefully we can jog some people's memories.'

'Natalie! Can we get a picture of you and Georgia together? Or you and Jo? *Two Sisters United In Grief*, that sort of thing. All very tasteful.'

'Natalie, we've got a budget for this. Can we talk?'

Finally, I reach the driveway, wishing we'd had a high electric gate fitted ten years ago. Theo and I had talked about getting one after it happened, but eventually decided it was too expensive. Now I wish we'd just done it because I hate the thought of all these journos getting an uninterrupted view of the house, even with the blinds closed.

Finally, I'm inside, and I lean back against the front door, catching my breath and trying to compose myself.

'Mum!' Georgia bursts out of the kitchen, tear tracks down her face.

'Oh, Georgia, are you okay?' I give her a huge hug, relieved to be here with her.

She nods and sniffs. 'Ollie came ten minutes after I called you.'

I look over her shoulder to see him come out of the kitchen, shaking his head in anger. 'Bloody parasites. I went out there and told them to piss off. To leave Georgia alone. Told them she's a minor and they shouldn't be harassing her.'

'You star,' I reply. 'Thank you. You got my message then?'

'Yeah, Jo's at work.'

'Thank you so much. Let's get away from the front of the house.' We all troop into the kitchen and I close the door behind us. 'I'll just message your dad and tell him there's no need to leave work early and give him a heads-up about the press.' I knock out a quick text and then turn my attention back to Georgia and Ollie.

'They were asking me about Elle at the ice rink,' Georgia says. 'It was so horrible. It felt like they were blaming me because it happened at my birthday party.'

'I could kill them,' I snarl. 'How dare they!' I'm already worried about my daughter's mental health and now the media have arrived with all their probing questions, uncovering all the upsetting memories and laying them bare. I'm petrified that this harassment could set her back again.

I give her another hug and kiss her cheeks. I want to protect my daughter from all of it, but it's too late for that. She's having to navigate this crap alongside the rest of us. There's no shielding her from it any longer.

'Mum?'

'Sorry, Gee. Shall we sit down?' The three of us sit at the kitchen table and I wait for my daughter to continue.

'That's not even why I was upset.'

'What do you mean?' I ask.

'I mean, I was already in a state when I got home. And then they all started crowding round me, making everything worse.'

'Why were you in a state?' Ollie says.

Georgia sniffs. 'When I came out of school, there was this woman.'

I tense up. 'What woman?'

'I've never seen her before.' Georgia's eyes are wide. 'But she came up to me when I was walking to my car and she shouted, "I know you know".'

I screw up my face. 'What does that mean?'

Georgia shrugs. 'No idea. But she was really intimidating. I thought she was going to hit me.'

'Georgia, that's terrible,' I cry. 'What did you do?'

'I just got in my car and drove away, but she was shouting after me. It was weird and really scary.'

My heart pounds with anger.

'"I know you know"?' Ollie repeats. 'Like she thinks you know something?'

'I think so, yeah. That's what it sounded like. Like she was accusing me of knowing something. Maybe about Elle?'

'Sounds like a crank,' I reply. 'I don't want you going anywhere on your own while all this media stuff is going on. Could she have been a journalist?'

'Don't think so. She looked like a regular person.' Georgia screws up her nose. 'A bit skanky though.'

Georgia's words trigger something in my memory and I think Ollie has the same thought as we lock eyes.

'What did she look like?' we ask Georgia in unison.

'Dark hair in a ponytail. She was wearing white joggers and a black puffer jacket and short Uggs.'

'Damn,' Ollie says.

'What?' Georgia looks from Ollie to me.

'It's the same woman, isn't it?'

'Sounds like it,' I reply.

'Can one of you tell me what you're on about?' Georgia asks.

'Last month, a woman who sounds similar was following Aunty Jo,' I say. 'I'll report it to the police again. Sounds like it wasn't a one-off.'

Georgia's face pales.

'But I don't want you to worry,' I add uselessly, because of course she's going to worry. We all are. 'Just, like I said, make sure you don't go out alone. Your dad or I will drop you at school and pick you up, until we find out who this person is.'

'What about your work?' Georgia asks me. 'Won't that make you guys late?'

'Work shmurk. It's fine,' I reply, hoping they'll be understanding.

'Jo and I can help too,' adds Ollie.

'There, see?' I say to Georgia with a smile I manage to conjure up from somewhere. 'We've got you covered.'

Georgia nods, but she looks so young and scared. And I'm putting on this brave face when inside I'm just as scared as she is.

Chapter Twenty-Four

THEN

'Mum, when's lunch?' Georgia asks, popping her head around the kitchen door.

'Veggie lasagne's in the oven. Should be ready in about five minutes. Are you all ready for school tomorrow? Do you want to lay your clothes out?'

'Done it.'

'Come here and give me a hug then.' I hold out my arms.

My daughter comes and squeezes me tight. 'Love you, Mummy.'

'Love you too, Gee-Gee. You know you give the best hugs, right?'

She squeezes me even harder and I pretend I can't breathe, making her giggle. A sudden wave of emotion threatens to drown me and I have to try really hard not to cry. It's the last day of the holidays and it's been the worst Christmas we've ever had. Elle went missing just over three weeks ago and there have been no sightings and no leads. We all feel utterly hopeless and useless, like nothing we do will bring her back.

I realise that, throughout it all, Georgia has been extra helpful and sweet, offering to do more chores and giving everyone extra hugs. I think it's been her way of dealing with things. I worry that we haven't been paying her enough attention and vow to spend some proper time with her, but the holidays are already over and she's back to school tomorrow.

DS Lucy Gilligan has been trying to keep our spirits up, but even her sunny, positive disposition has lost its potency. Especially since that day she recalled my husband to the station. Any trust Theo had in her was eroded that morning. Added to that, he and Jo have barely said two words to one another since. We also know that the chances of finding my niece are growing tinier by the day.

Theo and I are returning to work tomorrow. My company gave me a week's unpaid compassionate leave and I also took the rest of my annual leave. Theo had a week's *paid* compassionate leave and his company always closes between Christmas and New Year so he still has his annual leave intact. Not that we'll be taking any holidays anytime soon.

'Where's Aunty Jo?' Georgia asks, eventually pulling away from our extended cuddle.

I know she heard Theo and I talking about her this morning, worrying about her aunt's whereabouts. Jo went out last night and she's still not back. I've left messages on her phone but she's not replying. I've also messaged Ollie, but he hasn't replied either. I don't want to call our parents and stress them out unnecessarily. And Jo would kill me for getting them worked up. Dad would only start lecturing her on being responsible and, to be fair, he'd have a point. I'll contact them as a last resort.

'She's probably at home in her flat,' I reply, hoping that's the case. 'Can you find Dad and tell him lunch is ready?'

Georgia skips out of the kitchen and I start preparing a salad. Everything I do at the moment feels odd, like I'm acting a part. I don't think anything will feel real until we get Elle back.

Theo comes into the kitchen with Georgia and we sit down to lunch together. Our daughter chatters away about the new Disney movie that she went to see with Sasha yesterday. I'm trying to concentrate on what she's saying, but my mind is dull and anxious. Worrying about where Jo is, where Elle is. It all feels so desperate and awful. I put my fork down on my plate.

'Not hungry?' Theo asks.

'Not really. I'll save it for later.'

'Looking forward to school tomorrow, Gee-Gee?' Theo says.

'Yep. Me and Sasha are going to ask Mrs Lee if we can sit together this term.'

'I wouldn't count on it,' he replies. 'She knows what a couple of chatterboxes you two are.'

'We won't be. We'll tell her that if we sit together we'll really concentrate on our work.'

Theo raises his eyes at me with a grin, but I'm too distracted to smile back.

'Everything okay?' he mouths.

I get to my feet. 'I think I'm going to pop to Jo's flat. See if she's there.'

'What, *now?*'

I nod and grab my keys from the dish on the dresser. 'I won't be long.'

'I'm sure she'll be back soon.'

'I know,' I reply, turning back to him. 'But I can't relax.'

'Can we play Monopoly when you get home?' Georgia asks excitedly.

My heart sinks. I'm not in the right frame of mind for a board game. But it's Georgia's last day of the holidays so I dredge up some enthusiasm from somewhere. 'That would be lovely. You can set it all up while I'm gone.'

Georgia jumps up from her seat.

'*After* you've finished your lunch and helped me clear away,' Theo says.

'See you in a bit,' I say as I leave the kitchen, head out the door and get into my car.

As I drive over to Jo's place, I'm irritated by all the Sunday drivers pootling along the coast road and I have to stop myself from overtaking them. The last thing I need is to cause an accident. Jo says she hasn't been back to her flat yet. She didn't even want to go there to get her stuff. Ollie brought it back for her. He also let the police into her place and waited while they did a thorough search, hoping to find clues to where Elle is. But they didn't discover anything helpful. All they did was make a mess.

Finally, I pull up outside Jo's flat, a run-down red-brick Victorian conversion. I'm lucky to get a parking spot as it's always busy here at the weekends, being so close to the beach, and her flat doesn't come with a space. I let myself into the building with my spare key and check her pigeonhole for mail, stuffing a wodge of it into my bag. Then I head up the three steep flights of carpeted stairs.

Back when Jo was pregnant and looking for a place, our parents tried to persuade her to get a ground-floor flat, or somewhere with a lift, because they knew how awkward it could be to navigate stairs with a baby and a pram. But as soon as Jo saw this cosy little one-bedroom apartment in the eaves, there was no dissuading her.

Hers is the only apartment on the top floor, so she has the landing to herself, and treats it as an extension of her flat, with chairs, plants and a small shoe cupboard. Even from out here, I can tell that it's empty inside. It has that air of abandonment. A stillness and an absence of sound. But I press the bell anyway and hear it chime inside, willing Jo to come to the door. I knock and call out her name, pretending to myself that she really is here, but all I get in return is a deep, cold silence.

I insert the key with a sigh, open the solid wooden fire door and enter the apartment. It's cold and it smells musty. My eyes skim the hall and land on the coat pegs, where the sight of Elle's little coats and scarves makes my heart crack. I take a breath and call out my sister's name before heading into the living room, its dormer windows looking out on to the trees, their bare branches rattling intermittently against the single panes of glass. The room is surprisingly large, with a fake-leather sofa strewn with throws and cushions, an armchair, and a nook with a circular glass dining table and four chairs. I swallow at the sight of an over-decorated fake Christmas tree in the corner. Jo and Elle always love doing their tree and it's usually up by mid-November.

Lastly, I check the shower room, which is empty, and then the bedroom that Jo and Elle share. It too is deserted. My body sags with disappointment. Both beds are unmade – Jo's double beneath the window, and Elle's child-sized bed against the far wall. Jo's been worried about Elle wanting more privacy as she gets older. She didn't want to give up the flat for something bigger as – aside from two-bedroom flats being out of reach financially – they both love it here, so she was planning on giving her double bed to Elle, and taking the sofa in the living room. I try not to think about the possibility that it might never happen.

I take a deep breath, suddenly needing to get out of here.

Driving home, my thoughts are a blur and I can barely concentrate on the road ahead. Rationally, I know that Jo is probably crashed out on someone's floor, or in some guy's bed. But after Elle's disappearance, I can no longer rely on things being rational and predictable. Nothing has been normal for three weeks now.

Back in the driveway, my body feels heavy. I wish I could just stay sitting here for the next few hours. Doing nothing. Saying nothing. Thinking about nothing. But I haul myself out of the car and into the house.

'Mum, you're back! My tights have all got holes in them!' Georgia says as soon as I walk in the door.

'Your tights?'

'Yes, my school tights.'

I blink and focus. 'I thought you checked your uniform this morning.'

'I did, but then I remembered that all my tights were holey. I can't go in with holey tights on the first day back. Mrs Lee always checks our uniforms, and I want to get the most stars on the star chart this term because Cleo beat me by three stars before Christmas and she got to help decorate the tree in the main hall.'

Normally, we would have got Georgia's school stuff sorted days in advance of term starting, but unsurprisingly we've let everything slide this holiday.

'Any luck with Jo?' Theo asks, coming into the hall. 'Oh, and also, Georgia says her tights have holes in them.'

'Jo wasn't there,' I reply. 'I don't suppose you could take Georgia to Castlepoint, could you? I think the shops shut at four today, so you should be able to make it. I'd take her myself but I really need to find Jo, because I'm starting to freak out.'

'Are we going to Castlepoint?' Georgia cries, her eyes wide. 'Can we get a hot chocolate from Costa?'

Theo asks her to go upstairs for a minute because he needs to speak to Mummy.

'Are you okay?' he asks, once she's out of earshot.

'Not really. It all just hit me when I was at the flat – seeing Elle's stuff, and now not knowing where Jo is.'

'I know she's suffering, but would it kill her to text you?' Theo huffs, giving me a hug.

'She's out of her mind with fear. I'm not cross with her for not texting, but it doesn't stop me worrying.'

'I know.'

I pull back from his embrace. 'Anyway, you should probably leave if you're going to get there before the shops close.'

'Good point.' He kisses me and hooks his coat off the peg. 'Georgia!' he calls up the stairs. She comes rushing back down and I have the suspicion that she was eavesdropping. Nothing gets past my daughter, and we haven't exactly been discreet these past few weeks.

Once they leave and the door closes behind them, the house settles and I stand in the hall for a few moments. This is the first time I've been home alone since Elle went missing. It's so quiet. So still. Empty. Like Jo's flat. As much as Jo is hard to be around, I would give anything for her to come charging through the hall right now. Drunk, sober, I don't care. Just please let her be okay.

Chapter Twenty-Five

You thought this evening would be the hard part. That it wouldn't go to plan. That it would somehow all fall apart. But it didn't. The hand-off went well. In fact, it all went like a dream. No, this. This right here is the hard part. This is you doing it by yourself. Running the gauntlet.

Everything and everyone makes you nervous here. Back home, you're the confident one. The person who commands respect. But this place isn't your place. Here you're vulnerable and alone, except for the sleeping child in your arms. Here there are cameras and security, police with guns and dogs.

You don't have any luggage to check in. Just a backpack for you and a miniature version for her. A seed of excitement waits in your chest, but you can't allow it to bloom just yet. First you have to get through today.

Only then can you start to relax.

Chapter Twenty-Six

NOW

'Mum, don't worry, it's just a dress. I'll wear a different one.'

'I just can't believe it.' I throw my phone down on the kitchen table in disgust. 'That delivery company is useless. I know it was the one you had your heart set on. I'm so sorry it didn't arrive in time. I ordered it a month ago and they said it would be here last week.'

'Honestly, Mum, it's fine.'

'I hope one of those journalists out there hasn't swiped it.' I glare at the kitchen door in the direction of the journalists who, despite being ignored by everyone coming and going from the house, are still out there four days later, although there are far fewer of them.

'I'll borrow something from Cleo. She literally owns every dress that's ever been made and doesn't mind any of us wearing them. I'll message her and see if I can pop round in a minute. Actually, she loves lending us stuff, because whenever we get complimented, she lets people know it's *her* dress. So the compliment ends up being for her instead of whoever's wearing it.'

'Ingenious,' I reply. 'Kind of generous but selfish at the same time.'

'I know, right?'

We laugh, and I finally relax over the dress. I'm glad Georgia's so philosophical about it. I'm not sure I would have been at her age. Those sorts of things always seemed so important to me back then. But Georgia's been through a lot so I suppose a missing dress doesn't feel like much of a big deal.

My daughter has had to grow up way too quickly. She was only eight when Elle disappeared and, without ever having to be asked, she took on more responsibility for herself so as not to add to our burden. She also had to deal with years of helicopter parenting, constantly trying to put our minds at rest that she was okay. Looking back, I wonder if we became way too overprotective. I also think she must have buried a lot of her true feelings in order to make things easier for all the adults around her. The thought makes me sick with guilt. I know there are many more conversations to be had with her after today, but Theo and I wanted to give her some space to enjoy her eighteenth and to wait for the noise around the anniversary to die down before we raise all the difficult stuff again. That's if it does die down. Maybe the appeal will do its job, and someone will step forward with some real information about Elle.

I've just picked her up from sixth form and Theo's supposed to be back from work early so we can hand over her birthday present. But he's not home yet.

'Well, happy eighteenth, darling.' I stand up to give her a hug and kiss her cheeks. She's taller than me now and it still feels strange to reach up instead of down.

'Thanks, Mum.'

I hear the front door open, and I'm relieved to see Theo stride into the kitchen.

'Jeez, I'll be glad when they're gone!' He takes off his coat and folds it over one of the bar stools. 'I don't remember it being this bad before.'

'That's because it wasn't,' I reply. 'Or maybe we were all in such a state of shock that we didn't pay them as much attention.'

'It's horrible,' Georgia says, her good mood dipping.

Theo and I refused to be railroaded into talking to them while they were being so pushy and disrespecting our privacy. I also had to mute the landline and we all set our social media accounts to private. Thankfully, they tend to disappear after dark so at least we can get a little peace in the evening. Jo chose a couple of nationals to give interviews to, and she also crafted a press release with the help of the police, which was sent out everywhere else, so we're hopeful that, since all the stories ran today, things will quieten down.

'Anyway, enough about them,' Theo says. 'Is there a birthday girl in the house? He-e-ey! Happy birthday, Gee-Gee. Eighteen! You can start taking your old man down the pub for a pint now.'

'I can just see that. You and Georgia down the Flying Goose every Saturday night.'

'I don't think so,' she replies with a mock-horrified expression.

'Cheeky,' Theo says. 'So, party night tonight. You all ready?'

'It's only two o'clock, Dad. Anyway, I need to message Cleo about a dress. I think I'll ask to borrow the green one she got from New York. I don't think she ever wore it in the end.'

Theo gives me a look, and I nod, sidling over to one of the kitchen drawers and opening it.

'Before things get too hectic, Gee, your dad and I have got you a little birthday present.' I take a box out of the kitchen drawer and hand it to our daughter.

Her eyes light up in disbelief at the sight of the iconic blue box. 'Is that . . . ?' She presses the little silver button to release the catch, and the box opens, revealing a delicate gold bracelet studded with freshwater pearls. 'A Tiffany bracelet? I can't believe you got me a Tiffany bracelet!' Her eyes are wide and brimming with tears. 'Thank you so much.'

'Happy birthday, Georgia,' I say, thrilled with her reaction.

'Happy birthday,' Theo echoes.

'I always wanted a Tiffany bracelet. It's gorgeous.'

'We're glad you like it.' Theo gives her a hug.

'I love it. And I can wear it tonight. I can't wait to show Sasha and Cleo!'

Georgia's gift is a little over the top for us. We don't normally buy each other expensive presents. We're more about doing things together as a family. But this is such a special birthday, and Georgia has been through a lot recently, so we thought it would be nice to get her something memorable that she can keep forever and maybe even pass down to her children or her grandchildren.

Theo and I spoke to her a couple of weeks ago about the scars on her legs. When we brought it up, she started sobbing and apologising and we held her and said she had nothing to be sorry about, but that we'd really like to know if there was a reason for it, and if there was anything we could do to help. She said she was just overwhelmed by life. By her A levels and turning eighteen and having to be an adult. She said that when she cut herself, it stopped her worrying about stuff. It was a distraction.

Afterwards, I told Theo I thought she was holding something back, but he disagreed and said that she sounded sincere. I wonder if we should take her to see someone. But what if she was telling the truth and it's all behind her now? Wouldn't we be making things worse by making a big deal of it and bringing everything up again? I really have no idea what to do for the best. I think we need to wait until after the party, and then Theo and I can have a good talk about it again.

In the meantime, we took the advice we found online to recommend alternatives, such as screaming into a pillow or scribbling with a black pen on to fresh white paper. The website also said to avoid telling her she shouldn't do it. We should suggest the alternatives but then, if she still feels she has to do it, she should make sure she uses a clean blade. It sounds crazy to be recommending such a thing. But what's the alternative? To bury our heads in the sand and pretend it's not happening? Maybe if she knows she can trust us to be there for her, then she'll feel less alone, and be less likely to do it. I hope she feels like she can talk to us now.

Being a parent is like walking across a minefield. What works for one child might not work for another. One person's great advice could be the thing that blows up in your child's face. I think, as long as we move forward from a place of love, then that's all we can do. Every time I think about her cutting herself, my stomach sinks to my feet. I need to put it to the back of my mind. To focus on today. On celebrating my beautiful daughter's birthday.

One great piece of news is that Jo has said she wants to be there tonight. I'm absolutely over the moon that she's coming. It will mean so much to Georgia. I was dreading having to explain to my daughter that her Aunty Jo wouldn't be able to make it. I wonder if this could be a turning point in all our lives. A chance to lay the past to rest.

The next few hours are spent running the media gauntlet and picking up decorations, helium balloons and the birthday cake. Then, finally, once that's all been dropped off at the venue, Theo and I come home and start getting ready. Theo's parents FaceTime their granddaughter from Mallorca and let her know that they've transferred a little something into her bank account. They live there, but have a great relationship with us and we often go out to stay with them in their apartment, which overlooks the beach. Georgia is already trying to wheedle a girls' holiday over there next summer with a couple of her friends.

Cleo happily lent Georgia the green dress, and she and Sasha have come round to get ready at ours. I can hear them giggling in

Georgia's room, only popping their heads out for the pizza delivery that came an hour ago. Thankfully, the press cleared off. I'm hoping that this might be the last we'll see of them. That by tomorrow we'll be yesterday's news because the anniversary will be over. Maybe it's wishful thinking, but we could do with a break.

I try not to draw comparisons about this birthday party with the one ten years ago, but it's hard not to get little memories flying into my head. Like when Jo dropped Elle off at our house and she ran inside, flinging her arms around Georgia and wishing her a happy birthday, excited to be sharing in her big cousin's celebrations. It makes me wonder what she would have been like today. Would she and Georgia have been besties, getting ready together? I shake away the thought and get back to my attempt at mindfulness and concentrating on today.

I'm in my dressing gown, hastily applying some make-up – we're supposed to leave for the venue in forty-five minutes and I'm nowhere near ready – when the doorbell rings. If that's another journalist, I'll scream.

'Theo!' I yell.

The bell rings again and I look out of the window, where a woman is standing beneath the security lighting. It must be a delivery. It might be Georgia's dress! I put down my mascara and hurry down the stairs.

I open the front door to see a woman standing in the driveway staring at me, but she's not carrying a parcel and she doesn't look like she's on the verge of leaving, the way most delivery people do. This woman's arms are folded across her chest and her dark hair is tied back in a severe ponytail. She's wearing jeans, Uggs and a black puffer jacket. Something immediately clicks in my brain. Something unwelcome.

Chapter Twenty-Seven

THEN

'Ollie! I've been trying to get hold of you.'

'Hey, Nat. Jo still not back?'

I stand back to let him in the door and we walk through to the kitchen, where I put the kettle on. 'No. She went out last night and hasn't come home. It's been almost twenty-four hours and I'm trying not to freak out.'

'Sorry I didn't reply to your texts. I was out with friends up at Hengistbury Head and the phone signal's non-existent up there. I came straight round when your messages came through.'

'I was so hoping she'd be with you.'

'She was supposed to meet us in the car park. We waited for half an hour and then I left a message on my windscreen, in case she showed up. So she never came home last night?' Ollie's expression is gloomy. 'Bet she's hooked up with some rando. Sorry, that's probably not what I should be saying to her big sister, but she's on quite the self-destruct mission at the moment.'

'Tell me about it,' I reply, thinking back to a few weeks ago when she brought that stranger to the house. I don't mention it to Ollie, even though she probably told him herself. 'Tea or coffee?'

'I'm fine.' He leans on the counter. 'Just had a huge takeaway latte and it's given me the coffee jitters.'

'How about something herbal?'

'That would be great.'

I pour our drinks and we take them over to the kitchen sofa.

'How are you holding up?' he asks.

'Not good, to be honest. I can't seem to do anything to help her. I don't know what she would have done without you these past few weeks, Ollie. You've been her rock.'

'Thanks. But she's still so closed off though.' He shakes his head. 'You know, she won't talk about Elle at all. Just glares at me if I bring her name up. All she wants to do is smoke weed, drink vodka and reminisce about our school days or gossip about friends.'

'Really?' Hearing this makes me worry about her even more. 'I was sure she was opening up to you. Talking about Elle. Slagging me and Theo off for losing her.'

'She wouldn't do that.'

'Wouldn't she? I would if someone lost Georgia. Even if I knew it was an accident. I wish she would yell at us and tell us what awful people we are, but the minute I bring Elle up she shuts down.'

'I guess it's her way of coping right now,' Ollie says. 'It's such a . . . I don't know, such a big thing that it must be almost impossible to comprehend what's happened, if you know what I mean?'

'I do.'

He runs a hand through his hair and leans forward to take a biscuit from the tin on the coffee table.

We sip our drinks companionably and I feel a little calmer. 'I just wish I knew where she was though. My brain is making up all sorts of terrible scenarios. Same as for Elle.'

'They'll show up. Both of them.'

'I wish I had as much faith as you do.'

'I can't imagine a life without Elle,' he says. 'So that's how I know we'll see her again.'

That sounds like magical thinking to me, but I want so much to believe him.

'And as for Jo,' he continues, 'she'll come swaggering through the door any minute.'

'How do you know?'

'Because she will. She needs you, Nat.'

His words make my throat tighten and my eyes prick. I don't want to cry right now. It wouldn't be fair on Ollie, not when he's going through it with Jo right now.

'Can I ask you something?'

'Uh-oh.' He gives a wary smile and shifts position.

'No, it's nothing bad,' I say. 'Well, it's quite personal though.'

'Go on.' He looks at me with his trusting brown eyes and I feel like I shouldn't be asking this. But I can't help myself. It's something I've wanted to ask him for years, but I never thought it was appropriate. It still isn't. However, I feel like normal social rules have gone out the window.

'Do you know who Elle's father is?'

He looks surprised by my question, and a little uncomfortable. 'Um, no. Even Jo doesn't know who it is. I thought you knew that.'

'I did. I mean, I do know that, but I thought that was just something she told me because she didn't want me knowing the truth. I hoped she might have confided in you. I actually thought you might have been Elle's dad.'

'Me?' His eyes darken for a moment and then he looks sad. 'No. I'm not her dad, but I wish I was. Elle's always felt like a daughter to me, or at least a little niece.'

'Nuncle Ollie,' I say.

He gives me a soft smile. 'Yeah, she's stopped calling me that now, but I wanted her to call me Nuncle Ollie forever. It was the cutest.'

It's clear to me that Ollie's been in love with Jo for years. They once had a fling years ago, but Jo said it was a mistake. That she didn't want to lose their friendship. I think she was simply scared of falling in love with a nice guy. She couldn't see herself in the role of cherished girlfriend or wife. To be fair, Jo and Elle make a great team, just the two of them, and they certainly don't need anyone else in their family unit, but it would be nice for Jo to have a partner to share her life with. Ollie would be good for both her and Elle.

I check my phone, but my messages are all still sitting there unread. There's just one from Theo, saying he and Georgia are heading back from Castlepoint with the last pair of tights in her size.

'Anything?' Ollie asks.

'Nope. You?'

He looks at his screen. 'Nothing.'

It's growing dark outside and I don't think I can go through another night of wondering where Jo is and whether or not she's okay. I've been telling myself that my sister is a grown woman, that she can take care of herself. But these are exceptional circumstances. Jo isn't in a good state of mind. Despair is beginning to take root in my bones.

'You don't think she'd do anything stupid?' I ask.

'Absolutely not,' he replies.

'How do you know?'

'I just do. Trust me, Nat. She'll go on a dozen benders, sleep with a few strangers and then she'll crash and it will all come pouring out. And we'll just need to be here to catch her when she goes into freefall.'

My head swims at his words. They scare me. If this isn't Jo in freefall, then what's that going to look like? And, more importantly, will I be able to cope when it comes?

Chapter Twenty-Eight

NOW

I stand in the doorway of our house, facing down a heavily made-up woman in her thirties with violence radiating off her.

'I'm here to see Jo Warren,' she says aggressively.

'Who are you?' I ask warily, wondering if this woman is who I think she is.

'That doesn't matter. Are you related to Jo Warren?'

'Did you harass my daughter outside her school this week?' I ask.

'I never harassed anyone,' she retorts.

'I've reported you to the police, you know.' I fold my arms across my chest, not buying her denial for a second.

'Good for you,' she replies, 'but I haven't done anything wrong. Last time I checked, it wasn't illegal to talk to someone.'

I stand up straighter, wishing I wasn't still in my dressing gown. 'I'm not telling you anything until you tell me who you are and why you want to speak to Jo.'

'Who are you anyway?' she demands.

'I'm her sister,' I reply, immediately berating myself for telling her. 'Have you been following her?' My heart starts thumping loudly in my chest and my face feels hot despite the cold air that's creeping into the hallway.

'Does she live with you?'

'Either you tell me what you want with Jo, or I'm calling the police.'

I hear my sister call out from the kitchen. She must have just arrived from her flat, not realising I'm at the front door. 'Ollie and I are ready to go whenever you are, Nat. Shall we have a drink with the birthday girl first? Ollie's here. He's brought champagne. I'm going to put some music on for a pre-party party.'

Jo is ready uncharacteristically early. I usually have to chivvy her along. I think she's trying to make up for her drunken outburst at the pub a few weeks ago. She's been overly nice to me and Theo ever since. Which has been a welcome relief for everyone.

'Is that her?' the woman says to me, taking a step closer.

'Stay there,' I reply and push the door closed before turning to face my sister, who's coming towards me.

'I didn't know you were at the door. Who was that? Another journalist?' Jo looks gorgeous in pleather jeans and a grey silk top. Her hair cascades down her back in blonde waves and she's wearing diamanté-strip earrings and a necklace to match. I can't remember the last time I saw her looking so beautiful. I want to hug her and tell her how brave she is to be facing tonight with such positivity, but now isn't the time, even without a stalker on the doorstep.

The woman starts knocking on the door and ringing the bell again, which is bad because I don't want Georgia coming down and seeing her.

'Um, Jo, I think your stalker's here.'

'What?' The colour drains from her face. 'As in . . . *here.*' She nods towards the door.

'She wants to talk to you.'

Jo shakes her head and backs away.

'Maybe you should hear her out. Better to do it while we're all in the house than wait for her to sneak up behind you or Georgia again. If you don't speak to her, I will. I want to know where she gets off harassing my daughter.'

'You're right.' Jo pushes her hair back with a beringed hand. 'Okay.'

'Good.' I could really do without this – whatever *this* is – right now, but it's better to get it sorted. I wonder again if it's anything to do with Elle. It's a bit of a coincidence that this woman has turned up today of all days. If she levels any abuse at Jo regarding her daughter, I don't know what I'll do.

I stand back a little and my sister edges past me and opens the door. She doesn't sound scared at all as she faces her stalker. 'Who the fuck are you?' Jo asks.

I wonder if I should call for Theo to come downstairs. Safety in numbers, and all that. Thankfully, Georgia's bedroom is at the back of the house, so I'm hoping she hasn't heard anything. I don't want the arrival of this woman to spoil her big day.

If she shows any sign of upsetting my sister, I'm calling the police. It occurs to me that I should probably be recording this, in case she says anything nasty. I pat my dressing gown pockets, but they're empty. My phone must still be upstairs. I want to retrieve it, but I can't leave Jo alone with this stranger.

'Is your name Jo Warren?' the woman spits out.

'Who are you?' My sister repeats the question.

The woman scowls. 'My name's Justine.'

'Justine *what*? And why were you following me the other week? You scared the crap out of me.'

'Good. You deserved it,' Justine sneers, without offering her surname. 'I saw you leave work and I followed you. I wanted to see where you lived. I wanted to catch you both.'

'What the hell are you talking about?' Jo snaps. 'Look, you can see I'm all dressed up here. I don't have time for this shit. If you come anywhere near me or my niece again, I'll report you to the police for harassment, get a restraining order. Now just leave, okay?'

The woman hesitates, her confidence waning a little. I'm hoping that the threat of a restraining order will send her back to wherever she came from. But I also don't want her to leave like this. Not without telling us the reason she's hounding my family. Because what if she does start following Jo again? What if she catches up with her or Georgia while we're not there to protect them?

'Did you sleep with Ryan Mills from the Coach and Horses?' Justine asks, her eyes clouding with something like pain.

'*What?*' My sister tenses next to me. 'I don't know what you're talking about.'

My heart sinks. I can tell Jo's lying. What has she been up to? This isn't the way I thought this confrontation was going to go. Has she been cheating on Ollie? Is that what this whole thing is about?

'You did, didn't you?' Justine screeches. 'Casey told me it was the girl from wash-up he was seeing, and I wanted to find out before I spoke to you, but just looking at your face, I can tell – you slept with him, didn't you? Just admit it. Casey said she saw you both shagging in the car park. Apparently your niece was there too. That's why I wanted to speak to her. Find out what she knew.'

I grit my teeth at this news. So Georgia saw Jo sleeping with another guy? I feel nauseous at the thought. My poor daughter. She must have been keeping this a secret.

'Who's Ryan Mills?' I look at my sister.

Jo's face is pale. 'I work with him. It was just a one-time thing,' she says to me in a low voice. 'But I haven't told Ollie yet so—'

'He's my fiancé, you bitch!' Justine lunges for my sister's arm, pulling her out on to the driveway and ripping the sleeve of her top.

'Hey!' I cry. 'Get off her.'

Justine grabs a handful of Jo's hair with her left hand and then pulls back her right, making a fist.

'Oh shit.'

'What's going on?' Theo marches past me in his joggers and no top, his hair dripping wet from the shower. He grabs hold of Justine's arm just a fraction too late. Her fist has already collided with Jo's cheekbone and now that Theo has hold of her arm, she's kicking Jo's shins as well.

'Je-e-esus! Get off me, you crazy bitch.' Jo is holding her face and trying to back away from Justine's vicious kicks. 'You've wrecked my clothes!'

'And you've wrecked my relationship!' Justine yells, so loudly they can probably hear her all the way down the coast at Sandbanks.

'If Ryan's your fiancé,' Jo replies hoarsely, 'then I've just saved you from making a massive mistake in marrying the dickhead.'

With Theo having inserted himself between them, Justine stops attacking my sister for the moment, but her eyes are glittering with rage and I'm worried for both Jo and Theo's physical well-being. I hope she hasn't got any kind of weapon on her.

'I'm getting my phone to call the police,' I say.

'No!' Jo calls out to me. 'I'll sort this out. You and Theo carry on getting ready. It's almost time to go, isn't it? I don't want Georgia's party ruined because of this.'

I can't believe my sister's slept with someone. Ollie's going to be devastated. I can't bear the thought of her hurting him. It will be like kicking a puppy. But I'm more concerned with what Georgia must think of her aunt.

Ollie comes out of the house looking dapper in a navy suit, a bottle of champagne in his hand. His smile melts away. 'Jo! You're hurt.' He notices Justine. 'Who are you? What's going on?'

None of us catches his eye.

'This your boyfriend, is it?' Justine asks Jo with a smirk. 'Will you tell him, or shall I?'

160

Chapter Twenty-Nine

THEN

Theo and I are in the living room watching a movie about a mountain climber, but I can't concentrate on the storyline because my mind is on Jo and where she might be. It's been over twenty-four hours since we saw or heard from her and my whole body is on high alert listening out for the door, and checking my phone. I'm also nervous about returning to work tomorrow, having been away for a month. Normally, I'm really organised and have my week planned out ahead of me, but I have no clue what tomorrow will bring. Other than my boss, Lisa, being kind, but pushing me on targets, because if we don't bring in the funds then our small cancer charity could fold, and I don't want to be responsible for that on top of everything else.

'You okay?' Theo nudges my leg with his foot.

'Hmm?'

'You're not into this film, are you?' He pauses the TV.

'No, I am, it's just, I can't concentrate. I should probably go to bed, but I don't know how I'm going to sleep tonight if—'

'Shh.' Theo holds up a finger. 'What's that? Is that a key in the door?'

I lurch to my feet and leave Theo while he's still talking. In the hall, I watch Jo come in through the front door.

'Oh, hey,' she says warily.

'*Hey?*' I reply, knowing I should tone it down, but feeling a rising fury spread throughout my body.

Theo joins me in the hall, and I hate the way we feel like Jo's parents, standing in judgement, ready to send her to her room or ground her. I never wanted to take on this role.

'Have you never heard of a phone?' I say, squashing the urge to yell at her.

'Uh, sorry.' She looks down and edges past us towards the kitchen. 'My battery died and the . . . place where I was didn't have a Samsung charger.'

'Where were you? We were so worried.'

Theo points to the lounge to indicate that he's leaving us to it. I nod and follow my sister into the kitchen.

She grabs a clean glass from the cupboard, fills it with juice and gulps it down. 'I'm fine,' she replies.

'Yes, well, I can see that, but it might have been nice if you'd let me know, rather than disappearing for hours.'

'Oh, sorry.' She sounds anything but. 'I didn't realise you were my jailer. Would you like me to wear an ankle bracelet?' She says it lightly with a half-smile, but I'm not in the mood to be won over right now. I feel ragged and teary and relieved but so, so angry.

'That's not fair, Jo. I was sick with worry about you. I've been calling, texting. I went over to your place, terrified at what I might find. Ollie came over and tried to reassure me that you'd be fine. But he didn't know where you were either. You can't keep doing this!'

'Well then, what should I be doing?' she asks, putting her empty glass on the island and turning to face me across the expanse of quartz. 'Tell me. Because I sure as shit don't know. I have no clue what I'm supposed to be doing.'

I shake my head, words failing me.

'I'm sorry you were worried,' she continues, 'but I can't cope with worrying about you worrying. You need to let me breathe, Natalie! I need to not be thinking about your house rules or how I'm disappointing you or being crap, flaky Jo.' She grips the edge of the island and takes a shaky breath. 'Right now, all I need is your spare room and this houseful of people who love me but who will let me be. Can you do that? Because if not, I'll have to go back to my place, and I really fucking don't want to go back to that empty flat. Not without my little Elly Belly. I don't think I can do it.' She sits cross-legged on the tiled floor, tears streaming down her exhausted-looking face.

I sit facing her, and squeeze her knee, hating to see her so distressed. So lost.

'I'm losing my mind here, Nat, and I need my big sister to let me be a selfish mess. Can you do that? Can you let me be awful for a little while longer? Because otherwise I'm going to have to stop and look at what's happened, and I don't think I can do it. I really don't.' Jo is sobbing, her arms over her eyes.

I'm crushed by her words. A new level of guilt flooding me. 'I'm so sorry, Jo. Please forgive me. Of course you can deal with this however you want. I'm sorry. I'm really, really sorry.' I wrap my arms around my shuddering, sobbing sister. 'Of course you must stay here with us. We'll give you your space to come and go as you please, and I promise we won't hassle you or have any expectations. I promise.'

As I comfort Jo, I'm crying too, but I also can't help feeling a tug of relief that we're finally able to have a real conversation with real emotions. Seeing my sister like this breaks my heart, but I know she needs to do it. I'm surprised by how prescient Ollie was earlier. He said Jo would let it all out eventually, and he was right.

After a while, I help my sister to her feet and heat up a portion of lasagne for her. I tell her that she'll have the house to herself from tomorrow as Georgia's back at school, and Theo and I will be back at work. I reassure her that I'll back off and give her space, but that I'll be here for her if she needs me. To my surprise, she throws her arms around me and whispers 'Thank you' in my ear.

'There's nothing to thank me for.'

'I couldn't get through this without you,' she replies.

The words that come to my mind are *You wouldn't have to if it weren't for me*. But instead I just squeeze her tighter and kiss her cheek.

I've been in bed trying to get to sleep since 10.30 p.m. and now it's almost two. Every time another half hour goes by, I add up the number of hours' sleep I'm likely to get, and think about how exhausted I'm going to be at work tomorrow. My thoughts are zigzagging between Georgia going back to school and me going back to work. But my biggest concern is Jo. I don't know how I'll ever recover from the guilt of losing Elle, and the impact it's having on my sister. I know that the more time goes by, the less chance we have of finding and bringing my niece home safe. None of us have verbalised the possibility that she might not even be alive, but it's something that pulls on the edges of my consciousness every day. Something that is too terrifying to think about properly.

I wish I could talk to Theo about my anxieties. Let him soothe me to sleep with comforting words, like he did in those first days after Elle disappeared, but it wouldn't be fair to wake him up, not when he goes back to work tomorrow too. Instead, I get out of bed, slip on my dressing gown and slippers and tiptoe downstairs. The house is cold, the remnants of this evening's central heating long gone. I grab my laptop from the kitchen and take it into the living room, where I curl up on the sofa.

Over the past couple of days, I've been subconsciously formulating a plan. One that I hadn't really allowed myself to seriously consider, but one that I'm coming to realise is my only course of action. But I can't tell the police, and I don't even think I'll be able to tell Theo as I'm sure he'd try to talk me out of it. Maybe I'm not being rational, but I'm hovering on the edge of desperation. It feels as though every route we've taken to find Elle has been shut down, and this is the last one left. If I don't at least try this, I'll regret it. I open my laptop and start typing.

Chapter Thirty

NOW

My sister stares at me beseechingly while Justine nurses her fist, on the verge of spilling the beans to Ollie that Jo has been sleeping with her fiancé.

'Jo,' I say, not wanting to prolong the drama. 'Why don't you go back inside with Ollie and I'll sort this out.'

'What's she talking about, Jo?' Ollie asks, still clutching the champagne bottle.

'I'm talking about your girlfriend—'

'I think you've said enough.' I cut her off.

Jo doesn't waste any time bundling Ollie back inside the house and closing the door behind them before Justine can say any more.

'What's happened?' Theo hisses.

'Jo slept with this woman's fiancé.'

'Why am I not surprised? Wait a minute, is this Jo's stalker from the other week?'

I nod, cringing at the memory of how I defended my sister to Theo, saying we should be sympathetic and supportive.

The anger has drained from Justine's eyes and she starts weeping, her face in her hands. Theo gives me a look that encompasses everything I'm feeling. I'm dreading what he's going to say about all this. There's only so much I can do to stick up for my sister when she has so little regard for herself or anyone else. Only a few moments ago I was so proud of how she's been doing recently. Of how she's facing this evening with so much courage. Only for it all to come crashing down because of her own selfishness and stupidity.

I walk over to where Justine's now perched against the wall of our driveway, tears still running down her cheeks, streaking her make-up.

'Don't worry, I'm going,' she says, gulping back a sob and standing up.

'You should probably ditch that fiancé of yours. He doesn't sound very trustworthy.'

'No shit.' She sniffs and wipes her sleeve across her eyes. 'I wasn't sure if it was true. But now I know for sure. We're supposed to be getting married next month in the Maldives.'

'You should take a friend instead,' I tell her. 'Have a nice holiday.'

Theo comes over. 'It's getting late, and we're not dressed.'

'My hair's ruined and I haven't even done my make-up,' I reply.

'I'll get out of your way. Will your sister tell her boyfriend what she did?'

'I'll make sure of it,' Theo says.

Justine nods.

'Poor woman,' Theo adds as she stumbles away down the road.

'You might not say that when I tell you that she was the woman who confronted Georgia after school this week.'

'What? The one who yelled at her and made her cry?'

'Yep. At least Georgia didn't see her out here tonight,' I say. 'At least, I hope she didn't.'

'I don't believe it!' Theo's face is stiff with fury. 'I'm not going to talk about it now, Nat, but I want you to know I'm not happy about this.'

'You and me both.' I shiver as I realise I'm out here with no shoes on and just a dressing gown.

'Okay.' He nods, exhales and pulls me in for a hug. He's bare-chested and freezing.

'We should go in,' I say, relieved he's not cross with me. It's got to the point where I'm constantly worried about what my husband thinks of Jo. I'm always in the middle and it's not healthy. After all this, I need to do something about it.

Back inside the house, Theo hurries up the stairs to dry off and get ready. I head into the kitchen, wondering what Jo has told Ollie. They're sitting on the kitchen sofa, talking in a low tone.

'Jo, can I talk to you?'

'What?' She glances up at me, her face reddening. 'Oh, sure.'

Ollie looks confused and a little angry. I'm pretty sure she hasn't told him the truth yet.

'Sorry, Ollie,' I say. 'We'll be back down in a minute.'

I pull Jo up to my bedroom for a private chat, where she starts to thank me for covering for her.

I hold out my hand to stop her speaking. 'If you don't tell Ollie what you did, then I will.'

She nods. 'I will, I will. It was ages ago. A one-time thing. I'm so stupid. I love Ollie and I'm gutted about it.'

'Right now I don't care, Jo. What you did caused so much distress. That woman scared Georgia half to death, not to mention that, by the sounds of it, Georgia saw you and that woman's fiancé having sex in a pub car park. It's horrible. You need to talk to Ollie. It's not fair to keep him in the dark when Theo and I know about it. Maybe you shouldn't come tonight.'

Jo's face falls even further. 'You don't want me to come? What about Georgia? She'll think I don't care about her.'

'Well, you should have thought about that before you started shagging some bloke from work behind Ollie's back.' I plonk myself down at my dressing table and start aggressively applying mascara. Stabbing myself in the eye and swearing.

'I'll leave you,' Jo says quietly. 'I really am sorry.'

I don't reply, but I feel like screaming.

Chapter Thirty-One

THEN

'Can you get the garden sofa cushions out?' I ask Theo as he comes into the kitchen wearing shorts and a crumpled T-shirt. 'I thought it would be nice if we had coffee in the garden.'

'Good idea. They might be a bit damp though. They've been in the shed all winter.'

'I'm sure they'll dry in a few minutes. That sun's hot.'

Summer has crept up on us and it feels like the change in season has signalled the end of hope for finding Elle. While the weather was still cold and dreary, it felt as though we were in the same wintry time frame as when she disappeared. But now that June has blown in with its warm breezes and swallows flitting above the houses, it's like the whole world has moved on. Relentlessly marching forward with no pause button. No waiting around for Elle to get back on board. No waiting around for anything.

'Ooh, are you making coffee?' Jo comes into the kitchen with Ollie, who's just arrived. She looks different this morning, and then I realise what it is.

'You've dyed your hair again,' I say with a smile. 'Looks lovely.'

She flicks a few strands dismissively. 'Yeah. I was sick of looking at my roots so I've gone back to blonde.'

It may not seem much, but this feels like a momentous step towards getting the old Jo back – the fact that she's started caring about how she looks. Even so, it still feels very precarious. Like I'm waiting for a bomb to drop. She was out again last night and every time she comes home, I brace myself for some kind of drama.

Theo thinks I'm worrying over nothing. He thinks Jo will calm down and that she and Ollie will end up together, but I'm not so sure. I think that's just wishful thinking on his part. A neat solution to the problem that is my sister.

'Do you want a cup?' I ask them. 'I'll make a cafetière and do some frothy milk. Theo's getting the cushions from the shed.'

'I'll give him a hand,' Ollie offers. 'I brought doughnuts.' He hands me a small cardboard box.

'Thanks, Ollie. But you really didn't have to do that.' He's always bringing us little treats and has also started helping out around the house. I think he feels guilty that he spends so much time here. But as far as I'm concerned, he can come round as often as he likes. Jo is always in a better mood when he's around.

'Can I have a coffee and doughnuts too?' Georgia skips into the room and Ollie pretends to grab her. She squeals with laughter and dodges out of his way.

'You're too young for coffee,' I tell her. 'But I'll do you a hot chocolate, if you like?'

'I had a latte at Cleo's last week,' Georgia replies. 'Her stepmum lets us have whatever we like when we're round there.'

'Well, good for Cleo,' I retort, slightly annoyed that Rachel gave my daughter coffee. 'But here in *boring* town it's hot chocolate, water or juice, take your pick.'

Georgia laughs. 'It's not boring town.'

'Glad to hear it.'

'It is a bit boring town,' Jo adds, winking at Georgia, who giggles.

'Charming,' I reply with a smile.

If anyone came into our sunny kitchen right now, they would see nothing but a happy extended family without a care in the world. Five people enjoying a light-hearted, carefree Saturday morning. But looks can be deceiving. We all spend a lot of time pretending to be normal and happy, because the alternative would be too depressing. Too hard to keep going.

Jo is still living in our spare room until she finds her feet again, and we haven't spoken about any long-term plans. She gave up her flat without ever setting foot inside it since losing Elle. She also hasn't worked regularly and could no longer afford the rent and bills. But even if she could have afforded it, she said she never wanted to go back there. Even the mention of going there would get her shaking or retching.

Theo and I packed everything up for her and took it round to my parents' house, where they've said we can store it in their garage – as long as we cleared out said garage first. It took us many weekends, but we finally did it. I had to shut off my emotions while we packed up Elle's belongings. It was one of the hardest things I've ever done. I suppose we could have paid someone to do it, but that felt disrespectful somehow. And Theo and I both still carry so much guilt. It was the least we could do.

We take our drinks into the garden and sit on slightly damp sofa cushions, but no one minds because it's so lovely to be outside and feel the warmth of the sun on our faces.

'It's properly hot,' Theo says.

'Georgia, you need sun cream,' I say. 'Can you pop upstairs and get the sun cream from my dressing table?'

'Okay.'

'How's work, Ollie?' Theo asks.

'Good, but it's been hot this week. I keep asking the owner to install air con, but she says it's too expensive.'

'That's rough,' Theo replies.

'It's fine. I suit the bright red sweaty look.'

'Yeah, you can pull it off.' Jo smiles and takes a bite of her pastry.

'How about you?' Ollie asks Theo. 'How's the world of sportswear?'

'Scary at the moment. We've just been bought out by another company, so everyone's stressing about their jobs, running around, trying to be indispensable so we don't get made redundant.'

'That's not good.'

'No,' Theo agrees. 'Obviously don't mention anything to Georgia. I don't need her worrying about it.'

'You'll be okay though, won't you, Theo?' Ollie asks.

'I hope so, but it's all up in the air. It's the not-knowing. That and also worrying about the rest of the team.'

Theo earns a lot more than I do, so if he loses his job we'll be screwed. We're fairly confident he won't, and even if he does, I'm hopeful he'll get another job. But it's not a nice feeling to be at the mercy of others.

'Keeping everything crossed for you, mate,' Ollie says.

'You're quiet.' Theo nudges me with his foot.

'Am I? Sorry.' I feel everyone's eyes on me and I'm not sure what to say. I'm anxious about later, but it's something they don't know about so I can't talk about it.

Thankfully, Georgia returns with the sun cream, diverting their attention.

'How about you, Georgia?' Ollie asks. 'Everything good at school?'

'Yep.' She nods, plopping herself down between Jo and I and taking a sip of her drink.

Jo takes the lid off the sun cream and starts applying it to Georgia's arms, dabbing a bit on her nose and making her laugh.

'Got anything planned for the weekend, Gee?' Ollie asks her.

'Yep. I'm going to a hot-tub party at Sasha's today.'

'Is that where groups of hot tubs get together and dance around?'

Georgia rolls her eyes at Ollie. 'Uh, no-o.'

'Oh, that's a shame,' he says with a smile. 'Well, I hope you have a great time.'

'Thanks.'

'Once you've got that cream on, you'd better get your stuff ready,' I say. 'We'll have to leave soon.'

'Okay, in a minute, when I've finished my doughnut.'

There's a lull in the conversation as we sip our drinks. I'm anxious to get going, but I try to relax.

'Aunty Jo, do you think they'll find Elle?'

Georgia asks the question and it's as if time stops. As if the bees stop buzzing and the neighbour's lawnmower stops humming, the birdsong stills and even the breath in our bodies is quelled. The moment seems to last a lifetime and then . . .

'That's what we're all hoping for,' Jo replies softly.

'Because it would be nice if she was here too,' Georgia adds.

'It would, darling.' I put an arm around her and hold her close for a moment.

'Does anyone want another drink?' Jo asks, getting up abruptly and banging her leg on the table.

'I'll have a water,' Theo says.

My sister heads inside and I get that familiar sick feeling in my throat. I hope Georgia's question isn't going to set Jo off. I'm still so worried about her. I don't know what to do for the best. She refuses point-blank to talk to anyone, so I guess we just have to carry on being here to support her when she needs it.

'Right . . .' Theo gets to his feet. 'I'd better get ready too.'

'You off out?' Ollie asks.

'Yeah. Kite-surfing at Poole Harbour with some buddies.'

'Nice. Have a good one.'

'Thanks. You up to anything?'

'I've got today off,' Ollie replies. 'So Jo and I are meeting some friends in town. What about you, Natalie?'

I swallow, trying to appear nonchalant. 'Oh, not much, just a bit of shopping.'

'Not kite-surfing with Theo?'

'Definitely not.'

Theo laughs and I punch him lightly on the arm.

'Nat and kite-surfing don't get on.' Theo proceeds to tell Ollie the embarrassing tale of my one and only kite-surfing lesson, where Theo and I had a massive argument and I stormed off. We can laugh about it now, but at the time I wanted the wind to take him across the Channel to France.

Once we've finished our drinks and doughnuts, and Georgia is sun-creamed up, we all go our separate ways. Jo and Ollie leave first, and then Theo and Georgia head off. Theo's dropping her at Sasha's on his way to the harbour.

I grab my bag and keys, lock up the house and get in the car, taking a steadying breath before I start the engine and head towards the neighbouring town of Christchurch.

The roads are carnage because it's the first hot weekend of the year and everyone is going nuts trying to get to the beach or the river, probably via the supermarkets to stock up on picnic food and alcohol. I try to stay calm and not get wound up by drivers either tailgating me, cutting me up at roundabouts or just not indicating. The last thing I need is to get into an accident. Not when I have such an important meeting to get to.

At the beginning of the year, I felt so guilty and helpless. I wanted to do something positive to help find Elle. I kept thinking that there had to be something. Some way of finding out what had happened. And that's when I had the desperate notion to hire a private investigator.

The police were winding down their search, and my DIY publicity and search campaigns weren't yielding any results. I couldn't bear the thought that this was the end of the line. That we just had to hope Elle would turn up safe and well. Because it was looking less and less likely that it would actually happen. Not without some serious help.

I didn't want to tell Jo because I couldn't bear to get her hopes up, in case it didn't work out. I also didn't want to come across like I was doing some magnanimous thing. Some favour. I didn't want any thanks or praise or acknowledgement. I just wanted to find Elle.

I suppose it was the sort of decision I should have run past the police, but I thought they might be against it. I thought they might see it as a slight regarding their efforts. As well as my doubts around police approval, I was also fairly sure that Theo would be against the idea. Of course, he was desperate to find Elle as much as me, but the costs of hiring an investigator could run into thousands, and it was money we didn't have. So I made the decision on my own to take out a bank loan.

Now that Theo's job might be in jeopardy, I'm even more desperate to know if Tara Stiles, the PI I hired, has found anything. The loan has all been used up over the past few months and so today will have to be our last meeting. If Tara hasn't been able to come up with any leads, then I'll be paying back a loan over the next four years for nothing. It feels like this is our last hope at finding Elle, and my stomach is in knots. I'm praying that she's going to have good news, but it's not looking hopeful, because surely if she'd found anything she would have contacted me by now.

Chapter Thirty-Two

NOW

Surprisingly, once Theo and I have reached the venue, frazzled and a little bit late, with Georgia and her two best friends in tow, every single thing turns out to be just perfect. From the cosy venue, with its twinkling fairy lights and friendly bar staff, to the upbeat music, delicious canapés and the genuine warmth of all our friends and family. You can just feel that everyone is enjoying themselves, wanting to make it special for our daughter. The atmosphere is electric, with all Georgia's friends making a big fuss of her, and it's heartwarming to see her so happy. Even better, there isn't a journalist in sight.

After a couple of cocktails, I've calmed down a bit and am allowing myself to relax. Theo and I have based ourselves in a secluded corner with the other relatives and parents that have come along. My mum and dad, my mum's sister, Aunty Val, and her husband, Uncle Armand. Sasha's parents, Liz and Steve, are also here.

'You look lovely, Natalie,' my mum says, her voice raised to make herself heard above the music. She touches the billowing sleeve of my leopard-print dress. 'I love that style on you.'

'Thanks, Mum. You look gorgeous too. That dark green really suits you.'

'They had a sale on in Marks. Forty per cent off.'

'Bargain,' I reply.

'This is a lovely venue,' she adds. 'Although it's a bit loud. Difficult to talk.'

'Nowhere to park,' Dad says. 'The car parks in town are astronomical. It's why we never come in.'

'Where's Josephine?' Mum asks, looking around.

I brace myself. 'She's not coming.'

'Not coming?' Mum echoes.

'Why isn't she coming?' my dad asks.

'You know. Elle's anniversary. It's tricky.' I can hardly tell them it's because she slept with someone behind Ollie's back and had a fight with his fiancée outside the house.

'But it's Georgia's eighteenth,' Mum says. 'She should really be here.'

'Your mum and I made the effort.' Dad sips his pint. 'All she had to do was show her face for half an hour. Did you tell her she didn't have to stay the whole night?'

As they continue to question me, anger scrapes my throat and I can feel my blood pressure rising.

'You should have made her come, Natalie,' Mum continues. 'It would have been good for her. Especially tonight.'

'It's not healthy for her to be hiding away,' Dad adds.

'Why is it always down to me to look after everyone?' I snap. 'You could have spoken to her too, you know! I've had all this to organise. I've had work. I'm constantly worrying about Jo, about Georgia—'

'What's wrong with Georgia?' Mum asks.

'Nothing! Just . . . Sorry. I didn't mean to blow up. I'm just a bit stressed, that's all.'

Dad raises an eyebrow. 'Sounds like you and Theo need a holiday, just the two of you.'

'That's a good idea, Derek,' my mum says. 'A lovely break away from it all.'

'Chance would be a fine thing,' I reply. The only holidays we take are with Theo's parents in Mallorca. It's lovely seeing them, but it's never exactly a break as we usually end up helping them with chores like sorting out utility bills and putting together flat-pack furniture.

'We could have Georgia while you're away,' Mum offers.

'She's eighteen now, Mum. Doesn't need babysitting anymore.'

'Well, you know what I mean. The offer's there.'

Too little too late, I think to myself. They've also conveniently ignored my point about Jo, like always. 'Thanks,' I reply through gritted teeth. 'Anyway, I'd better go and mingle.' I head over to the bar, attempting to soothe my fractured nerves.

'Mum, this is amazing!' Georgia comes up to me, her brown eyes shining, her long dark hair cascading in waves down her back. 'Thank you so much for organising it.'

Her joyful smile is exactly what I need to restore my equilibrium. 'You're welcome, darling.'

'I wasn't sure about a party at first,' she says, 'because it's quite a responsibility, isn't it? Making sure everyone has a good time, and that it's not too lame and everything. But it's honestly just perfect.' She takes several large sips of her drink.

'I'm so pleased to hear that. Go easy on the cocktails though, won't you? I know you're eighteen now but they're quite strong. Maybe alternate with mocktails.'

'I will, don't worry.'

'Cleo's dress looks gorgeous on you,' I add.

Georgia does a little twirl. 'She said I can have it as a birthday present.'

'Really? That's generous of her.'

'I know, right? Where's Aunty Jo and Ollie? Are they here yet? I thought they were going to come early with us. All my friends think Jo's so cool. I want to have a dance with her.'

I swallow, trying to remember the cover story I made up in the taxi over. But my mind has gone blank.

'Mum?'

'Sorry, but Jo's not feeling too well. She said she'll try to come later if she can.'

Georgia's face drops. 'But I saw her earlier and she was all dressed up. She looked amazing and so did Ollie. He was wearing a suit and everything. I've never seen him in a suit before.'

'I know it's disappointing, Gee, but it came on suddenly.'

'Is it because of . . . you know, Elle?'

'What? No, nothing like that. She's just got a bit of a migraine. Now, go and have fun. Your Aunty Jo wouldn't want you worrying about anything on your birthday, especially not her.' I kiss my daughter's cheek, hoping I've reassured her enough to get back to enjoying her night. Theo and I decided not to mention Justine's visit earlier. We'll tell Georgia about it at a later date, just to put her mind at rest that Justine won't be bothering her again.

'Georgia-a-a-!' Two of her friends, Naomi and Faye, come over to drag her on to the dance floor, pressing a fresh cocktail into her hand. She lets herself be taken off, but I can see that the light in her eyes has dimmed a little at the news that her aunt won't be coming.

I'm trying to put the events from earlier out of my head, but it all still feels so surreal. Was there an actual fight on our driveway? Thank goodness the media weren't there to see it all. Despite the whole thing happening because of Jo's actions, I can't help feeling sad that she's missing out on tonight. I'm suddenly overcome with the urge to call her. To tell her to come to the party. Aside from Georgia wanting her here, I really believe that Jo should be here too, celebrating with us. At the end of the day, this is the ten-year anniversary of when her little girl went missing. And here I am celebrating my daughter's eighteenth without either of them. It feels wrong.

Theo comes over to me with a pint in his hand. 'I know that expression. You want to call Jo, don't you.'

'I really do. Am I a pushover?'

'I could throttle her,' he says, taking a sip of his beer, 'but I agree she should be here.'

'What if she's told Ollie the truth already. They might be fighting. Or he might have left her.' I take a gulp of my cocktail. 'I really do think she should be here, but I can't deal with any more drama tonight.'

Theo's brow creases for a moment. 'Okay, instead of calling, why don't you message her. Tell her not to talk to Ollie yet, but to come tonight for Georgia's sake. That way, if it's already gone tits up then at least you won't have to deal with it over the phone.'

'I think I will.' I place a hand on Theo's arm. 'Thanks, Mr Edwards, you're a good husband.'

'I have my moments.' He smiles and places a kiss on the side of my head. 'Right, I'm off to dance with my daughter. Don't be long sorting things out with Jo. I want you on the dance floor pronto.'

'Deal.' I take myself off to a corner and WhatsApp my sister, suggesting she come to the party, and hoping that she can make it. I'm selfishly hoping she hasn't had that talk with Ollie yet. I send the message, put my phone back in my bag and head to the dance floor to celebrate with my family.

As the evening progresses, it's clear that Georgia's good mood is deteriorating. Her face is drawn and she keeps disappearing off to the loos. She's also knocking back the alcohol at an alarming rate.

I check my phone periodically, but my messages have not been read. So either Jo hasn't seen them, or she's ignoring them. I don't know which is worse. I tell Theo that Jo hasn't responded, but he shrugs and says, 'Well, you asked her to come, the ball's in her court now. Just enjoy tonight, okay?' He goes back to talking to Steve about work and I drift over to the edge of the dance floor, trying and failing to take my husband's advice, while scanning the packed venue for Georgia.

'Great party.' Liz comes by and stands next to me. 'Such a good space too. I think I might book it for my fiftieth.'

'Fifty?' I gasp. 'You're right. I guess that's the next milestone birthday for us, isn't it? In . . . six years.'

'Four years for me,' she says. 'Georgia enjoying herself?' I can tell by Liz's tone that she's spotted my daughter's deflating mood. But I don't want to make a big deal of it.

'I think so,' I reply. 'She's a bit overwhelmed.'

'They're so up and down, aren't they?' Liz's eyes are full of concern. 'Not like my Finlay. His teenage years were a breeze compared to Sasha's. But then he was a nightmare toddler. They all have their moments, don't they?'

I nod and smile, but I'm finding it harder and harder to relate to friends when they haven't been through what we have. I know everyone has their problems, but I feel so alone right now.

Liz is still talking, but I can't focus on what she's saying. My mind is crowded with thoughts of the fight on our driveway, and of the marks on Georgia's legs, of her downcast expression when I told her Jo wasn't coming tonight, of poor Ollie, of Jo's troubled life, and – it hits me in the chest like I only just remembered – of Elle, who went missing ten years ago today. And suddenly I feel like I'm drowning in a dark, empty, silent pool.

Chapter Thirty-Three

THEN

I try not to show my irritation as Jo comes into the kitchen and tells me she's 'just going to borrow the sugar bowl'. I wouldn't mind, but she has a habit of helping herself to things and not bringing them back.

'Hang on a sec,' I say, searching in the cupboard for some kind of dish or cup that I don't mind going missing. I linger over a really ugly pink mug that Georgia – aka Theo – bought me for Mother's Day last year, but I decide I shouldn't part with it yet and instead settle on a bowl with a chip on the rim. 'Here, pour some into this.'

She does so without so much as an eye-roll, which makes me instantly suspicious. 'You seem very chipper this morning,' I add. 'And since when do you have sugar in your tea or coffee?'

Her face reddens. 'I just fancied some, that's all.'

'Have you got a man in there?' I ask quietly, conscious that Georgia might be down any minute.

'What?' She gives me a quick scowl before relaxing a little and suppressing a smile. She puts the bowl down on the counter and sits on one of the stools.

'Who is it?' This whole conversation reminds me of when we were younger, before relationships and kids made things more serious. There's a five-year gap between us so we were never super-close in terms of sharing this kind of stuff, but there was a short time when she was in her late teens and I was in my early twenties when it was fun to talk about boys together.

'I'll tell you,' she replies hesitantly, 'but you have to promise not to make a big deal out of it.'

I'm trying not to feel too worried that she's brought someone back with her. I thought her days of bringing random men back were over. It's been almost two and a half years since Elle went missing, and it's been rough. But recently, these past few months, things have felt a little calmer, a little easier. After that first Christmas without Elle, that first birthday, all those milestones we had to navigate, things now feel a little less brutal.

I didn't know how we would all get through those first months, but somehow, we did. Battered and bruised, tired and still disbelieving. I don't think time has healed any of us, it's just made things softer around the edges. Less sharp. Jo has become less angry and self-destructive, thank goodness. It's helped that we recently had the garage converted into a little self-contained apartment for her so that she now has her own space, yet she still has our support on hand if she needs it.

'Well?' I prompt.

'Promise you won't overreact first,' she replies.

'Fine, I promise.' I stare at her across the kitchen island, wondering why she's being so coy about this. She never has before.

'Ollie stayed over,' she says.

I frown, wondering what she means. She's always said there's only friendship between them, nothing more, so if she means what I think she means, then this is huge.

'He's been here for me through all of this. I mean, obviously so have you and Theo, but Ollie has been the absolute best friend I could have wished for. And last night I just thought *What am I waiting for? Why am I holding back?*

I'm holding my breath, hardly daring to hope that this means what I think it does. 'So . . .' I begin tentatively. 'Does this mean that you and Ollie . . . ?'

She nods. 'We're going to give it a go.'

I want to squeal with excitement for her, but I'm scared to show too much support, as she's likely to back off. 'I'm so happy for you, Jo. Seriously, you two will be great together.'

'I hope so.' She gives me a nervous smile. 'I just don't want it to ruin our friendship. I made him promise that if it all goes wrong, he'll still be my best friend.'

'It won't go wrong,' I reply. 'It's perfect. You could do with something good in your life right now. Can I give you a hug?'

She shrugs and nods, and I walk round to where she's sitting on the stool and wrap my arms around her. 'Honestly so happy for you, sis.'

'Thanks, Nat.'

My brain goes into overdrive, picturing the two of them moving in, getting married, maybe even having a family together. I know Ollie would be up for all of that, but he'll need to tread softly around Jo because if he comes on too strong, she'll get spooked and back off.

'Anyway . . .' She slides off the stool and picks up the sugar bowl. 'Better get back with this or Ollie will be late for work. He doesn't normally work Wednesdays but Cassie's off sick. So annoying. What are you up to today?'

'Easter holidays so I'm working from home. I've got a couple of Teams calls this morning.'

'Want me to look after Georgia?' she asks. 'It's gorgeous out there. We could go to the park.'

'That would be great if you don't mind?' I reply, buoyed by her request. Jo loves her niece, but it's been hard on my sister, living in such close proximity to Georgia while her own daughter is missing. There's this very slight distance between the two of them that never used to be there, but it's not something I ever felt I could draw attention to. I would love it if they could rebuild their relationship. Georgia's a bit old for the park these days. She's ten going on sixteen, but I don't want to put a dampener on Jo's offer.

'Hi, Aunty Jo.' Georgia comes into the kitchen in her pyjamas.

'Hey, Gee,' Jo says. 'Fancy coming to the park with me?'

'The park? Uh, yeah, sure.'

'Or we could do something else?' Jo amends, picking up on the less-than-enthusiastic vibe.

'No, the park sounds fun, actually. They've got a new zipwire that Naomi said was awesome.'

'Okay.' Jo claps her hands. 'You get dressed and I'll meet you back here in half an hour. We can get an ice cream or a coffee after.'

'Yesss!' Georgia skips back upstairs.

'You've made someone happy,' I say.

'Cool,' she replies. 'Okay, now I really have to get this sugar to Ollie before his coffee goes cold.'

My heart is warm with possibilities for a better future for all of us, but especially for Jo. Could this be the turning point for my sister? The moment when her life stops being so bleak? I really, truly hope so. I can't wait to tell Theo about Jo and Ollie when he gets home from work. He always thought they'd get together. Looks like he was right.

An hour later, and I'm in the living room having just come off my first call with a new client who could potentially bring a lot of business in. I close my laptop, stand up and stretch my arms out. This morning feels like it couldn't have gone any better. I'm still riding high off Jo's news, and now this. I started my new job in January, working for a big hotel chain, so I'm keen to show them what I can do. I'm looking forward to telling my boss about this potential deal. If the client decides to book his conferences with our chain, I'll get a decent bonus, which will really come in handy, especially after we had to remortgage to pay for the garage conversion.

I glance out the window, hoping Jo and Georgia are having a lovely time. I sneak a peek at the Find My app, but Georgia's location is only showing from two hours ago. I'm sure they're fine. I just have time to make myself a quick cuppa before my next call with another potential client – an upmarket wedding planner. I don't think she's that keen because she tends to use more quirky boutique hotels rather than large chains, but I'm determined to give it my best shot.

Twenty minutes later and I'm in full flow, giving the woman my best sales pitch as to why she should recommend our hotels to her happy couples.

'And of course,' I say, 'we can give you incredible discounts, depending on how many weddings you can refer to us each year.'

As she gives me her lukewarm response, I hear the back door close and footsteps rushing along the hall. I told Jo and Georgia I was going to be working in the living room, so I hope they don't disturb me.

I glance up in annoyance as the door flies open, and I look over my laptop to see Georgia standing there with tears streaming down her face.

I realise I need to end this call.

'Um, so sorry, but I have a bit of a home emergency, do you mind if I reschedule?'

The woman looks a bit miffed. 'Fine. When do you want to—'

'I'll email you. Thanks.' I end the call and look up at my daughter, trying not to panic. 'What's happened?' I get to my feet. 'Did you fall off the zipwire?'

'No.'

'Where's Aunty Jo?'

Georgia crosses the room and huddles into the far corner of the sofa, still crying.

'Georgia?'

She doesn't reply. I poke my head out of the door and peer down the hall through to the kitchen, but I can't see my sister, so I return to Georgia and crouch down in front of her. 'What's happened?'

'Aunty Jo g-g-got upset.' Georgia manages to stutter out the words.

'Upset? Do you mean she got sad, or she got angry?' I ask, a million-and-one scenarios flying around my head.

'S-sad. And so I brought her home.'

'Oh, darling. Where is she now?'

'I took her into her new flat and she got into bed.'

'Do you know what happened to make her sad?' I move up to the sofa and put my arm around my distraught daughter, bringing her in close.

'We were having fun and going on all the stuff at the park, but we never managed to get on the zipwire because there was a queue. And then we sat on the bench next to this woman and she and Aunty Jo were talking, and the woman thought she was my mum because she said that Aunty Jo looked just like her daughter, and I think she meant me.' Georgia stares at me for a moment, reliving the shock, before continuing: 'Aunty Jo didn't reply. She just stood up and started walking off towards the trees. So I followed her and saw that she was crying.'

As my daughter recounts what happened, my body grows heavier and a sick feeling lodges itself in my chest.

Georgia continues, 'And she was just standing there, not moving, just crying and crying. And I didn't know what to do. I was too scared to ask if she was all right. So I just took her hand and brought her home. Was that okay?' Georgia looks up at me again, her brown eyes wet with tears.

'That was the perfect thing to do,' I reply. 'Well done, Gee-Gee. That was so grown-up and thoughtful.' I kiss my daughter's head and wish more than anything that that woman had kept her thoughts to herself. Only moments ago, I'd been happy that things were moving in the right direction. That Jo might have actually turned a corner, but now all the progress she's made has been undone by a few well-meaning words from a stranger. And my poor daughter has been caught in the crossfire. I don't know how to cope with this anymore. Just as I think we're getting back to some semblance of normality, we're catapulted back to square one. Is it always going to be like this?

Chapter Thirty-Four

NOW

I know I'm being rude when I cut Liz off mid-sentence and excuse myself to go to the loo. I'm actually going to look for Georgia, who's been missing from the party for a while now. She's definitely not on the dance floor, she's not at the bar or outside on the terrace with the vapers and smokers, and she's not with my parents in the corner.

Normally, she and Sasha are joined at the hip, but it looks like Sasha is 'getting' with a boy, as the kids say. They're kissing in a booth that's slightly set back from the dance floor. Not sure if Steve will be thrilled about that, but that's their problem. I've got enough of my own right now. I head to the bathroom, worried but hoping that Georgia is hiding away in here. But she's not.

Unwanted echoes of the past billow around me as I search the crowded venue for my daughter, just like I searched the ice rink for Elle. *Don't be silly, this is nothing like that.* This is probably just my daughter having had too much to drink. Or maybe she's also getting with a boy.

I stop outside the loos to check the Find My app. After last month's broken-curfew debacle, I made Georgia reinstall it on her phone. The circle spins while it tries to locate her. And then it zooms in. She's not here in the Hearts Club, she's a few buildings down the road in what appears to be a shoe shop.

I head for the exit, hurry down the stairs, through the busy restaurant and out into the chilly street. It's Friday night, but the cold weather is keeping most people inside. There's a group of women staggering through the town, dressed up for a hen do, and a homeless man sheltering on the steps of a closed-down bank. I turn right and walk up the street, shivering in my silk dress.

Georgia is vaping in the doorway of a shoe store, crouched down, her coat pulled around her. She looks up when she sees me, but she doesn't seem surprised and she doesn't try to hide the vape. Her face is streaked with tears, but she's crying silently. She looks very old and very young at the same time. Fear clutches at my heart. There's something wrong with my daughter.

I reach down to take her hand and she lets me pull her up to her feet. I wrap my arms around her and she stiffens before letting go and sobbing into my shoulder.

'Come on,' I say, keeping my arm around her.

'I can't go back in,' she says, resisting.

'No, we'll go in there.' I point to a pub up the road.

She hesitates for a moment, and then nods.

Inside it's warm and calm, just the clink of glasses and some gentle chatter. An older-person's pub. No cool kids in sight. I settle Georgia at a corner table, go up to the bar to get us each a pint of Diet Coke and then sit opposite my daughter, passing her a tissue from my bag to wipe her eyes.

After a few sips of our drinks, Georgia starts talking. She says she's worried about her Aunty Jo not coming tonight. 'Is it because she blames me for what happened to Elle?'

'Blames you?' I'm horrified that my daughter thinks any of us might blame her in any way for what happened. 'Of course not. What would make you think that?'

'Because Elle disappeared at my birthday party. I wanted to go there. I wanted to go ice-skating and if we hadn't gone, then Elle would still be here. So it's obviously my fault.'

'It's absolutely not your fault,' I manage to say. 'And I can categorically state that Jo has never and will never think that. She adores you.'

'That's not true.' She stares into her drink.

'But it is true. Look at me, Georgia.'

She reluctantly looks up.

'What's all this about?' I ask. 'You know that Aunty Jo loves you and would be here tonight if she could. You've never mentioned these thoughts before. What's brought this on? You were having a nice evening and then—'

'I didn't want Elle at my party!' she cries. 'I just wanted my friends. I was annoyed that she was tagging along. If I'd been nicer to her, then maybe she wouldn't have gone missing. I'm a horrible person and I don't deserve this party tonight.' She blinks furiously and grits her teeth.

As I look at my daughter's distressed features, the sounds of the pub recede, and all I can hear is my heart beating. I'm gutted she's been blaming herself like this. 'Georgia, that's not true. You loved your little cousin. You were so happy when you heard she was coming to your birthday.'

'No, I wasn't,' she insists. 'Because I remember Cleo asking why my baby cousin was coming to my party, and I felt embarrassed. I was embarrassed that she was there. I really am a horrible person.'

'But that was Cleo making you feel bad,' I say. 'That wasn't you. You were the sweetest cousin. I promise you. And if you got irritated with Elle from time to time, well that's just normal, isn't it? That's the same for all families. Take me and Aunty Jo. Sometimes we fight like cat and dog, but that doesn't mean I don't love her.'

Georgia stares at me, trying to work out if I'm telling the truth. Trying to see into the past, to get the answers she needs to absolve her from this terrible misplaced guilt she seems to be carrying. How have I never seen this before? Has she been keeping all this locked inside for a decade? I wish I could make her remember the truth – that she was a wonderful cousin. That she adored Elle and loved having her round to play. Somehow she's latched on to one or two isolated incidents, and has created a past that paints her as the bad guy. Something else occurs to me.

'Can I ask you something?' I say to my daughter carefully.

She nods warily.

'Those marks on your legs, were they anything to do with how you were feeling about Elle?'

She hunches for a moment, chewing her thumbnail, and then she nods again, this time more vehemently. 'Yes,' she squeaks. 'I hadn't really thought about Elle for years. Not really. I knew this terrible thing had happened in the past, but it was like it had happened in a movie, not in real life. And then, as it got closer to my eighteenth, I realised that it was ten years since she went missing, and I saw that Aunty Jo was sad and she wasn't really being herself, and that she wasn't really talking to me much anymore, and I thought she blamed me. I thought you all blamed me, but because I was a kid, you couldn't really say anything, and it all got jumbled in my head.' The words are tumbling out of her now and I don't want to interrupt so I let her keep going, even though I'm heartbroken by what she's saying.

'So I took the razor,' she continues, 'and I thought I'd try it just to see. Every time I thought about Elle, I would do it and it made me forget for a bit. But later, when I saw the scars, I got scared and thought how will I be able to go to the beach and wear a bikini because everyone will see, and they'll know what I've been doing. And they'll know I did it because it was my fault Elle went missing.' She finally stops, her breath coming in short gasps. 'But I deserve the scars, because it was my fault.'

'Listen to me, Georgia.' I stare into my daughter's beautiful brown eyes and take both her hands in mine. 'Your Aunty Jo loves you to pieces and her sadness or quietness has nothing to do with you. You have nothing to feel guilty about. You were a brilliant cousin. I saw you taking Elle's hand and helping her to skate. You and Sasha absolutely loved looking after her that evening.'

'You're just saying that.'

'No I'm not. On my life, I'm not.'

'Really?' She sounds dubious.

'I promise you. Can't you remember? You were excited to have your cousin there.'

She frowns for a moment. 'I . . . I think I remember,' she says. 'I do! I'd forgotten about it. All my friends wanted to skate with Elle, but she wanted to skate with me, and I felt proud. Cleo was annoyed because Elle chose me and Sasha to hold her hands. I . . . I don't know how I forgot that.'

'You were eight years old, and it was such a traumatic night. You must have blocked part of it out, and then over time it's easy to misremember things. But I can tell you with one hundred per cent certainty that you were a wonderful cousin and you loved Elle very much. You looked after her so well that night. But it wasn't your responsibility to keep Elle safe. Your dad and I were the grown-ups in charge. If anyone should have kept a better eye on her, it should have been us.'

Georgia squeezes my hand. 'But Sasha slipped and then we all got distracted.'

'Exactly. It was nobody's fault, other than the person who took her.'

Georgia tenses. 'Do you really think someone took her?'

I shake my head. 'I don't know. I don't think we'll ever know. Not now. But the main thing is, we need to keep on living our lives the way Elle would have wanted us to. We can't blame ourselves for something that wasn't our fault.' As I say the words, I realise I'm saying them as much for myself as for Georgia. I stifle a sob.

'Are you okay, Mum?' my daughter asks, concern etched across her brow, mascara smudged beneath her eyes.

'I'm fine. It's you I'm worried about.'

'I feel a little bit better after talking to you,' she says. 'I think I just let everything get on top of me. I built it all up in my mind. I can't quite explain it properly.'

'I know what you mean,' I reply, feeling like a terrible parent for not realising my daughter's been going through this inner turmoil. Now that she's spoken about it, it seems obvious that we should have made sure she was mentally okay afterwards. But we didn't. We were all living in our own personal hells.

'So, Aunty Jo really does have a migraine?' Georgia asks, giving me a penetrating stare.

I don't want to lie to my daughter, but it's not my place to tell her what happened, so I tell Georgia some of the truth: 'She had an argument with Ollie.'

'Oh.' Georgia looks surprised. 'You should have told me that in the first place.'

'I know, but I didn't want to worry you.'

'Well, that worked out well.'

I choke out a laugh. At least she's feeling well enough to make jokes. But there's something else I need to ask her.

'Gee-Gee, did you . . . did you see something in a pub car park a few weeks ago?'

My daughter's face flushes a deep crimson.

'It's okay if you did. You can tell me.'

'How did you know about that?' she says. 'It was two people having sex in the car park where Aunty Jo works.'

'Did you see who it was?' I ask, holding my breath.

'No. Why?'

I exhale in relief, hoping she's being truthful. I'd hate to think of her seeing Jo like that. Of her knowing how her aunt went behind Ollie's back.

'I was meeting Cleo and Naomi in the pub that night,' Georgia continues, 'and I bumped into this older girl, Casey – you don't know her – in the car park. We said hello and that's when we saw that couple having sex. Why are you even asking about it?'

'To put your mind at rest about that woman who confronted you after school.'

'Oh. So was it her in the car park?' Georgia asks. 'Did she see me that night? Is that why she was mad at me?'

'No. It was her fiancé and . . . someone else. That's why she was so angry. She thought you knew who it was. Anyway, I set her straight.'

'Oh.' Georgia nods, her shoulders relaxing. 'Well, that's good then. I mean, not for the woman whose fiancé it was, but I mean it's good that I know why she was so angry with me.'

'I know. So hopefully you can put that horrible episode behind you now.'

'Definitely,' she replies. 'I'm glad I know what it was about. But what about Aunty Jo and Ollie? Is it a serious argument? Will they be okay?'

'I don't know. We'll have to give them some space to work it out.'

'Poor Aunty Jo.'

Poor Ollie, I think to myself.

Georgia yawns. 'I'm tired.'

'Me too,' I reply, suddenly feeling the weight of everything.

I wish we'd never planned this birthday party in the first place. I think it's all been too much. I wanted everything to come good without taking the time to fix things properly. But that's not how things work. I didn't want to face up to the fact that nothing is right. That our family has been fundamentally broken by what

196

happened ten years ago. Me, Theo, Georgia, Jo, my parents – we're all still dealing with this shit. I tried to paper over the past with this party, hoping that would mend things, but it's all come oozing through the cracks anyway. It seems the more I try to force things to work, the further back we fall.

As I gaze at my daughter's face, I wonder if we'll ever truly be able to heal properly.

Chapter Thirty-Five

NOW

Highcliffe is a pretty beach suburb just up the coast from Christchurch and it's where I'm headed right now for an unexpected meeting that has my heart racing and my hands clammy on the steering wheel.

It's been almost a week since Georgia's birthday party and we've all been pretty exhausted in the aftermath of her breakdown. After our talk in the pub that night, Georgia finally felt strong enough to return to the party and ended up having a pretty good time with her friends. I could see she was emotionally exhausted, but at least she looked happier, more relaxed.

This week, Theo and I persuaded Georgia to go for some counselling. Georgia said she didn't need it, that she felt a million times better after our chat, but we asked her to give it a go anyway. We don't want to take any more chances. Theo says we should probably all have got counselling years ago.

Predictably, Ollie has forgiven Jo for her transgression with Justine's fiancé. Honestly, in his eyes, Jo can do no wrong. He was obviously hurt by it, but they seem to be fine now, and Jo is being super-nice to him as if that can make up for everything. But it's their relationship, so I'm not getting involved. Well, as much as I'm able to not get involved when there are disgruntled girlfriends showing up at my door and fights on the driveway.

Today is bright and sunny, but the traffic is light and I'm making good time. Luckily, I had a work meeting that ended early, so I'm able to whizz up to Highcliffe before heading home. My curiosity is in overdrive, but I can't allow myself to get my hopes up.

Tara Stiles, the private investigator I last spoke to ten years ago, left me a voicemail this morning and I could hardly believe it. Hearing her voice instantly took me back to that terrible time when I had pinned all my hopes on her finding Elle. When I first met Tara, I had a really good feeling. I had been quietly optimistic that she would be the one to succeed where the police had failed, even though she warned me not to get my hopes up.

She even turned me down at first, explaining how unlikely it would be for her to find Elle. That's one of the reasons I liked her – because the other two investigators I'd spoken to had been overly confident, promising me that they would get my niece back. Afterwards, when Tara's search ended in disappointment, reaching dead end after dead end, I cursed myself for choosing the wrong PI. Maybe one of those two confident men would have been the better choice. But when I reapplied to the bank for a further loan, they turned me down.

So now I'm wondering what it is that has her getting in touch after all these years. Elle would be sixteen now, almost unrecognisable from the little girl she once was. The police reconstruction for the anniversary appeal created a teenager that looks a little like Georgia and a little like Jo, but would anyone really be able to recognise her? Has Tara discovered what happened? I suddenly feel sick at the thought of what she might be about to tell me. I glance in my rear-view mirror and pull into a lay-by, turning off the car and taking deep, steadying breaths. I've tried not to think about all the awful things that could have happened. Now that I'm faced with a possible answer, I'm not sure I want to hear it. If it's bad, maybe we'd be better off not knowing. But that's not my decision to make. I need to find out whatever it is for Jo's sake.

I press both hands to the centre of my chest and hold myself still, trying to push out all the negative thoughts. A tiny voice in the back of my head creeps in to tell me that it could be good news. This little spark of hope gives me the boost I need to get back on the road.

Ten years ago, Tara lived in a small flat in Christchurch, but now I find myself turning into a leafy avenue. I park on the road outside a double-fronted arts-and-crafts house, two roads back from the beach. It would seem that the PI business is booming.

Now that I'm here, I wonder again if this meeting is going to be more successful than our previous one. Last time, Tara told me that all her leads had reached a dead end and that even if I'd had the funds – which I didn't – there wasn't any more she could do. She had seemed genuinely upset. I know she wanted a more successful outcome. That she was emotionally invested. She said it was different to her usual adultery and financial cases. Even her missing persons cases hadn't struck a chord the way that this one had. We parted ways, and I haven't seen or heard from her since. Until now.

I never told anyone that I hired an investigator and I'm glad now that I didn't because it would have been another crushing disappointment. Not to mention the fact that I spent years paying back the loan. But that doesn't mean I enjoyed keeping it a secret from Theo. By the time we were more financially secure, I felt that too much time had gone by to let him know what I'd done.

I get out of the car and smooth down my work suit before heading across the block-paved driveway to the pretty pale-green front door adorned with a real holly-and-ivy wreath. I tug a charming iron pull-bell and hear it chime inside. A dog immediately starts barking and footsteps approach.

A woman answers the door and I almost don't recognise her. Tara's changed a lot in ten years. Gone are the glasses and frizzy brown hair, the scruffy leggings and sweatshirt. Now, she's immaculately groomed with sleek chestnut locks, a navy wrap dress and expensive-smelling perfume.

'Natalie,' she says warmly. 'Thank you so much for coming.'

'Hi,' I say a little uncertainly.

'Come in. Do you mind dogs?'

'No, I love them.'

'Great.' She opens an interior door and a little black spaniel comes out to say a boisterous hello. 'Get down, Pepper. Come through, Natalie. We'll chat in the lounge. It's mayhem in the kitchen.'

I hear the sound of multiple children laughing and chattering from the back of the house, but she shows me into the room the dog just vacated. There's a gentle fire burning in the grate and she gestures to me to sit on one of the overstuffed sofas.

'Can I get you a drink? Tea, coffee? Or there's fresh water in the jug.' She gestures to a low glass coffee table with a tray of water and two glasses.

'No thanks, I'm fine.'

She sits opposite me on one of two cream club chairs.

'I have to say, I was surprised to get your message,' I begin. 'It's been a long time since we spoke.'

'I know,' she replies with a dip of her head. 'I'm not even in the business anymore.'

'You're not an investigator?'

'No. I gave it up quite soon after your case, actually. I work in the music industry now. Live half the time in London, half the time here.'

'Wow, that's quite a change,' I reply. And then I'm suddenly overcome with a wave of sickening disappointment that maybe she hasn't contacted me about Elle at all. I realise I must have got my wires crossed and she wants to talk to me because I manage events. I'd assumed she had some news about the case. How could I have been so stupid? It's been a decade, so of course this meeting isn't about Elle.

Tara must have noticed something in my expression. 'Are you okay, Natalie?'

'I . . . sorry, can you tell me what this is about? I'm a bit confused.'

'I can imagine. I apologise for the cryptic message, but I didn't want to talk to you about this over the phone. I thought it should be an in-person conversation.'

My pulse thrums as I wait for her to elaborate, allowing a spark of hope to reignite.

'The thing is,' she says, 'I know it's been years since Elle disappeared, but I've come across what I think might be a promising lead.'

Chapter Thirty-Six

Warm air wafts over your skin as you exit the plane and walk down the metal staircase, the sleeping girl a pleasing weight in your arms. The familiar mixed aromas of melting tarmac, blocked drains and hot tamalitos comforts your senses. The sound of your native language cloaks you with relief. All these things you've missed. But you can't relax yet. You have one more hurdle to get through. One more barrier between you and the life you're meant to live.

You already love her more than anything. You already know you would lay down your life for her. You try not to think about the heartbreak you've left behind because it's too late to have misgivings now. You've done it. It's been agreed. There's no going back.

Chapter Thirty-Seven

NOW

I settle myself on the plane, having been allocated a window seat. If the departure gate was anything to go by, the flight will be full. An elderly couple come to a stop near me, making a bit of a to-do about which bags to place in the overhead locker and which to put under the seats until the steward comes along to help them out. The woman then settles herself next to me with a smile, looking like she wants to chat. I return the smile politely and transfer my gaze to my phone, hoping that will deter her. I usually enjoy making small talk, but I want peace and quiet right now. I need to be able to think.

When I told Theo I was going on a business trip, he was pretty surprised. I've never been abroad with work before, but I explained that my hotel chain is having a training seminar in Gran Canaria and I've been asked to attend. He pointed out that it's really last minute and that it's a bit off to expect me to drop everything and go the week before Christmas. But I told him it's just for a couple of days and anyway, I'm not mad about getting some warm sun on my face. At one point, he suggested coming with me – making a mini-break of it – and the thought was so lovely that I almost came clean about why I'm really going. Only I stopped myself in time and dissuaded him by saying that one of us should stay to keep an eye on Georgia as she's still a bit fragile.

I'm still shaken up by what Tara told me. She stressed that it might not be anything. But she knew she had to tell me. To give me the chance to see if it was real or not. So here I am on this last-minute flight to the Canary Islands on what is, in all probability, a wild goose chase.

It's a four-hour flight so I open my Kindle app and start reading chapter one of the book I downloaded this morning. But after I've read the first page three times without absorbing any of the words, I give up and look out of the window instead.

The plane taxies down the runway and takes off from a grey and drizzly Bournemouth, cruising up beyond layers and layers of rain clouds into a sparkling blue afternoon. We're due to land in Gran Canaria at 5.20 p.m., which means I probably won't get to my hotel until at least seven-ish. I'm still hazy on exactly what I'm going to do when I get there. I have a vague plan, but the whole thing is quite terrifying. Ever since I spoke to Tara, I feel as though I'm in the grip of some kind of madness. The secretiveness and potential danger of this trip surely isn't something any sane person would do. But as the fasten-seat-belts sign clicks off, I realise I'm right in the midst of it now. There's no backing out.

The flight simultaneously seems to take forever and yet goes by in the blink of an eye, and before I know it, I'm exiting the plane into blinding sunshine, a warm breeze sweeping across my dehydrated skin. I head down the metal staircase on to the runway, gripping my small carry-on case, the scent of hot tarmac and drains assaulting my nostrils. A pleasing garlicky smell makes my stomach rumble and I try to remember the last time I ate something. I had a coffee at Bournemouth Airport, but I don't remember having breakfast, and I didn't fancy the plane food.

Without any checked-in luggage my trip through the airport is relatively smooth and quick, and I soon find myself outside climbing into the back of a taxi. The driver is a young guy who doesn't look too much older than Georgia. He isn't the chatty type, which suits me fine, but he has the radio turned up loud at a frequency that's giving me mild earache. I put up with it but feel relieved when he finally drops me at my budget hotel on the outskirts of Las Palmas.

As I check in, I'm antsy, wanting to go straight to the address Tara wrote down for me, but I need to be patient. Showing up after dark, tired and hungry, is not a good move. I'll be sensible and go first thing tomorrow morning.

After dumping my bags in my little room and messaging Theo to say I've arrived, I find a charming little restaurant along the road from the hotel and let the waiter recommend whatever he likes. He brings me a delicious stew made with chickpeas and potatoes and I absolutely wolf it down, feeling instantly revived. Afterwards, I walk back to the hotel, the nerves kicking back in. Maybe I should have had a glass of wine with my meal to help me relax, but I wanted to keep a clear head.

It's only nine thirty, but I think I'm going to go straight to bed. The sooner tomorrow comes, the sooner I'll know. The sheets are clean and crisp despite the warmth of the room. I fiddled with the air con earlier but I couldn't get it to come on, and I didn't have the wherewithal to speak to the man on reception about it.

As my eyes close and sleep comes for me, I wonder again if I'll find what I'm looking for. I make a promise to myself tonight that if this turns out to be a dead end, I'll let it all go. I've lived too long with guilt and remorse. After tomorrow, I'll move on.

◆　◆　◆

'Are you visiting friends?' my cab driver asks as we travel inland, further from the centre of Las Palmas. He's an older gentleman with a weather-worn face and a kind smile.

'Yes,' I reply, unable to think of another answer.

'It's a nice neighbourhood, Tafira Alta,' he says, trying to engage me in conversation.

I nod but don't say anything more, and thankfully he takes the hint and retreats into silence.

It's half past seven on a Tuesday morning and the roads are busy. But it's nothing like rush hour in Bournemouth. At least the traffic is moving and I'm not on any timetable. I wasn't sure what time of day I should get there. Supper time would have probably been the best chance of catching people at home, but I can't wait that long because my brain is going into overdrive already and if I had to kill time back at my hotel for a whole day, I think I'd end up a nervous wreck. Instead, I've opted to arrive around 8 a.m. Morning feels less scary than evening to confront a stranger.

After only fifteen minutes, we pull off the main road and it's a world away from the city of Las Palmas with its wide streets and mix of houses, high-rise blocks and office buildings. Out here, it's greener and more hilly.

'Tafira Alta.' The cab driver gestures to our surroundings.

How can we be here already? My stomach is in knots.

We're driving through a genteel suburb of tree-lined roads with large ivy-covered villas painted in all shades of terracotta, pink, white and grey. Behind walls and security gates, I catch glimpses of date palms, willows, swimming pools, terraces and verandas. This is a wealthy area. The driver turns down a clean, narrow street with high walls concealing huge houses. He stops opposite a pair of black gates set into a high whitewashed wall dripping with lush greenery. I ask if I can sit in his cab for a while, obviously with the meter still running. He's happy to oblige and takes out his phone, settling in for an easy fare.

The road is quiet. A woman walks her dog, and a car pulls out from behind a pair of electric gates further up the lane, but I don't see anyone else. As I wait, trying to compose myself, I remember how desperate I was to get a lead from the police or from Tara or a member of the public, and how for so many years there's been nothing but silence. But now, after all this time, I'm sitting within sight of this tiny sliver of hope. I don't want to let myself believe it could be anything meaningful. But what if it is? What if the answers to all our questions lie behind that set of black gates?

I should be terrified that I'm here alone in a foreign country, facing who knows what kind of people. But, strangely, right this second, I'm not scared. I'm nervous but determined to confront this person or people. *Who are they?*

Just as I'm working myself up to leave the cab, the black gates slide open. My heart is in my throat as I wait to see who is about to come out. What if they drive off and I've missed my chance to speak to them this morning? I curse myself for not ringing the buzzer earlier.

But it's not a car leaving the property, it's a girl. A girl of about fifteen or sixteen with dark hair and brown eyes. *And she looks just like my sister.* I realise I'm shaking and tears are sliding down my cheeks as I watch Elle leave the house and walk away up the road.

Chapter Thirty-Eight

NOW

Am I dreaming? As I watch the girl leave the house, there is absolutely no doubt in my mind that this is Elle. She's a younger version of Jo, same nose, eyes, everything. Like me, Jo is naturally dark-haired with dark eyes, but she's dyed her hair blonde since she was sixteen. Elle has the same colouring and I know with every cell of my being that a DNA test would come back positive that this is my niece.

My first instinct is to leave the cab and run up to her. To throw my arms around her narrow frame and tell her who I am and that we've been searching for her for years. But I stop myself. Elle hasn't seen me since she was six years old. I doubt she even remembers me. Can she even still speak English? I think this is going to be harder than I thought. Has she been living here in this house the whole time, while we've been going out of our minds with grief and guilt? While our lives have been imploding?

I can't believe she's alive. She's actually here. I should tell Jo immediately, but I need to find out what's going on first. I need to speak to whoever else is in that house. Are they the bad guys? Or could they have innocently adopted her? I'm still shaking, quietly crying.

'Are you all right?' the taxi driver asks as he catches my eye in the rear-view mirror.

I rummage in my bag for a tissue to wipe my eyes, but I don't seem to have one so I use my fingertips to stem the flow.

'Here.' He passes me a clean cotton handkerchief. 'Keep it.'

'Gracias,' I reply, dabbing at my eyes.

'You don't want to go inside?'

'It's . . . complicated.'

'Ahhh,' he says knowingly. 'A boyfriend.'

I shake my head. 'No.'

'You take your time.'

His phrase jolts me out of my paralysis. I don't want to take any more 'time'. It's been too long already.

'Do you have a business card?' I ask. 'So I can call you later to come back?'

'Si.' He passes me his card and I pay my fare, giving a generous tip. Then I step outside into the warm morning air and walk across the road towards the black gate.

I vaguely hear the taxi start up behind me and drive away. Maybe I should have asked him to wait. What if no one else is home?

Before I lose my nerve, I press the buzzer. After a few moments, a woman's voice comes on the intercom. 'Hola?'

'Hola,' I reply. 'I have a delivery for you to sign.' I hope she understands English.

'Okay, one moment.'

The gate slides open and I see a petite dark-haired woman about my age walking down the front steps of a beautiful white house with a wide veranda. From the corner of my eye, I notice a jewel-green lawn to my right and a sparkling blue swimming pool with sun loungers along the edge. The woman is wearing wide-legged navy linen trousers and a plain white top, with gold jewellery.

My heart is beating so loudly that I'm amazed she can't hear it over the sound of the sparrows chattering in the trees. My body feels numb as I open my mouth to speak.

'You have a delivery?' she interrupts before I can say anything. She's staring pointedly at my hands, which are clearly empty.

'No, I'm sorry,' I reply.

She frowns and comes to a stop at the bottom of the steps. 'I don't understand.'

I swallow. 'Who was that girl who just left here? Is she your daughter?'

The blood drains from the woman's face and I instantly realise that she knows I'm something to do with Elle. *She knows.*

'Please leave,' she says.

'Is she adopted?' I ask.

'I told you to leave.' She throws a glance over her shoulder and calls out, 'Mateo!'

The same name that Tara Stiles gave me.

'Mateo!' She turns and stumbles up the steps back into her house and slams the door.

I feel dizzy with discovery. With shock and fear and excitement and every other emotion I can think of. Heat thrums in my head. Fury that these people have stolen my sister's life from her. They've stolen *all* our lives. Who the hell do they think they are?

I march across the gravel path, up the terracotta steps and across the tiled veranda with its wicker furniture and potted plants. And I bang on the door with the end of my fist. I'm too angry to ring any doorbell. Only pounding the door will do. I want to batter the bloody thing down. 'Open the door!' I cry hoarsely. 'Open the door and speak to me!'

I step away after a while and stand there waiting, straining to listen for any sound that might be emanating from behind the walls. But all I can hear is the hiss of the sprinklers and the gurgle of the swimming pool. I think my yelling must have scared all the birds away.

For a moment, I worry that she might call the police. But then, if they've taken Jo's daughter, the police would be the last people they would call. They might, however, have other shadier contacts. Why the hell did I come here alone? I should have told Theo about this, but it all seemed perfectly reasonable when I was back in the UK. I quickly bang out a message to Tara:

I'm at the address in Tafira Alta.

If you don't hear from me within an hour,

please call the Spanish police.

Thank you, Natalie.

She replies almost immediately:

Are you alone?

Yes.

Not a good idea!

I know but I'm here now.

I'll text you in a bit to let you know I'm okay.

Text me within 30 mins.

Okay. Gotta go x

The door opens and a good-looking man with salt-and-pepper hair stands in the doorway. The woman, who I'm presuming is his wife, stands a little way behind him.

'My name is Mateo,' he says. 'And this is my wife, Isabel. Would you like to come in?'

Chapter Thirty-Nine

NOW

I hesitate on the veranda. Now that they're willing to talk to me, I wonder how safe I'll be going into their house. But I've come too far to be nervous now, so I step inside the cool, airy hallway and follow them into a large square living room. A beautiful arched window dominates one end, and a floor-to-ceiling bookcase the other. There are three sofas arranged in a U-shape, but I don't feel like sitting in any of them. I don't feel like being civilised at all.

The couple are visibly nervous. They keep shooting glances at each other and the woman looks almost unrecognisable from the poised, cool character she was when I first arrived. Again, I wonder if I might be in danger. I still have my phone in my hand, ready to dial Theo or Tara if I need to.

None of us sit down and I wonder what was the point of them bringing me into this room. I'd have felt safer in the entrance hall. I edge closer to the door in case I need to leave in a hurry.

'Why are you here?' Mateo asks. 'How did you get this address?'

I don't feel like answering his questions. I want him to answer all mine first. I still can't believe that Tara actually found Elle. And that she's alive and well after all this time. It's a miracle. I wonder if I'm dreaming.

The lead that Tara discovered was a long shot. She made it clear to me not to get my hopes up too much, but thought it was worth following. She said she'd always felt terrible that she wasn't able to help find my niece. That it had been the one big regret in her working life. And with all the stuff in the media about it being the ten-year anniversary of Elle's disappearance, she was having thoughts about her again, especially as she now has three young children of her own. Back when she'd been working as an investigator she always ran on gut instinct, and right then instinct was telling her to review Elle's case.

So she brought up Elle's file and read her notes to see if she could possibly have missed anything. Nothing stood out to her at first, and she was going to close it all down and try to forget about it, but then, in a newspaper article, she noticed something so small that she'd missed it earlier. It was a quote from one of Elle's friends' parents. She said that Elle was a sweet little girl who loved to dance. Tara did some digging and managed to discover that Elle took dance lessons on Saturday mornings.

The dance instructor was a local woman who said she had already been interviewed ten years ago by the police, and that she sadly had no new information or knowledge about what had happened to Elle. But after some probing questions from Tara, she remembered that there had been a visiting instructor from Mexico who had showed the children some traditional dances. She said she often had visiting dancers and instructors as it made things fun and interesting. She remembered he had said that Elle was very talented for her age. But he had flown home a few weeks earlier and so she didn't think it was relevant.

Tara couldn't believe the instructor had left out that information during the initial investigation. It could have been nothing, but surely it was worth following up. So Tara discovered the instructor's name and, although he was indeed Mexican, she managed to trace him to Gran Canaria. She then discovered that he had a daughter the same age as Elle would have been now. That was when she messaged me.

Even when I was on the plane, I knew I might have just wasted my money on a flight to discover another dead end. But I had to try. And now, standing here in these strangers' house, I'm so glad I did.

'Please,' Mateo says. 'Tell us who you are and why you asked my wife if our daughter is adopted. Are you from England?'

'Ten years ago, my six-year-old niece, Elle, disappeared from Bournemouth in England.'

Isabel gives a gasping sob.

'But you already know that, don't you?' I clench my fists. 'Otherwise why would your wife be crying? It should be me who's crying, not you! Elle went missing from my daughter's ice-skating party and we've spent the past ten years in hell, not knowing what happened to her.'

Mateo covers his face with his hands for a moment and also lets out a sob. 'We should never have gone along with it, but I can't regret what we did.'

'Along with *what*? Did you abduct her? Or did someone else do it for you? Was it planned right from when you went along to her dance lessons?'

Mateo takes a breath and tries to compose himself. 'You know about that?' he asks. But Isabel is gripping the back of the sofa, still crying like she's suffering a bereavement. Mateo takes a step towards me and I wonder again if they might try to harm me to keep me from telling anyone. To keep me from taking Elle back home to Jo, where she belongs.

216

I square my shoulders. 'My husband knows where I am and so does the private investigator I hired to find you, so if anything happens to me . . .'

Mateo shakes his head. 'Of course nothing will happen to you, what kind of person do you think I am?'

I choke out a bitter laugh.

'I don't know what you think will happen here,' he says. 'I'm Adela's father and she lives here with us. She's happy.'

'Her name is Elle,' I snap. 'And she's only happy because she doesn't know the truth. She doesn't know what you did. She doesn't know you're not really her father.'

'But I am,' he says. 'She's my daughter.'

'I know you might have raised her for the past ten years, but you've done it under false pretences. You've—'

'No. You misunderstand. She really is my daughter.'

'What are you talking about?' I reply, getting a bad feeling.

'We need to tell you the truth about what really happened,' the woman says, tears still sliding down her cheeks. 'Because I don't think you know.'

I put my hand against the door-frame to steady myself because I'm scared to hear what they have to say.

'Will you sit down?' Mateo asks, gesturing to one of the sofas.

My first instinct is to say no, but my legs feel soft and my head is woozy. Gingerly, I cross the room and perch on the edge of the sofa waiting for them to explain, hoping I can recover some strength.

They both sit opposite me, Mateo grasping his wife's hand as he opens his mouth and begins to talk.

Chapter Forty

NOW

The room is silent apart from a ticking clock and the hum of the air-conditioning unit. It's chilly and I rub my arms.

'Can I tell you the story from the beginning?' Mateo asks as Isabel cries quietly by his side.

I shrug and nod. That's what I'm here for, after all. But this whole thing is much harder than I could have imagined. Could Elle really be this man's daughter? I stare at his features and realise that she could.

Mateo glances at his wife and wipes a tear from her cheek before turning back to me and continuing. 'Seventeen years ago, when I was twenty-five, a friend and I saved up enough money to go travelling around Europe for a year. We found ourselves in England and spent a while in Bournemouth, where I started seeing your sister, Jo. We had fun. Your sister liked to party.'

I grimace. That sounds like Jo.

'Anyway,' he continues. 'One day, after we'd been together for a few months, she came to me, agitated, and told me she was pregnant, and that the baby was mine. I'm ashamed to say that I wasn't nice about it. I knew she liked me a lot and I had a suspicion she might have done it to keep me in England. I had more travelling to do and a real-estate career to get back to at home in Mexico City. I didn't want to be tied down. I ended up leaving without saying goodbye.'

'Nice,' I mutter. 'You've got yourself a real gem there,' I say to Isabel. But I don't think she understands my sarcasm.

'You're right to be disgusted,' Mateo says. 'I treated Jo badly. There's not a day goes by when I don't regret how I behaved in that situation.'

I think back to that time and I don't recall Jo mentioning anyone called Mateo. But my own daughter had been born a year earlier and I was in the throes of new motherhood. I wasn't really focused on Jo's love life, which had always been erratic. I hadn't known she'd had a crush on this guy, but I can see why – he's incredibly handsome and charismatic. Jo always maintained that she never knew who Elle's father was but if Mateo's to be believed, then that was a lie.

I wonder why my sister never told me about him. Probably because I was too absorbed in my own life. She might have thought I'd be judgemental. But I wouldn't have been. I would have commiserated with her about Elle's father leaving her in the lurch. The more Mateo tells me his story, the more I detest him. And why didn't Jo tell the police about him? If she had, they would have found Elle immediately.

'If what you're saying is true, that you ran out on my sister and you didn't want anything to do with Elle, then why are we in this situation? Why do you now have my sister's child?'

Mateo continues with his story. 'A year later, back in Mexico, my career was going well, and I met Isabel at the local college where I went to give a careers talk to the students. She was teaching there on an exchange programme from Spain. We fell in love and got married, but sadly we were unable to conceive. We tried for three years to start a family, but it just didn't happen. It was a heartbreaking time.'

I think I can see where this is going. And it's clear that Mateo wants me to feel sorry for them. But I don't. The more he talks, the more angry I feel. I want to tip over the perfectly placed coffee table and yell at them both that they're selfish pricks. But I don't. I sit here, well-behaved, on the sofa and I keep listening to his sob story.

'Around that time, I tried to contact Jo,' he says, 'to see if she kept the baby, but she'd blocked my number and had also blocked me on social media – not that there was much of it back then. We were only on Facebook, I think. Anyway, I'd made a few friends in Bournemouth from that time, and so I made some discreet enquiries. I discovered that Jo had a four-year-old daughter – my daughter.

'I knew that Jo didn't have a husband or boyfriend, and I wondered to myself if she might let me have shared custody. I could help out financially and build a relationship with my daughter. But when I spoke to Isabel about it . . .' Mateo gives his wife an apologetic look. 'She said that it wouldn't be easy with us living halfway around the world. So I left it.'

'At the time, my relationship with Mateo deteriorated,' Isabel says quietly. 'I think he resented me for pouring cold water on his idea. I didn't want to stop him seeing his daughter, but he was more focused on that relationship than on us creating our own family. I was upset. I wanted to adopt, but Mateo was frustrated that he had a biological daughter out there who he'd never seen. He didn't give adoption a chance.'

'Isabel and I loved one another,' Mateo says, 'but we were on the verge of breaking up. That's when I received a message from Jo. She had a proposition for me.'

'Jo contacted you?' I say, thunderstruck.

'Jo wanted me to take our daughter.'

'You're lying.' I rise to my feet, a chill sweeping across my skin. 'She would never do that.'

Mateo and Isabel stand too. He holds his hands out placatingly. 'I know how it sounds, but I can assure you it's true.'

'If she "gave" her daughter to you, then why was she snatched from the ice rink? Why wasn't it all done legally and above board?'

'Those were my questions too when she first told me what she wanted to do,' Mateo says. 'But Jo explained that she couldn't cope with being a single mother. That she was struggling and alone. That Adela would be better off with a wealthy family like ours.'

'But she loved Elle!' I cry. 'Jo was a good mother. The two of them were a team. She was devastated when Elle disappeared. I was with her. No one can fake that kind of distress.'

'Just because she arranged it doesn't mean she didn't love her daughter,' Isabel says, her tears now dry. 'She probably *was* devastated to give her up, even though she knew she was doing it for her daughter's sake.' Isabel gestures to her surroundings. 'You can see that we're giving our daughter a privileged life. She has a beautiful home here, with many friends.'

'There's more to life than a nice house!' I snap. 'And Jo wasn't some charity case. She had a nice apartment and lots of help from our family. She and Elle were happy.'

'I can only tell you what she told me,' Mateo says.

'You still haven't explained why Elle was taken like that.' I push my hair out of my eyes. 'It was terrifying. We had search parties; the police were involved. It was an extreme situation.' My phone buzzes and I see that it's Tara checking in. I message her back, letting her know I'm okay and that we'll speak soon.

Mateo waits for me to finish texting and then he continues. 'Jo said that it would be easier for her if Adela was snatched.'

'That makes no sense,' I reply, trying to get my head around this outlandish story.

'I think it does, if you look at it from Jo's point of view,' Isabel says. 'The way Jo explained it to my husband was that she would be ashamed if people knew she'd willingly given custody of her child to the father. Her family wouldn't understand. And they'd understand even less if they knew she'd been paid to do it.'

'You gave her money?' I stiffen.

'Fifty thousand dollars,' she says with a curl of her lip to let me know what she thinks of that. 'But Adela is worth more than a million times that. She's our life.'

'So you went along with this plan to take her from the ice rink?'

'I refused at first,' Mateo says. 'But Jo said that her plan was the only way I was getting Adela. She told me to take it or leave it.'

'So you took it.'

'I felt I had no choice. Adela was the answer to our prayers of having a family. I put myself in danger and paid a fortune to get forged documentation for her and we managed to bring her back to Mexico with no trouble, even though I was terrified the whole way. I told my family most of the truth – that I'd discovered I had a child from a previous relationship and the mother couldn't cope so we were now raising her. But when we read about the police hunt for my daughter in the UK, we were nervous that they might somehow trace her to Mexico. So we moved to Gran Canaria.'

I suddenly remember something. 'The investigator I hired found you because she spoke to Elle's dance teacher. You went to her studio and spoke to Elle weeks before you took her.'

Mateo's face pales. 'The teacher spoke to your investigator?'

'Yes,' I reply.

'Well . . .' Mateo composes himself again. 'I couldn't just take Adela without her knowing who I was. I had to build up a relationship with her first. So I came over to Bournemouth beforehand. I used to compete as a dancer when I was younger, so it wasn't hard to volunteer my services as a visiting instructor.

After that first lesson, Jo and I decided that Adela would stop going to her regular teacher and would come to me instead. Adela and I built up a great rapport over that month and I fell in love with my daughter. I knew there was no way I was going to back out of the plan now. I came back to Mexico for two months, and then returned to Bournemouth to bring my daughter home.'

'And she's at school today?' I ask woodenly, trying to absorb everything he's telling me. Trying to align this new information with what's gone on before.

'Yes,' Mateo answers warily, and Isabel tenses in her seat.

'I want to see my niece properly. I need to speak to her to see that she's okay.'

'Look . . .' Mateo holds up his hands, as though trying to ward me off. 'I realise that now this is out in the open, you'll want to see Adela. But can you please let us speak to her first? You should also speak to Jo because this was her idea, not ours. She might not want Adela's life turned upside down like this. Our daughter knows that I'm her real father and that Isabel is her adoptive mother, but we explained that her biological mother wasn't well enough to look after her. I don't want to upset things if Jo doesn't want to have a role in her life. Please think about this from your niece's point of view.'

I sink back down on to the sofa, trying to process what they've told me. Trying to work out if it's lies or if it's the truth. But he seems so sincere, and their story seems too crazy to be a lie. In this terrible, awful moment, I don't know what to do. If I call the police, then what will happen to Elle? What will happen to Jo? It's all too much. I feel like crying. I need to get away from here. From these people who say they're Elle's new parents. I need to clear my head. I think I have to go home.

Chapter Forty-One

NOW

The early-morning journey back to England was exhausting. Overwhelming. The whole time, I felt as though I were floating outside of my body. And now that I'm back in Southbourne I don't feel much better. In fact, I feel physically sick.

I dump my case on the bedroom floor and sit on the end of my bed, still stupefied by what Mateo and Isabel told me. I can barely believe it's true. How can it be? Because if it is, then I've been living with a monster. A liar. But not for much longer. If what Mateo says is true, then my sister can pack up her things and move out. Can this really be the conclusion to a decade-long search?

Theo is at work right now, and Georgia is at school, and I feel sick that I'm still keeping this secret that Elle is alive. Knowing they deserve to know that she's safe. That their worst nightmares were just that – nightmares and nothing more. I'm desperate to tell them the truth. But first I have to confront my sister.

I'm presuming she's in our garden flat. I still don't want to believe it's true. How could she do that to us?

I left Isabel and Mateo's house without seeing Elle again, even though it felt wrong. But when Mateo told me to think about it from Elle's point of view, I had to listen. It's enough for now that I know where my niece is. I don't believe they'll do a runner. Mateo has a thriving property business in Las Palmas and Isabel is a college lecturer. They're normal people, not hardened criminals. But they still did a really bad thing. Even if it was with my sister's blessing.

Before I do anything, I need to speak to Jo. I'd like to be clear-headed when I do it, but right now I have so much boiling anger in my chest that I feel as though I'm going to explode. I think about how many years of our lives have been ruined by their scheme. How it's affected my marriage. How much guilt Georgia has suffered, to the extent that she harmed herself. Maybe my sister does deserve to go to prison. Maybe it's the only answer. Even if it will break my parents' hearts and throw our family life into turmoil yet again.

Could she really have done this thing? Mateo said it was because Jo didn't want to admit she couldn't cope as a single mother. That she didn't want us to judge her. But to have done something this extreme is outrageous.

And what did she do with the money? Fifty thousand dollars is a lot of nights out, a lot of clothes and booze and drugs. Theo and I never asked her for any rent or bills because she hardly earns anything. I've never seen her spend much and she's never really been money-oriented. Unless maybe she was in debt and needed the cash to pay it off. That's the only thing I can think of that would make any sense. But to willingly give up her daughter after six years . . .

I could understand if she felt overwhelmed and unable to cope, but then why didn't she just ask me for help? She knows I would have given it. Why resort to kidnap? She could have simply said that she'd discovered who the father was and they'd decided to share custody.

Over the years, I've always stood by Jo's side. I've constantly defended her against Theo, often to the detriment of my marriage. Sorrow for Jo's loss mingled with guilt at having taken my eye off Elle has made me forgive my sister time and time again. I've never once asked her to move out, no matter how hard things have got. So to discover she's betrayed me like this is sickening.

I take a leaf out of Georgia's book, grab one of my pillows off the bed and scream into it until I'm hoarse. But it's not enough. I unplug my bedside lamp and I hurl it across the room, watching the ceramic base smash into pieces against the wardrobe. I do the same with Theo's lamp and then I throw myself face down on the bed and I sob. But the fury and hurt is still fizzing through my body like poison. I know it won't dissipate until I've had this out with my sister. I can't put it off any longer.

I go to the bathroom and splash my face with cold water. In the mirror, I see a tired, middle-aged woman with puffy eyes and dry skin. I turn away from my reflection and head downstairs, my stomach churning.

In the kitchen, I pour myself a glass of water and gulp it down before opening the back door and making my way to Jo's flat. The garden is damp and drizzly. Everything feels grey and sodden. Me included. I haven't decided exactly what I'm going to say to Jo. Whether I'm going to accuse her straightaway, or give her the benefit of the doubt. The trouble is, my sister hasn't always been the most truthful person. I wouldn't call her a liar, but she has a tendency to omit things.

Outside the bifold doors, I take a breath and knock. Maybe she's got a shift at the pub. That could be good. Give me more time to compose myself. And I should probably eat something. But just as I'm about to head back to the house, I see the shadowy figure of Jo coming towards the glass doors. She's wearing her dressing gown, her hair tousled, her eyes half closed.

'Nat?' she says, opening the door. 'It's a bit early, isn't it?'

'It's half ten.'

'Is it? Shit, I've overslept. I'm supposed to be meeting Petra for coffee at eleven. How was your work trip? Can we talk about it later? I've got to get ready.'

'No,' I reply. 'I need to talk to you.'

'Sounds serious.' She gives me a fake worried look that turns to genuine concern when I don't smile. 'Everything okay?'

'No,' I repeat, walking into the flat without waiting to be invited. It's an open-plan kitchen-living-dining area, compact but really nice, with pale wood furniture and white-and-cream furnishings. She's added a few little touches over the years, but not much – a few plants, a couple of photos of Elle, and the other bits and bobs are mainly gifts from friends and family. 'Sit down,' I say, turning one of the wicker dining chairs to face the living space and taking a seat. She sits opposite me on the settee, pulling her legs up under her and hugging a fluffy cushion that's seen better days.

'Why do I feel like I'm in trouble?' she says.

'Do you know where I've been?' I ask.

'Theo mentioned something about a work trip abroad. Was it sunny?'

'I've been to Gran Canaria.' I look at her face closely for any kind of reaction. I realise now that I should have asked Mateo if he was still in contact with Jo.

'Nice,' she replies.

'But I wasn't there for work,' I add.

'Oh, okay.' She's not giving anything away. Her expression is curious but not nervous. Maybe she hasn't been in contact with Mateo since he was in Mexico. Maybe she doesn't even know her daughter is living in the Canary Islands now. 'So why were you there?' she prompts.

'I got a tip-off from a private investigator.'

'A *what*?' Her face pales and she gets to her feet, still hugging the cushion. 'You've been talking to an investigator? About . . . about . . .'

'About Elle, yes.'

'Oh my God! What did he say? Does he know where Elle is? Is she in the Canaries? Why the hell didn't you tell me!' Jo's eyes

227

are wild, but I can't tell if she's genuinely clueless or if she's terrified that I've found out what she's done.

'Tara, the investigator, told me about a man in Gran Canaria who has a daughter the same age as Elle. He was a visiting dance instructor in Bournemouth back when Elle was having dance lessons. Is this ringing any bells?' I ask.

Jo ignores my question. 'Are you telling me you saw Elle? Was it her? Why are you being so weird, Nat? Tell me what you know.' She's crying now and I'm getting the feeling that maybe she doesn't know about Mateo and Isabel. Either that, or she's a better liar than I thought.

'I went to the address that Tara gave me and, yes, I saw Elle.'

'You saw her? My daughter's there? What the hell?' She drops the cushion and runs both hands through her hair, her face a mask of shock. 'Where is she now? Did you call the police? Oh my God!' She gives a manic laugh and then goes back to disbelief. 'Why didn't you bring her home with you? Why didn't you take me with you in the first place?'

My sister seems stunned, but is that because this is news to her or is she babbling to cover up the fact that she's been caught?

'Natalie, why are you being weird about this? We need to get my daughter. We need to get Elle!'

'The couple I spoke to said that you arranged the whole thing. That you sold Elle to them for fifty thousand dollars.'

'They said *what*? Well, they're fucking liars and surely you didn't believe them.'

I don't reply.

She gives a disbelieving cough. 'You actually believe that I would do that? That I would sell my own daughter? Are you mad? I mean, I know I might not be the most respectable and perfect parent in the world, but I'm not evil! Jesus, Natalie. I'm your sister.

I thought we knew each other. How could you . . . never mind, just tell me everything you know from start to finish. Right now.' She marches up to me, staring unblinking into my eyes with hope and fury blazing. And as I stare back, my stomach churns with the fear that I might have made a terrible, terrible mistake.

Chapter Forty-Two

NOW

My sister drags over another dining chair and sits opposite me, ordering me to tell her everything, and so I do. Starting with my meeting with Tara.

'But why didn't you tell me you'd hired a private investigator?' Jo asks.

'I didn't want to get your hopes up.'

'Does Theo know?'

I shake my head. 'I didn't tell anyone. It was expensive and I had to take out a loan.'

'Okay, go on,' she prompts.

'As you know, I went to Gran Canaria. I took a cab to the address that Tara gave me, and was literally there for ten, fifteen minutes when the gate opened and Elle walked out.'

'How do you know it was her?' Jo fires back. 'It was ten years ago. She will have changed loads. That girl could have just been someone who looked a bit like her.'

'It was her,' I insist. 'She looked just like you, Jo. The spitting image.'

'If it was her, then why the hell didn't you just grab her and bring her home?'

'Jo, I wanted to, but I didn't want to freak her out. She hasn't seen me for ten years. She probably wouldn't even know who I was.'

Jo gets to her feet again and walks around the flat, blowing air out through her mouth, her whole body trembling. I want to hug her. This should be a joyous occasion, but I still don't fully trust that she's telling me the truth. Maybe the reason she's acting this way is that I've discovered what she's done. This is one of the worst situations I've ever been in.

'Anyway,' I continue. 'I waited until Elle was out of sight and then I rang the buzzer and managed to get them to open the gate. There was a posh-looking woman about my age and I cut to the chase and asked if her daughter was adopted. She gave me this look of horror and bolted back to the house and shut the door.'

'So do you think they used some kind of, I don't know, some kind of illegal adoption agency to get Elle?' Jo asks.

'That's what I thought at first. But, no. When they eventually let me into their house—'

'You went in there on your own?' She stops pacing for a moment.

'Yes. I went in and they told me that she was Elle. But she's now called Adela.'

'Adela?'

'They changed her name.'

'Bastards! Her name is Elle. It's Elle, not Adela.' Jo's voice cracks and she buries her face in her hands, her shoulders shaking. After a couple of seconds, she removes her hands and sucks air in through clenched teeth. 'So they straight up admitted that it was her? That it was Elle?'

'Yes, because they said you knew about it. They said it was you who contacted them in the first place and wanted them to have custody.'

'I don't understand,' Jo cries. 'Who are these people?' She throws her hands in the air.

'His name's Mateo Romero Garcia and his wife is Isabel—'

'Wait, did you say *Mateo*?' Jo freezes.

'Yes.'

'Mateo?' she repeats, almost whispering the name to herself.

'So you do know him,' I say.

'You said they live in Gran Canaria. Is that where he's from?'

'Yes,' I reply. 'I mean, not originally. He said he's from Mexico.'

Jo crouches down and starts shaking. 'You saw Elle? My Elle?'

'I told you I did. She's the spit of you, Jo. It was her; I'd bet my life on it.'

'Oh no, this is . . . I can't believe this. How did he even get her out of the country?'

'He said he had fake documents made. They were living in Mexico City at the time, but his wife was from Spain. They thought it would make more sense to move to Gran Canaria where no one knew them.'

'Okay, this is too weird. I feel weird, Nat, I feel weird.'

I go over to where she's crouching next to the sofa and I put my arms around her. Whatever she's done or hasn't done, she's my sister and she's not okay. 'It's okay, Jo,' I say, stroking her hair. 'Whatever's happened, we'll get to the bottom of it. We'll sort it out, I promise.'

She sits on the rug, hugging her knees to her chest with her back against the sofa. 'Did you really see Elle?'

'I did.' I sit next to her. 'And she looked well. Happy.'

'Okay, that's it. I need to book a plane ticket and get her. Did you fly from Bournemouth?'

'I flew out from Bournemouth, but had to come home via Gatwick. They only fly out from here a couple of times a week. But, look, we need to tell the police first. We can't just rock up and tell her you're her mum. We need to do this properly.'

'She won't even know me, will she?' Jo cries. 'It's been so long.' She takes a shuddering breath. 'I missed all that time.'

'You can make it up. You can get to know her all over again. You're her mum, Jo.'

'But this woman, this . . . what was her name?'

'Isabel.'

'This Isabel. Elle thinks she's her mum.'

'She knows Isabel isn't her real mum,' I reply. 'But Mateo told her he's her biological father. Is that true?'

Jo nods and bites the inside of her lip as it trembles. 'I was seeing him for a while. He was pretty much the love of my life. When I told him I was pregnant, he was shocked, obviously, but then he just upped and left the UK and I never heard from him again. I was gutted.'

I kiss the top of Jo's head. 'He told me he was ashamed that he'd treated you so badly.'

'So he should be,' she says.

'Why didn't you tell the police about him when Elle went missing? We could have got her back straightaway.'

Jo frowns. 'I told you! He disappeared when he found out I was pregnant. Didn't want anything to do with us. He was the last person I thought would take her. Why would he, when he couldn't get away fast enough? There was no reason to drag him into the situation.'

I shake my head at my sister's reasoning. I don't agree with her logic, but what's done is done. There's no point berating her over it, so I continue. 'He said he tried to contact you a few years later, but you had him blocked.'

'Too right. I never wanted to hear from him again. Not after he left me in the lurch.'

'And then he says you messaged him the same year Elle went missing.'

'He said that?' Jo turns to look at me.

'He said you wanted him to have custody of Elle. That you couldn't cope being a single mother.'

'What a liar!'

'You never said that?'

'I never contacted him, full stop.'

'He said the abduction was your idea. That you told him the only way you'd give him custody was if he paid you fifty grand.'

'Do I look like I've got fifty grand?' she says. 'Would I be living in my sister's garage and working in crappy pubs if I had that kind of money?'

'He also said that you made him take Elle from the ice-skating rink.'

Jo grasps both my hands in hers and stares into my eyes. 'I swear to you now, Nat, on my life. I never contacted Mateo. The last time I had contact with him was when I was pregnant.'

'Shit.' I exhale. This time I really do believe my sister, and I feel terrible for giving credence to Mateo's story. It must have been a fabrication. A twisting of the truth to stop me from calling the authorities. I feel like such a sucker.

'Do you think he'll still be there, at his house in Gran Canaria?' Jo asks. 'Can we fly back today?'

'I think we should call the police first,' I say.

'You don't think he'll have done a runner, do you?'

'I really hope not.' My phone buzzes in my pocket and I check the screen.

Jo gets to her feet. 'I need to get dressed, pack a case. Check my passport's in date.'

'Hang on.' I hold out a hand for Jo to help me up off the floor. 'I've just had a voicemail from Tara. Let me call her back.'

'Tara? You mean the investigator?' Jo asks.

'Yeah.'

Tara answers straightaway. 'Hey, Natalie. Thanks for calling back. Did you get my message?'

'Hi, Tara. No, I didn't listen to it. Can I put you on speaker? I'm with my sister.'

'Yes. Sure. So, you finally told her about me then?'

'I did. And it's all a lot more complicated than the quick version I gave you last night.'

Jo and I sit beside each other on the sofa as I hit the speaker button.

'The main thing is that you found Elle,' Tara says.

'Well, technically, you found Elle,' I reply.

'Thank you, Tara,' Jo says. 'We're going to fly back there today. I can't believe you found my daughter after all this time. I'll never be able to thank you enough. You've given me my life back.'

'It's my pleasure,' Tara replies. 'I'm absolutely over the moon for you both. But I'm guessing things are going to get tricky now. Have you told the police?'

'Not yet,' I tell her. 'But we'll be contacting them this morning.'

'Good call. You probably should have done that before you went to Gran Canaria. I worry that Mateo and his wife might flee with Elle again. Although it will be harder this time, now that we know who he is. If you want to talk anything through with me, I'll be happy to give my opinion, for whatever it's worth. But first I have some new information that might or might not be of interest.'

'Really?' I'm surprised to hear that she's still looking into this for me. 'I feel bad that you're spending so much time on this when you're not even in the business anymore.'

'I want to,' she says. 'It's been weighing on my mind for years. So, are you both listening?'

'Yes,' we reply. I glance at my sister and she takes my hand, grasping it tightly.

'Again,' she says, 'I want to reiterate that this information might not be relevant. Especially as it seems you've now found Elle anyway. But I thought I'd pass it on. It's actually nothing, really. I'm not sure why I'm telling you. After I found that last lead, I got hooked on the case again and started trawling through social media from that time. I came across a post of someone wearing that dog costume at his son's fancy-dress birthday party.

'I messaged the guy about it and he told me he still had the costume. I asked if he'd had it on the night of Georgia's party and he said he couldn't remember that far back, but that if it was the first weekend in December, then it was probably at the dry cleaners because he took it in the day after his son's birthday, which was on the Wednesday. And he didn't pick it up until the following week.'

'Oka-a-y,' I reply. 'So you think this guy might have had something to do with Elle's abduction too?'

'Not really,' Tara says. 'I mean, no one could even conclude that the person in the dog suit had anything to do with it. But I remember you saying that your sister's best friend worked at a dry cleaners and so I wondered if that was relevant.'

My skin goes cold and my brain starts clicking, trying to slot the pieces together, but I don't want to reach the conclusion that's screaming out to me.

'Tara,' Jo says woodenly. 'You wouldn't happen to know the name of the dry cleaners, would you?'

'Sure. It's quite near you guys. It's called Dry Your Eyes.'

Chapter Forty-Three

NOW

My husband pinches the bridge of his nose and shakes his head. I got back from the police station an hour ago and called Theo at work, asking him to come home as soon as possible. Georgia is out with friends after school, so at least I don't need to worry about her coming home in the middle of all this.

Theo and I are sitting in the living room, where I've just told him everything that's happened. He's stunned about Elle, and he cried when I told him we'd found her. But it's clear he's hurt that I kept such huge secrets from him. That I went behind his back and took out a loan. That I put myself in danger by going to the Canaries alone. The seriousness of the immediate situation means we'll talk about what I did at a later time, but I don't blame Theo for being pissed off with me. I would be too, in his position. I just have to hope that some part of him will understand.

Jo, Tara and I spent a couple of hours at the police station earlier, giving statements to DI Lucy Gilligan. She was incredibly surprised to see us, and listened carefully to everything we had to say – from Tara's first discovery of Mateo to her latest bombshell about Ollie, and of course my trip to Gran Canaria.

After our conversation with the DI, she immediately contacted the Gran Canarian police, who sent a squad car over to Mateo's house. Thankfully, he and Isabel were still there and they've both been taken into the station for questioning. Elle is safe and staying with a friend. My heart aches for her. She must be worried sick about her 'parents'. But Jo and I had no choice. The truth needs to come out. And we need to get Jo's daughter back.

'So what's going to happen with Ollie?' Theo asks. 'It's just unbelievable. It's *Ollie*. I always thought he was one of the good guys. Are we sure it was him?'

'The exact same dog costume was at his dry cleaners during the week Elle went missing. It's a bit of a coincidence, don't you think?'

Theo shakes his head. 'I just don't want to believe it was him.'

'I know. He's always felt like part of the family. Mum and Dad are going to be so upset.'

'How could he do something like that, and then carry on in our lives like he didn't cause all this pain?'

'I guess he did it for the money,' I reply bitterly.

'Not being funny,' Theo says, 'but fifty grand isn't even that much. Even less in dollars. I mean, obviously it's a lot. But it's not like you can retire on it, or buy a house or anything. And why did he stick around with Jo afterwards?'

I shrug and shake my head. 'Jo and I couldn't make any sense of it. She's devastated.'

'Let's hope the police can find out the truth. I can't believe you've found Elle. It's a miracle.'

Despite the incredible news of Elle being found, my heart is heavy with the thought of Ollie's betrayal and I can't help hoping that we've somehow got it wrong. That there's another explanation. That perhaps it was one of his work colleagues or perhaps there was another dog costume out there and this is just a terrible coincidence.

'How's Jo holding up?' Theo asks.

'So many emotions. She's desperate to see Elle, obviously. But she's gutted about Ollie.'

'Will she be able to keep her cool with him when he gets here?'

'I don't know,' I reply. 'But she promised the DI that she'd act like nothing's wrong until they arrive.'

Ollie is on his way over now. I called him to say I wanted to talk to him about Jo. He has no idea that once he arrives, the DI and her officers are going to come and arrest him.

'I wouldn't put it past Jo to do something drastic,' Theo says.

'I don't think so. All Jo's worried about right now is getting Elle back. She won't jeopardise that.' Theo and I thought it would be best if Jo stays in her flat and keeps out of the way. But she wants to see Ollie arrested so I don't know if she'll keep to the plan.

Theo and I freeze as a car door slams out front. We get to our feet and look out through the slatted blinds to see Ollie stepping out of his car and walking towards the front door.

'Shit,' I mutter. 'I don't know how I'm going to be able to hold back from punching him in the face.'

'You and me both,' Theo replies, his expression as dark as thunder.

Chapter Forty-Four

THE DAY OF THE ICE-SKATING PARTY

He heads back up to the Triangle at the top of Bournemouth town centre via the back roads. He's calmer than he should be, considering what he's just done, but he almost feels robotic in his actions, like all emotions have fled his body. It's just as well, because he's going to need to stay focused and not panic once Jo realises what's happened.

As he strides along the pavement, he reviews the events of earlier in his head. The dog costume was a stroke of genius on his part. First, it covered him from head to toe and was lightweight enough to stuff in a bag. Second, the ice rink already had cartoon characters so he didn't draw too much undue attention. And third, no one will be able to trace it back to him, as he doesn't actually own the suit. He borrowed it from the dry cleaners where he works. They're always getting various costumes in to clean and this one was perfect. Someone brought it in earlier in the week. It had an ice-cream stain down the leg, but it's as good as new now. He'll make sure to give it another deep clean before it's returned to the owner.

Elle came with him so easily. Like a dream. Even so, he didn't want to take any chances. Once she started to get a bit tearful about leaving the party, he gave her a mild sedative in some cola. That made things a lot easier.

Mateo will be on his way to the airport with Elle by now. Ollie made sure not to let Mateo see his face. The handover was in an unlit corner of the car park, and his baseball cap was pulled down low. As far as Mateo knew, Ollie was just someone Jo trusted to make the trade. Ollie had briefly met Mateo previously when he dropped Elle off at her dance classes on Saturday mornings as a favour to Jo, who didn't realise that Elle was now attending a different dance session – one with just her and Mateo. One where they were getting to know each other. Where she was learning to trust him. It was hard for Ollie to watch, but he knew that it would be the best outcome for everyone. Mateo will have his daughter, Elle will have her father, and Jo will come to realise that Ollie is the only person she can rely on. The only person she can turn to. She will eventually fall in love with him and they can have a family of their own. That's all Ollie has ever wanted. A family with Jo.

He checks his watch and picks up his pace, hurrying along a deserted alley behind Westover Road. Rushing to get back to the bar where he's meant to be meeting Jo and the rest of their friends. He's just picked up his regular phone from his car, where he left it earlier – just in case it could have been tracked. And he dumped the bag of cash, rucksack and ice skates under the front seats of his car, along with the burner phone he's been using to message Mateo. It's not ideal, leaving it all in his vehicle where, by some fluke, they could be discovered or stolen, but he has no choice. He needs to be at the bar with his friends as an alibi and he can't take the stuff with him. He can't dump the rucksack either. He'll have to return the dog suit and destroy the burner phone and ice skates, as well as

Elle's pink coat and hat. It's taken a lot of meticulous co-ordination, but it will be worth it.

Ollie has been in love with Jo Warren ever since he can remember. They've known one another since they were four. Since Mrs Howman's class. They weren't really friends until senior school, but he was always drawn to her vitality. Jo was always just herself. She never seemed to worry about what others thought of her. Not like the rest of them who, as they grew, became more self-conscious. More aware of how others perceived them. But not Jo. Never Jo.

Ollie wasn't short of friends. He wasn't overly popular, but he wasn't disliked either. He just sat somewhere in the middle. Whereas Jo was an outsider. A bit quirky and rebellious. She didn't have many girlfriends, but for some reason, she liked Ollie. So they became this unlikely duo. And they've stuck together through thick and thin ever since.

It was hard though, watching as she had flings with friends and random hook-ups with strangers she met in clubs. And all the while, Ollie had to act like he didn't care. He had to pretend that he didn't want to kill all those boys and men who didn't deserve to put their hands on her. Because she only saw him as a friend.

He's had a few girlfriends over the years, but none of them compared to Jo. Their lights were dim compared to Jo's firework-bright energy. And he couldn't open up to them the way he could talk to her. Mostly he went out with them to try to make Jo jealous. But it never worked. She just teased him about them and eventually he would break it off.

And then there was one incredible time when he and Jo had a drunken night together and he'd stupidly assumed that it meant their relationship had moved to the next level. But she acted mortified afterwards and begged him not to let it affect their friendship. That should have been when he declared how he felt. But he held back. He couldn't have borne it if she'd rejected him and it had made things awkward. So time ticked on and the moment passed.

When Jo told him she was pregnant, Ollie hoped that it might be his. But she assured him that the dates didn't match. She'd been seeing a Mexican guy called Mateo and, according to Jo, things had been getting serious. Ollie put two and two together and realised the baby was Mateo's, even though Jo denied it. It was a blow to Ollie's heart to see that she had fallen in love with him.

But, to Ollie's relief, Mateo left Bournemouth and Jo never heard from him again. Ollie tried to console her, to get her to open up, but she didn't want to talk about it. After her parents kicked her out, he thought she'd turn to him and they could rekindle their brief romance, but then Nat swooped in to take their place, the two of them bonding over the pregnancy. The biggest surprise was that Jo wanted to keep the baby in the first place. He'd been convinced she wouldn't. But she embraced motherhood, ditching her old ways and focusing all her energy on Elle.

Ollie made himself indispensable, helping out with errands and trying to be a father figure to Elle. He thought that over time he and Jo would naturally become a couple. That the three of them would be a family. Her family certainly thought so too. But when he voiced it in a jokey way to her one evening, she said her priority was Elle and that she didn't want a relationship with anyone. That she needed friends in her life, that was all.

This new maternal Jo was different to the Jo he had fallen for. Of course he still loved her, but she was less fun, more tired, just not like her old self. The sassy, fun, outrageous Jo had been subsumed by nappies and bottles and exhaustion. He missed her.

It got him thinking in an abstract way that if Elle was out of the picture, the old Jo might return and he might be able to get closer to her. If Elle disappeared, he could be the shoulder she cried on. Initially, it wasn't a serious thought, but his love for Jo was like a physical ache, and over time the idea grew and took shape. He couldn't shake it off. Until one day he decided to put it into action.

As far as the plan to take Elle was concerned, Mateo assumed that he had been making these plans with Jo. But he hadn't. It had been Ollie who was messaging Mateo. Ollie who had been using a burner phone for weeks now. Orchestrating it all. While Mateo believed he'd been messaging Jo. Though recently Ollie had begun to wonder if Mateo didn't care whether it was Jo or not, he just wanted his daughter, and was prepared to pay handsomely for her. Fifty thousand dollars in cash, to be precise. Ollie will have to get it changed into sterling somewhere out of the area in small batches. But he's not worrying about the logistics of that right now. One step at a time.

He's almost at the bar now. He slows his pace and rubs his icy hands to warm them. His friends will already be drunk and won't know the exact time he showed up. Hopefully, Jo won't have heard about Elle yet. The longer they're all there at the bar having fun, the better. He'll tell her to put her phone away and just enjoy being out with her friends. He wants her to have a good time this evening. Because after tonight there's going to be a period when things aren't so great.

Chapter Forty-Five

NOW

With my heart pounding, I answer the front door to Ollie's smiling face.

'Hey, Nat. How was your work trip? Jo said you went abroad. Hope it was a bit nicer than this!' He gestures to the rain pattering down on his head.

'It was good, thanks, interesting. Come in.' I swallow bile and have to turn away. 'Can I make you a cuppa?' I force out the words. Force out a bright tone as we head into the kitchen.

'Coffee would be great,' he replies, perching on one of the stools at the island. 'You said you wanted to talk to me about Jo?'

I ignore his question as Theo walks into the room. 'Hey, mate,' my husband says. I can hear the sarcasm in his tone as he says the word 'mate', but Ollie doesn't notice anything amiss.

'Hey, Theo. You're home early.'

'I've got an important appointment,' Theo grinds out.

'Oh yeah? Where's that?'

'Here,' Theo replies.

I shoot my husband a warning glance, reaching for a couple of mugs.

'Like a video call or something?' Ollie asks vaguely.

'Yeah, something like that.' Theo trails off, his hands clenching and unclenching by his sides.

I hear car doors slamming from the front of the house and my pulse speeds up. My wrists are shaking and the mugs wobble in my hands until I set them down on the island.

'Everything all right, guys?' Ollie asks, getting to his feet. 'You both seem a bit weird.'

The back door opens and Jo comes into the kitchen, her gaze focused on Ollie. Or should I say *un*focused, because her expression is glazed and I really don't like the look of it.

'Hey, Jo,' Ollie says to her uncertainly. 'Everything all right? I didn't realise you were here.'

'You bastard,' she hisses. 'You evil bastard.'

Ollie takes a step back and raises his hands. 'Hey, what's going on?'

The doorbell rings, but I'm scared to leave Jo in case she does something she shouldn't.

'That will be the police,' Jo spits. 'Here to arrest your evil fucking arse for taking my child.'

'The police?' He looks genuinely confused. 'I don't know what you're—'

'Save it,' she says. 'Tell it all to the cops. I hope it was worth it for fifty grand. I hope they lock you up and throw away the key.'

'Jo. I don't know what you're accusing me of, but you *know* me. You can't honestly believe I'd do anything to hurt you or Elle.'

'Liar!'

'I don't have Elle, I promise you,' Ollie replies, his eyes darting from her to me and Theo.

'No, but Mateo does!' Jo cries. 'He's had my daughter for the past ten years and you gave her to him! You watched me crumble.

You stood by while my life collapsed, and you were the reason for it all! How could you do that?'

The doorbell rings again and this time it's accompanied by a sharp knocking. 'Hello. Police, can you open up, please.'

'I'll go,' Theo says.

'Wait!' Ollie calls to my husband. 'Let me speak to Jo first, before the police come in.'

'It's too late for that, Ollie,' I say, my voice tight with anger. 'You've had ten years to speak to my sister.'

Theo gives him a disgusted sneer before leaving the kitchen.

'Shit,' Ollie mutters, his head down, shoulders slumped.

Suddenly, he makes a break for it, but Jo is blocking the back door and I watch, shocked, as he shoves her out of the way, tearing around the side of the house. Jo stumbles, but she doesn't lose her footing, steadying herself on the wall. She swears, turns and chases after him and I follow behind, already breathless.

Ollie doesn't get very far. He runs straight into the broad figure of a uniformed officer who's stationed on the other side of the gate.

'Going somewhere?' the officer asks, catching hold of Ollie's arm and leading him around to the front of the house, where we're met by a cluster of police vehicles with flashing lights and various officers positioned on the pavement and on our driveway.

'Oliver Camilleri,' DI Gilligan says as the officer leads Ollie towards her, 'I am arresting you on suspicion of child abduction and conspiracy to kidnap. You do not have to say anything, but it may harm your defence if you do not mention when questioned something which you later rely on in court. Anything you do say may be given in evidence.'

'No,' Ollie says, panting, his face red. 'There's been a mistake.' One of the officers handcuffs Ollie as he starts crying. 'Jo, tell them they've made a mistake. You can't believe I had anything to do with this.'

But Jo has fallen silent, glaring at him and rubbing her shoulder where he knocked into her.

Ollie is led towards a police car, his shoulders hunched, his hair damp from the rain, which is coming down hard now. I still can't believe that lovable, kind, sweet Ollie was responsible for destroying our lives. How is it possible that we didn't know him? That it was all just an act. He's a monster.

The DI guides Ollie into the back seat of the police car while Theo, Jo and I stand together on the driveway. Jo wanted to witness Ollie's arrest, but she's now shaking uncontrollably. The shock is all too much. I take her hand and squeeze it tight, as much for me as for her.

After years and years of sadness and silence, of not knowing what happened to my niece, these past few days have been a shocking unravelling of the truth. Meeting with Tara last week, flying out to Gran Canaria, and then finding Elle and discovering what Ollie did – it's all happened so fast that my brain has hardly had time to catch up. If I'm feeling like this, then goodness knows how my poor sister is holding up.

'Are you okay?' Theo asks, putting an arm around her.

'No,' she replies. 'I'm not okay. But I will be.'

Chapter Forty-Six

SEVEN MONTHS LATER

Our sprawling encampment seems to take up half the beach. We have a gazebo, parasols, beach chairs, a windbreak, rugs, towels, cool boxes, portable barbecues and plenty of beach games. We're bedded in for the day.

'It's a real scorcher,' Mum says. 'Good job putting up the gazebo, Theo. It's lovely and cool under here.'

'Yes,' Dad echoes gruffly from behind his newspaper. 'Good job, Theo.'

'Put that down for a bit, Derek,' Mum adds. 'You're being antisocial.'

'It's okay, Mum,' I say. 'He's relaxing. Shall we go for a paddle?'

'Oh, I'd love to.' She gets to her feet, dons her wide-brimmed straw hat, and we link arms, walking across the soft sand in our flip-flops as it's too hot to go barefoot.

'How are you doing, Mum?'

'I'm fine, darling. Isn't this just wonderful?' She gestures to the sea, where Jo, Georgia and Elle are swimming and splashing about in the shallows.

My heart fills at the sight. 'It's incredible, Mum.'

'I never thought I'd see the day,' she says. 'Truly, it feels as though this year has been a blessing.'

Contrary to the perfect visions we all had of Elle coming to live back here with Jo, she's still living with her Spanish family in Gran Canaria. I was upset at the unfairness of it all. Why should Mateo and Isabel have Jo's daughter when they already stole so many years from her? But, after numerous meetings with police and social workers in both countries, Jo said we had to look at it from her daughter's point of view. As far as Elle is concerned, Mateo and Isabel are her parents and Jo is a stranger. Of course, Jo doesn't love the thought of Elle having new parents, but it's better than the alternative. It's better than thinking she was dead or worse. To know that she's been living a lovely life is some consolation for the trauma Jo suffered.

◆ ◆ ◆

It's not all bad news – thankfully, Elle is bilingual and she and Jo have been getting to know one another again over the past few months. Mateo rented a studio apartment for Jo nearby so that she could see Elle regularly, and she says it's been the best time of her life. Apparently, the two of them are as thick as thieves, laughing and giggling constantly. Elle doesn't really remember her life in Bournemouth, but when she first saw Jo, memories of her mother started to return, and they had a very gentle, but emotional reunion.

Elle is still known as Adela by her Canarian friends and family, but she was happy for Jo to call her Elle, as it isn't so different from her nickname, Ela. Now that they're comfortable with one another, my niece has come over to Bournemouth to spend half the summer with Jo and the rest of us.

The loveliest surprise is how well Georgia and Elle get along. Only fifteen months apart in age, they're more like sisters than cousins. Georgia has loved introducing Elle to all her friends, who can remember that terrible evening at the skating rink. Many tears were shed when they all met up again for the first time in ten years, along with many of the parents and friends who joined the search parties. My daughter is like a new person. It's as though a weight has lifted from her shoulders. She's more confident, more at ease, happier. Elle says that Georgia will have to come and visit her in Gran Canaria and now that Georgia's A levels are done, they're already planning dates and flights.

'Come in! Swim!' Elle calls out to me and Mum as we reach the shoreline.

'We're just having a paddle,' Mum calls back, removing her flip-flops and rolling up her Capri pants.

Elle dives beneath the water and pulls Georgia under and they both emerge laughing and spluttering.

'Those two are a menace,' Jo says, coming towards us with a smile. 'No chance of a relaxing swim with them in the water.'

Jo has changed too. A lot. She's calmer and not so defensive. It helps that she and I have had some space from one another while she's been in Gran Canaria. The other big change to her life is that she's starting uni in September to study nursing. I spoke to Mum and Dad about how Jo is really getting her act together now and they've agreed to help her out financially, giving her this boost to get her life back on track. Yes, it's too little too late, but at least it's something. And it takes some of the burden off Theo and me, at last.

Of course, Mum and Dad are overjoyed at Elle's return. It's given them a new lease of life. I can't help being resentful at how they left me and Jo to cope without their help for so long, but I don't want to be bitter. I want to move on with peace in my heart. Some days are better than others on that score.

My parents will never change. They were great when we were younger, giving us all the love and attention we needed, but they couldn't cope when things started to get tricky and simply let us fend for ourselves. I see now that I stepped into the parenting role for Jo, which wasn't great for either of us. Maybe now we can get back to being sisters again.

I hope Theo and I will always be here for Georgia, no matter how hard things get. But I already feel as though I failed her on many levels after Elle disappeared. I guess we're all just doing the best we can, and I'm learning to forgive myself as well as everyone else.

Surprisingly, Jo doesn't blame Mateo for what he did, because he thought he was doing it with her consent, but I don't think Jo is Isabel's biggest fan. I guess that's to be expected as she's been a mother to Elle for all the years that Jo missed out on. Though Jo said that both Mateo and Isabel have been really warm and apologetic towards her. Giving her all the time she wants with Elle. Which is something.

Because of the media interest, they had to tell Elle the whole truth about what happened rather than glossing over some of the facts like they wanted to. But the main thing from Elle's perspective is that her parents weren't to blame. It was Ollie who orchestrated it all. And maybe one good thing to come out of it was that Elle got to know her father, which she may never have done otherwise.

When it all first came to light, the Mexican authorities wanted Mateo for questioning over his procurement of a fraudulent passport for Elle. At one point, he thought he was going to be extradited from Spain to Mexico and end up imprisoned there. But he was able to avoid extradition by co-operating with the Spanish and Mexican authorities to bring down the criminal gang who supplied his fake documents. The Mexican authorities kept Mateo's anonymity and arrested twelve people in connection with almost two hundred fraudulent passports. It was quite a coup for them, and a huge relief for Mateo and everyone else, especially Elle.

Every time I think about Ollie, I feel ill. The hell he put Jo through when he claimed to love her. He said afterwards that he thought he was doing what was best for her. That he knew she struggled with looking after Elle alone. But I've learned that struggle doesn't mean we want to opt out. Struggle means we care. Deeply. That's the whole point of it.

Ollie is in prison and he'll be there for a long time. After that awful day when he tried to do a runner from the police, they took him in for questioning and he crumbled. He admitted everything. How he wore the dog suit to abduct Elle. How he took Mateo's money. How he pretended to be Jo.

My sister decided that, as much as she never wanted to set eyes on him again, she needed to speak to him one last time. To find out why he did it. At first, Ollie refused to see her in prison, but eventually he gave in. Jo said he didn't even seem that remorseful. He was more defensive than anything, saying that he'd made sure Elle never suffered, that she was with her real father, who he knew would look after her. When Jo asked him why he did it, he said he did it for Jo, because he loved her. There was no real guilt. He'd built this logic in his brain where he truly believed he was doing something noble.

When Jo asked him what he'd done with the money, he said he'd spent it on the two of them. On meals out and little treats, bottles of wine and a few luxury nights away. The thought that he'd used that blood money to woo her had sickened Jo. Ten years of what she'd thought were little kindnesses from her best friend and then lover had been hideously tainted.

Despite knowing the truth and that it really is Ollie's role in all this that set off this chain reaction, I'm still furious about what Mateo did. He knew there would be family members affected by Elle's abduction, not to mention the huge police investigation he triggered, and yet he feels justified because he 'thought' Jo knew. Personally, I think Mateo got off lightly. Too lightly. No one took into account how ten years of my family's lives have been ruined by his actions.

But, for Elle's sake, Jo has asked us to move past all that. To forgive Mateo in order that she can have an uncomplicated relationship with her daughter. Which I think is very big of her.

Because I'm not sure I could have done it. I'm not sure I could ever be in the same room as that man ever again.

Jo and Mum walk back to the gazebo but I stay with my feet in the cool water, reluctant to leave, focusing on the happiness I feel watching the girls together.

'Hey.'

I turn to see Theo, a warm smile on his face. He stands next to me and squints out across the sea to where Elle and Georgia are floating on their backs, chatting. Calm for once.

'Hey, yourself,' I reply.

After we found Elle, I begged Theo for forgiveness for keeping him in the dark about Tara and for lying about my 'work' trip, but he said that we had beaten one another up for too long. That there had been enough blame and division, and could we just draw a line under all of it and move on. Be happy for a change. I don't know what I did to deserve such an amazing husband, but I give thanks every day. I lean in to give him a hug and a kiss, enjoying the feel of his arms around me. Maybe it's easier to forgive because there's been a happy outcome. I'm not sure what would have happened if my secrets had all led to a dead end. Thankfully, I don't have to find out.

Even when things are good, nothing is perfect. I know that. Georgia will be going off to uni soon and we'll have to deal with empty-nest syndrome. My work is okay, but I don't love it. My sister is still living with us and probably will be for at least the next five years while she's studying. But these things are all part of my life. The ups and the downs, the traumas and the elations, the monotony and the anxieties. All of it. And what I've learned is that while the sun is shining and the sand is warm beneath my toes, I have to soak it up and hold on to each second. To never take for granted the preciousness of these moments. And to hug my loved ones tightly while I can. Because, really, that's all that matters.

Epilogue
EIGHTEEN YEARS EARLIER

The bus pulls away from the stop and Jo half-heartedly starts to run but soon gives up, she's too far away to make it in time. She doesn't have enough money for a cab and doesn't want to wait an hour for the next bus so she'll have to walk home. Even though it's started raining and she feels like crap.

It's fitting really, after the day she's had. I mean, what did she expect? That he'd be over the moon, declare his undying love and suggest they get married? Maybe.

She only met him a few months ago. She was picking litter on Bournemouth Beach – a summer job that was actually pretty good fun – when he came up and asked if she wanted to get a drink later, in that gorgeous accent of his. She thought he was someone famous, like an actor, or a rock star, because he had that quality about him. That ultra-confident, good-looking swagger that not many people can pull off without coming across as arrogant.

But Mateo wasn't like that at all. He was sweet. Thoughtful. With his dark wavy hair and hint of stubble, and eyes that were almost black. Why did she even have to meet him in the first place? She'd never felt like this about anyone before and she hated how it made her feel so out of control. Jo had always prided herself on never falling in love. But now, at the ripe old age of twenty-two, it had finally happened. And she wished like hell it hadn't.

After that first evening, Jo and Mateo spent most of the summer together. She could tell that his friend, Rafael, was a bit pissed off with their relationship. The two of them were college buddies who were supposed to be travelling around Europe together, but Mateo extended his stay in the UK for Jo. She was flattered, excited by the possibility of the two of them having a long-term commitment. He even invited her over to Mexico City. He was going to show her the sights, introduce her to his friends, his family.

And now it's all gone wrong.

She crosses over Bath Road and trudges up the hill, trying to avoid being sprayed by the uncaring traffic. Although she's already soaked through, so it wouldn't make much of a difference.

This afternoon started so well. She'd arranged to meet Mateo in the gardens. It was a clear day with blue skies and a late-August sun. She'd hopped off the bus, crossed over the road and headed down into the gardens where the hot-air balloon was tethered. He'd treated her to a ride in it last month and it had been amazing. They'd been able to see for miles over the whole town and across the sea. The balloon has been in the gardens for six years already, but that was the first time she'd ever actually been up in it. So she thought it would set a good tone, to meet there today. To remind him of the fun they were having.

He was a little late, well, half an hour late to be precise, and he wasn't in a very good mood when he finally showed up. Apparently, he and Raf had a bit of an argument. Jo tried to kiss him out of his bad mood, and pretty soon it started working. He laughed and took her hand and they ambled down to the beach and along the pier.

Her heart started to pound at this point and she felt quite nauseous. All her hopes and dreams were pinned on whatever happened next. They marvelled over the old photos of the pier in its heyday during the

Victorian era, and sat on one of the benches, where he kissed her again. But she really felt quite sick just then, so she pulled away.

'What's up, JoJo?' he asked. He always called her that and she liked it. Although she wouldn't have tolerated it from anyone else.

'I'm pregnant.' She hadn't meant to blurt it out like that, but she hadn't been able to think of any other way to say it. She looked at his face and knew instantly that this wasn't going to be the outcome she wanted. The light had gone out of his eyes and he immediately looked away. Her heart felt like it had been replaced by a rock. It still does.

As she walks home, her whole body feels heavy with sadness. Heavier than it's ever felt before. She passes the Russell-Cotes Museum, yet another place they visited together. She realises her home town is going to be a constant reminder of him.

After she told him her situation and confirmed that the baby was his, he told her that he and Raf were travelling up to Scotland next week, and after that they were going to Norway to see the fjords. So a baby wasn't really something he had planned for. She told him that it wasn't something she had planned for either. So he took her hand and said he was sorry. Jo doesn't even know what he meant by that. Sorry? What did that mean? Sorry you got pregnant? Sorry, it's not my problem? Sorry I ever met you?

Jo felt stupid, duped. She thought Mateo had loved her. She thought he might have offered to stand by her. To get through it together. But he hadn't. And now she was heartbroken. But maybe deep down she knew he was flighty, and hoped that telling him about the baby might have pushed him to stay. The fact that he wasn't even the father wasn't the point. Mateo didn't know that. As far as he was concerned, the baby was his. But he still didn't want it.

Fuck! Why had she slept with Ollie that time? If they hadn't had stupid sex that stupid one time, then she wouldn't be pregnant now and everything would be sunshine and rainbows with Mateo. Instead, she's walking home in the rain feeling horribly sick and horribly tired.

Well, there's no way she's telling anyone who the father is. Ollie is great as a friend, but she doesn't want to be stuck with him as the dad. With him wanting to play happy families. That's not the life she envisions for herself. If she's going to keep it, then she'll do it alone. She'll be a single mum with a cute kid. That will rattle everyone's cages.

Another Southbourne bus passes her and pulls in at the stop up ahead. They must have put on an extra service. Jo waves at the bus to hang on, and picks up her pace, hoping the driver will see her. She's not sure she has the energy to walk all the way home. Thankfully, the bus waits and she manages to hop on this time.

Despite her heartache over Mateo's rejection, she's starting to feel a little stronger. It would probably have been wrong to pass her kid off as Mateo's anyway. And if he discovered what she'd done further down the line then that would be pretty bad. No, she'll simply tell everyone she has no idea who the father is, and that way no one will get hurt, and things will work out okay. No harm done.

Still sad, but also a little relieved that it's decided, Jo finds a seat near the back as the bus lurches out into the flow of traffic and carries on down the road.

NOW

RE: Elle Warren – Disclosure Order

To: Penny Rashid <PRashid86@ prinkandcosolicitors.com>

Dear Penny,

It was great to meet with you again this week after the judge's findings.

I just wanted to thank you for using the Public Interest Immunity against revealing Elle's paternity. I really don't think her paternity was relevant to the case and would only have harmed Elle when she's having to deal with everything that's come to light. Knowing that her biological father was the one who abducted her would have been crushing to everyone involved, and I certainly didn't want him finding out and laying some kind of claim to Elle. She's been through enough.

I was shocked when I heard that Ollie's DNA had pinged up as a hit with Elle's on the national database. Especially as I'd never believed he was the father. Mateo was especially gutted. But I'm so thankful the judge saw it our way. I don't mind admitting that I was terrified going into that closed-chambers meeting.

Elle has lived the majority of her life thinking Mateo is her dad and so, for now at least, both Mateo and I would like to keep it that way.

Huge thanks again. I'm incredibly grateful to you and the team.

Jo Warren

ACKNOWLEDGEMENTS

Thank you to my fantastic editor Sammia Hamer. As always, it's a joy to work with you. Huge thanks to my developmental editor Victoria Oundjian for all your brilliant suggestions to make this story shine. Thanks a million to Eoin Purcell, Rebecca Hills, Nicole Wagner and the rest of the fabulous team at Amazon Publishing who helped bring this book into the world. I'm forever grateful.

Thank you to Sadie for doing a fantastic job on the copy-edits, and to the wonderfully thorough and eagle-eyed Jenni Davis for an excellent proofread.

Thank you to The Brewster Project for my beautiful cover. Huge thanks also to Jonathan Pennock and the team at Brilliance Publishing for another incredible audiobook.

Endless gratitude to author and police officer Sammy H. K. Smith for advising on the police procedure. As always, any mistakes and embellishments are my own.

I'm so thankful to my beta readers Julie Carey and Terry Harden for always having the time and enthusiasm to comb through my books with such care. Thanks as ever to my lovely readers, bloggers, reviewers, sharers, recommenders and posters – none of this would have been possible without you!

As always, huge gratitude to my friends and family for your constant love and support, especially my husband, Pete Boland, who's the first person to read my books and to reassure me that they don't belong in the shredder.

Thanks to my children, who always inspire me, especially in the case of this book where, on my daughter's ninth birthday, one of her friends went missing at the skating rink. It was nightmarish for an hour until we discovered that the friend had been collected early to attend another party without our knowledge. That hour of hell resulted in this book, so silver linings and all that.

A LETTER FROM THE AUTHOR

I just want to say a huge thank you for reading my twentieth – twentieth! – psychological thriller, *The Birthday Party*. I hope you enjoyed it.

If you'd like to keep up to date with my latest releases, just sign up to my newsletter via my website and I'll let you know when I have a new novel coming out. Your email address will never be shared and you can unsubscribe at any time.

If you enjoyed my book, I'd be really grateful if you'd be kind enough to post a review online or tell your friends about it. A good review absolutely makes my day!

Shalini xx

ABOUT THE AUTHOR

Author photo © Shalini Boland 2018

Shalini Boland is the Amazon and *USA Today* bestselling author of twenty psychological thrillers. To date, she's sold over two million copies of her books.

Shalini lives by the sea in Dorset, England, with her husband, two children and their increasingly demanding dog, Queen Jess. Before kids, she was signed to Universal Music Publishing as a singer/songwriter, but now she spends her days writing (in between restocking the fridge and dealing with endless baskets of laundry).

She is also the author of two bestselling sci-fi and fantasy series as well as a WWII evacuee adventure with a time-travel twist.

When she's not reading, writing or stomping along the beach, you can reach her via Facebook at www.facebook.com/ShaliniBolandAuthor, on Bluesky via @shaliniboland.bsky.social, on TikTok via @ shaliniboland, on X via @ShaliniBoland, on Instagram via @shaboland, or via her website: www.shaliniboland.co.uk.

Visit Shalini's website to sign up to her newsletter.

Follow the Author on Amazon

If you enjoyed this book, follow Shalini Boland on Amazon to be notified when the author releases a new book!
To do this, please follow these instructions:

Desktop:

1) Search for the author's name on Amazon or in the Amazon App.
2) Click on the author's name to arrive on their Amazon page.
3) Click the 'Follow' button.

Mobile and Tablet:

1) Search for the author's name on Amazon or in the Amazon App.
2) Click on one of the author's books.
3) Click on the author's name to arrive on their Amazon page.
4) Click the 'Follow' button.

Kindle eReader and Kindle App:

If you enjoyed this book on a Kindle eReader or in the Kindle App, you will find the author 'Follow' button after the last page.